SEDUCTION

JAYMIN EVE and JANE WASHINGTON

Copyright 2017 © Jaymin Eve and Jane Washington.
All rights reserved.
The authors have provided this book for your personal use only. It may not be re-sold or made publically available in any way.
COPYRIGHT INFRINGEMENT IS AGAINST THE LAW.
Thank you for respecting the hard work of these authors.

Eve, Jaymin
Washington, Jane
Seduction

www.janewashington.com
www.jaymineve.com

Edited by David Thomas
www.firstreadeditorial.com

ISBN-10: 1981477802
ISBN-13: 978-1981477807

GLOSSARY

click – **minute**
rotation – **hour**
sun-cycle – **day**
moon-cycle – **month**
life-cycle – **year**
minateur – **soldier**
bullsen – **domesticated work-beast**
sol – **dominant race**
dweller – **serving race**
minatsol – **world of the dwellers and sols**
topia – **world of the gods**
blesswood – **the center of Minatsol**
dvadel – **the first ring**
soldel – **the second ring**
tridel – **the third ring**
swimmer – **fish**
pantera – **winged horse**
flame-rash – **nothing you need to know about**

TABLE OF CONTENTS

Chapter **One**	1
Chapter **Two**	19
Chapter **Three**	34
Chapter **Four**	52
Chapter **Five**	70
Chapter **Six**	78
Chapter **Seven**	97
Chapter **Eight**	113
Chapter **Nine**	131
Chapter **Ten**	148
Chapter **Eleven**	168
Chapter **Twelve**	188
Chapter **Thirteen**	202
Chapter **Fourteen**	218
Chapter **Fifteen**	239
Chapter **Sixteen**	262
Chapter **Seventeen**	281
Chapter **Eighteen**	293
Chapter **Nineteen**	309
Also by Jane Washington	233
Also by Jaymin Eve	234
Connect with the Authors	327

For Jane: This book isn't dedicated to you.
Also for Jaymin: This book is dedicated to me.

CHAPTER ONE

THE strange thing about life was that some sun-cycles it gave you reasons to rise above your station and change the world around you, and some sun-cycles it just made you want to punch a girl in the face. That sun-cycle was now, and that girl's name was Emmanuelle, formerly known as Emmy.

"Did you just re-name me to my original name?" Emmanuelle demanded, her pretty brown eyes narrowed as she jumped up from the bed and stalked toward me.

"Did you just read my mind?" I shot back, sounding just as angry as she had sounded, except that I was mostly just scared and pretending not to be.

Ever since Cyrus had stolen my soul-link from the Abcurses and started reading my mind, I had developed a completely rational fear of people suddenly growing the ability to hear my thoughts.

"No, Willa," Emmy was almost groaning now, her hand rubbing over her face. Her posture was somehow both rigid and exasperated. It made her look like she couldn't decide whether to slump back onto her bed or shake her fist at me. "You were speaking your thoughts out loud again. I haven't magically learnt how to read your mind in the last five clicks."

"You wouldn't be the first one," I grumbled. "It's happened at *least* twice … that I know of."

She ignored that statement, her eyes still steadily narrowed, her hands still firmly planted on her hips. "Why are you revoking my nickname?"

"I saw you with that guy." I could feel the pout that had started to tug down my lip, and I tried to stop it. I tried really hard.

"Are you jealous?" she asked dryly. "You know I'm allowed to have other friends, right?"

"No," I returned sulkily.

"*Seriously?*" She tossed her hands up and fell down onto the mattress beside me. "He's *just* a friend, Will. I haven't forgotten Atti already. I'm dealing with my—"

"You're not." I jumped up just as quickly as she had sat down, spinning to face her and adopting her earlier posture, my hands against my hips and my eyes narrowed. "You're keeping yourself so busy you barely even have time to sleep, let alone grieve properly, and you're hanging out with that *friend*—what's his name again?"

"Fred."

"Stupid name. He's stupid. You're hanging out with him way too much. You're *avoiding*. It's bad for you."

"You're not my mother." She jumped up again, and the mattress seemed to squeak a little in protest this time. "You can't tell me what to do! That's my job!"

I tried to stop the sigh from escaping, but I was pacing and rubbing my temples and before I knew it, I was sighing like I really was her mother. "You're acting out," I reasoned aloud. "I get it. You went through something terrible. You lost—"

"Stop trying to fix it." Emmy's voice had turned cold, almost flat.

She wasn't even looking at me as she walked to the door and pulled it open. She glued her eyes to the wall beyond, gritting out a goodbye from between her teeth before disappearing altogether. I wanted to scream, or pick up the little sundial that she had left behind and violently throw it at the rough, stone wall ... but I wouldn't do either of those things, because my sun-cycles of being immature and throwing fits to deal with my problems were over. If Emmy was going off the rails, I needed to be responsible.

I needed to ... stalk her.

Responsibly.

I marched out of the room, swiping the sundial as I went and shoving it deep into my pocket. I could see her blonde hair through the scattering of dwellers that remained in the underground section of the dweller residence, and I hurried to catch up to her. I didn't bother trying to hide myself from Emmy, because she was striding ahead with far too much purpose for me to think that she would turn around at any point—but I did keep my head down and my expression hidden from the other dwellers. I didn't need anyone calling out my name and alerting her to the fact that I was *maturely* keeping an eye on her. Like a responsible sister. Like an adult that doesn't throw fits. Like a dweller-sol-hybrid who knows how to weigh up pros and cons and save enough tokens to buy a little hut one sun-cycle halfway between Minatsol and Topia.

It didn't surprise me in the least to spot Rome in the corridor right above where Emmy's dorm room would have been on the lower floor. Even though I'd barely felt the tug of the soul-link while I had been in the room, moving toward the staircase had been a lesson in agony. We had figured out this trick a few sun-cycles ago, when I needed to speak to Emmy but refused to drag a contingent of Abcurses down into the dweller-dorms with me.

"Why are you walking like that?" Rome asked, running a broad hand through his short hair, his glittering green eyes flicking down my legs before settling on my face.

"Like what?" I asked, as he fell into step beside me.

He was starting to blow my cover a little bit, because every person—dweller or sol—in our immediate vicinity seemed to be covertly sneaking glances at him as though they were too terrified to look him squarely in the eye. I understood the dilemma. He was kind of huge. Looking him in the eye was difficult, because his eyes were so far up.

"Like you're scared of the ground," he replied on a snort. He had taken a micro-click too long to answer, which meant that he had probably been entertaining himself with my thoughts again.

More specifically, my thoughts about how tall he was.

He might be tall but everything else about him is utterly unimpressive, I thought, as loudly as I possibly could.

He smiled, cutting his eyes sideways to look at me again. "Watch out, Rocks, you know what we say about multitasking—"

But it was too late.

One click I'd been walking along in perfectly acceptable sleuth-mode, and the next click I was colliding with another body and causing a domino-effect of toppling sols, books, dwellers and trays. The noise was jarring, as was the elbow in my stomach and the knee in my back. I had no idea how anyone had even managed to fall on *top* of me, since I had been the one to start the momentum and I had started it in a forward direction, but ever since the guys had told me their theory of me being Rau's Beta, I had been forced to embrace the irrationality of my own personal brand of Chaos.

"We really need to stop meeting like this," a voice rumbled out from beneath me.

I flinched, because the voice was familiar. I distinctly recalled shouting something embarrassing at it a moon-cycle ago, while attempting to disguise the fact that I had been hiding in a supply closet with five oversized gods and two unconscious sols. I had shouted because Yael had *forced* me to shout. Because Yael was an Abcurse. And the Abcurses didn't like it when other boys touched me. Which made the fact that I was currently sprawled over Dru's chest a particularly awkward fact.

"Yeah," I mumbled, pulling my head up to try and spot Rome through the mess of tangled bodies. "We *really* should. For your sake."

Rome was the only person in the hall still standing. He was up against the wall, his arms crossed over his chest, his foot pushed back against the stone, a small smile on his face as his eyes crawled over the people now struggling to get to their feet. He was enjoying the Chaos. I liked that. It was my Chaos after all. I wasn't very good at making it happen on command, but I was *excellent* at making it happen by accident.

Dru started to grab me around the hips to help me up, but I quickly scrambled off him and leapt over the nearest fallen dweller. The mountain-sized sol seemed surprised to see me leaping around, all uninjured and unfazed. That made two of us.

"Can I walk you to class or something?" he asked, jumping to his feet and following me over the dweller.

I took another few steps back, until I felt an arm hook around my front. I glanced down, seeing a big hand settle across my right hip, fingers digging in. A bolt of heat travelled right through my body, and I tensed up and pushed back all at once, eliciting a small grunt from the body behind me.

"No," I croaked out, before clearing my throat. "No, that's okay! Thanks, though … Ah … I'll see you later, alright?"

"Right." He was frowning, apparently displeased that Rome had interfered, though he really should have been used to it by now. "Sure. See you."

He turned, and I watched him walk off as the rest of the fallen people managed to find their feet and recover their dropped items. Rome didn't release my hip until Dru was out of sight, and even then, it was only to spin me around to face him.

"You should—"

"Stop talking to boys," I interrupted. "Yeah. We've had this talk before. It's irrational. I can't avoid *all* males."

"Just the sols." He frowned. "And the dwellers. And the gods."

"So just … all males, then?" I arched a brow at him.

He nodded, once, short and sharp—as though we had just figured out our differences and come to a mutual agreement, and then he took my arm in hand and started to march me in the wrong direction. Wrong, because I was supposed to be following Emmy, who was now out of sight.

"Shit!" I pulled out of Rome's grip, spinning around and quickly scanning the people again to see if I could spot her.

She wasn't there, so I started off in the direction I had last seen her. She was going to see the stupid guy with the stupid name. I was sure of it. I wasn't sure how I was going to stop it once I discovered that I was right, but that was a concern for Future Willa.

"Where are you going?" Rome fell into step beside me, but luckily didn't grab me to turn me in the other direction again.

Luckily for *him*, because he would have been too strong for me to resist and it would have forced me to use my super special Beta-God abilities on him … or throw a tantrum. Always have a backup plan.

"I'm following Emmy," I whispered, hurrying to the end of the passage and then kicking into a run toward the dining hall.

It seemed like the sort of place a guy named *Fred* would ask to meet a girl, because it was the most obvious and unoriginal meeting place in the whole of the academy, and I didn't have very high hopes for Fred's originality or subtlety.

"You're stalking her," Rome corrected. "Following is far too innocent a description for the look on your face right now."

"This is the face I wear when you shouldn't mess with me because I mean business."

"Ri-ight." He drew the word out, but the smile was back. I liked it. I was pretty sure I wanted him to smile all sun-cycle. I was pretty sure I would do *almost* anything to keep the smile there, just so that I could keep looking at it.

The smile grew.

I mean who needs a fancy smile anyway, I thought, even louder than before. *It's just a smile. Lots of people have smiles. That guy has a smile. That guy has a smile. Oh that guy is—*

"Pay attention to where you're walking," Rome snapped. "We don't need another accident happening."

We were back to the bossing around, apparently. Well, two could play that game.

"How about you pay attention for me, and that way I'm free to multitask and maturely follow my sister around to make sure she's not doing anything stupid."

"What level of stupid are we talking here?" Rome asked, ignoring the first part of my bossing. "Are we talking stupid like a Beta who can't seem to stop talking to other males, forcing me into 'crusher' mode, as she so eloquently phrases it? Or is it more like Trickery when he decides that his little amusements are more enjoyable than letting us all know what he's up to?"

My feet tangled up again, but I managed to right myself before falling. *Progress*? *Damn right it was*! I knew Rome was referring to my latest rebellion against the Abcurses, during which I had walked around the halls of Blesswood semi-naked. Only … they didn't *know* that I had been walking around semi-naked, because Siret had used his Trickery to mask the fact.

"Coen almost put Siret through a wall!" I burst out. "Are you telling me that is the lesser level of stupid?"

What was he going to do if I didn't stop talking to other guys? *No, Willa!* A small part of me was suddenly determined to find out, but that was almost definitely the Chaos part, right?

Rome was nodding, his eyes locked on me. "Yes, he went easy on the bastard. I would have put him through ten walls."

With a shake of my head, I started walking again, hoping I would forget the last conversation we'd just had. The violence of his words and actions stirred something inside of me, almost as though it was calling to the budding Chaos contained within me. Either that, or I was hungry and my stomach was trying to tell me to eat.

The dining hall was reasonably empty when we entered, which meant that it wasn't quite lunchtime, yet. There was no sign of Emmy—no, *Emmanuelle*. She was most definitely not earning her nickname back until she returned to the rule-loving, responsible, solidly-upstanding dweller that I knew her to be.

I could pretend to be mature and rational for a little while, but it definitely wasn't the best long-term solution. The real me would break through at some stage and go on a rampage to get back at the mature, rational me for locking her up for so long. The *real* me was a wild animal, and she needed space to ... roam. Or hunt. Or sleep on tree branches. Or just space to not be forced into a polite, sol-driven social structure.

Rome let out a small bark of laughter at my side, which I ignored. I actually had a good grip on my ability to shut the Abcurses out of my head ... though it only worked when I really wanted them to stay out—which wasn't right now. We'd already come far too close to losing our soul-link, and I needed the comfort of knowing that the connection was still there.

"Doesn't look like she's here," Rome surmised, his amusement growing with each word. "Where to next?"

My snort of annoyance acted as an answer, until my brain had a chance to catch up. "If you're not going to be helpful in this situation, maybe you could … like, give me a bit of space. Everyone is staring and you're ruining my cover."

The breath knocked out of me as he stilled and locked those unnatural eyes on me. His irises were even more gem-like than usual. They were almost glimmering, and it made me uneasy, for just a moment. I had never been able to afford rare things before. Or glittery things. Not that I was considering purchasing Rome's eyes … because that would require some kind of underground, organ-harvesting group of eye-collectors and I wasn't sure I could handle any more secret groups or secret meetings after the dweller uprising.

"That's the only reason you wouldn't want my eyes harvested?" Rome grunted, a little disbelieving.

I shrugged. "Like I said: they're staring. Maybe if you were dissembled into little packages or something, they wouldn't be staring and I'd be able to carry out a full sleuth mission uninterrupted."

"The other students aren't staring at me, Willa." The blunt words were just so Rome.

He never wasted his breath, and he didn't particularly like to chase me down the tangents I often entertained. For a long time, I had considered myself a burden to him and his brothers, but we'd reached a turning point recently, after he declared that he wanted to keep the soul-link. I was pretty sure that we were friends now.

Large hands wrapped around me as he pulled me close to his chest. "What I actually said was that you are ours. I've claimed ownership of you, Willa Knight."

I wanted to shove against him. Maybe kick him in the shins ... but I knew that either option would be both futile and painful. Instead, I started calling him every curse I could think of, which had his huge chest shaking with laughter in no time.

Far more gently than I would have expected, he pushed me back to arm's length. "We're yours also, you know that. This isn't a one-way thing."

Oh. My. Gods. He had never said anything like that before. That was almost ... sweet.

I let out a shriek as he tossed me over his shoulder and took off. "Don't get used to it. I have a limited supply of *that*, and I just used up all of it to get you to stop looking at me like you want to stick a fork in my eye."

"Put me down, you giant pain in my ass!"

So much for stealth-mode. My shrieking alone was enough to draw the eye of every single dweller in the kitchen area we had just entered. Rome ducked his head so that both of us weren't clobbered by the large rack of cast iron pans hanging from the ceiling, before he continued to deftly manoeuvre through the room. We broke out into a garden outside, and passed through it, into another one.

"I know where your dweller-Emmy is." His words penetrated through my annoyance, and mild panic.

"It's Emmanuelle now," I said, all snooty like.

"I don't care," he replied smoothly. Which didn't surprise me at all.

The Abcurses weren't big on giving a crap about dwellers or sols. Which made sense, since they were gods.

Without my link to them, I would die. If I died, I would *maybe* become a Beta god of Chaos, which would give the current *main* god of Chaos a lot of power—power that he would most likely use to take over Topia, the world of the gods; and Minatsol, the land of mortals.

"It'd just be better all-round if I didn't die." I must have muttered the last part out loud without realising it, because Rome ground to a halt and lowered me down to my feet.

"No dying," he growled.

I was about to quip something back at him, but it died off when I finally noticed where we were.

"This is where Emmanuelle is?" I took a step closer, the freaky eyes of the god-statues most definitely following me.

Rome shrugged, before he pointed across to a sol hurrying toward the Sacred Sands arena. "I'm sure enough that I would bet that guy's life on it."

I followed the sol for a beat, before turning back to Rome. "So you have no idea, and you aren't sure at all."

He tilted his head to the side and hit me with that smile again. The one which should have been banned anywhere near a Chaos sol, or Chaos dweller ... or whatever I was now. The point was, if he didn't stop looking at me like that, Chaos was going to start happening. That was the only explanation for the tight pressure suddenly assaulting my chest.

Just when I was sure I couldn't take another moment of it, Rome gently shoved me along the path, and we were walking beneath the statues of the gods outside the temple. Just like the last time, I could feel prickling across the back of my neck, and I had the same sensation of being watched. One of the statues was ... *paying attention*. My first guess would have been Rau, the Chaos god, but he wasn't the only god who was now paying attention. It could have been Abil, the Trickery god—and the father to my Abcurses—or even Staviti. Sure, Staviti was the great Creator and probably had a really busy life making new flowers and other things, but for some reason I felt like he might have been very interested in all of this new stuff going on between both of the worlds.

Cyrus. His name brushed across my mind, and with a heavy shove, I locked it back down again. The Neutral God ... was an enigma, and I didn't have time for one of those.

Rome led me along the same path we had taken to the secret dweller meeting last time, and we were both silent as we descended the stairs. This time I managed to stay on my feet, which was a bonus. Low voices filtered through to me the moment I landed on the lower level, stepping out into the darkness.

"How did you know she was here?" I murmured, knowing his god-hearing would pick it up.

His voice was as low as mine, his breath brushing across my cheek as he leaned down. "We've been keeping an eye on her for you, she's been seen around the temple a few times."

My heart warmed at those words, because I knew how much they would have hated 'lowering' themselves to spying on a dweller.

He then straightened, and his hand wrapped around mine, lacing our fingers together as he started leading me. Ever since I had been hit with the curse from Rau, my senses had become heightened, and when Aros and Coen had stirred the Chaos into exploding out of me, my senses had improved even more. This meant that I could see where we were going just fine, but there was really no need to tell Rome that. Most probably he held my hand so that *he* wouldn't trip and fall over. I was the one doing the guiding, so I needed to keep holding his hand just in case he had any accidents.

Once I had finished reasoning that out in my head, I felt much better about tightening my grip and clinging to his strength.

I wasn't sure what I was expecting, but judging by the direction of the voices, whoever was down here was back in the same secret meeting place that everyone seemed to use. Rome and I squeezed in behind the shelves that we had used to spy on the previous secret dweller meeting; he was forced to contort himself into a painful-looking shape to fit inside, but he managed it. Standing on my tiptoes, I found a nice little gap to peek through, and if Rome hadn't managed to slip his free hand over my mouth, the gasp which I released when I saw the scene would have definitely blown our cover.

It was Emmy. And Fred. And Scrawny Dweller Number Two. Plus Slimy Dweller Number Three.

Emmy plus three guys? What the hell was happening? What were the worlds coming to?

Okay, so they weren't having four-way sex or anything, and I was in no way curious about how she was going to manage sex with three guys at all. I mean, why would I need to know that?

My eyes strayed to Rome and my heart began to perform a complicated pattern of stopping and starting. He was so huge he was like three guys all on his own. Which made sense, since you don't get to be the god of strength at a hundred pounds soaking wet. Which was definitely all that Scrawny Dweller Number Two was.

He was barely as tall as *Emmanuelle*—my best friend and sister who needed a serious lesson in how to pick a rebound guy. Or guys. Not one of her companions could hold a candle to Atti, which, come to think about it, was probably the reason she chose them.

Another sliver of my heart broke for her. I'd been losing slivers at a pretty frequent rate as I watched her grieve over the past moon-cycle—or *not* grieve, which was even worse.

She was shedding pieces of herself in her quest to run from the pain, and I needed all the pieces of Emmy. I needed her to be whole and bossy and smart. We were a team and I would not let her take herself out of the game like this.

"Didn't think the dweller had it in her." Rome whispered this in my ear and I found myself pressing closer to him, soaking up his warmth and the way our soul-link purred like a kitten at the contact. "Do you know who those three sols are?"

I was immediately paying attention—well, most of me, bar that small part still pressing against Rome. "Who?" I breathed.

"You've got the sons of three very powerful sols right there. Their fathers are all competing for the position of Vice Chancellor here at Blesswood, while the current Vice Chancellor takes over the role of Chancellor."

Sols? Those creepy slimeballs were sols? I should have known. Only a sol would have a name like *Fred*.

Rome's words reminded me that our school was in the midst of a change. The fight where Emmy had lost her love was the same fight that had seen the end of the last Chancellor of Blesswood. Afterwards, there had been pure chaos—much to Rau's delight, I was sure.

In the end, Yael had used his Persuasion to calm the fighting down, but now there was a significant race to bring new leadership to the top academy in Minatsol, which of course meant that every sol with an ounce of power was crawling out of their rat hole, and had entered their name into the race.

They all wanted a chance. They all thought that running Blesswood would increase their own chances of becoming a god when they died. Or grooming future gods and thereby receiving power for their family in that way.

"When do they make the final decision?" My voice got a little loud, and I thought I saw Emmy pause, but then she just went back to quietly chatting with one of the trio. The other two were pressed very close to her. Actually, all four were standing in a tight circle, and too many parts of their bodies were touching. A lot of touching.

Before Rome could answer, I let out a great huff, and pushed my way free from the bookshelves.

This crap with Emmy had gone on long enough.

CHAPTER TWO

"AND that would be my sister, Willa," Emmy announced, her voice suddenly raised enough to carry all the way over to me. I froze, but she kept talking. "You three know Willa, I'm assuming?"

"Everyone knows that ... girl," one of the guys replied, glancing over Emmy's shoulder to lock his eyes on me.

The fact that he was talking about me with even a small amount of disdain meant that Rome hadn't been able to un-wedge himself enough to follow me—or else he was deliberately not following me, which actually made more sense. If I wasn't forced to live inside myself and back up my own decisions I probably wouldn't follow me either.

"Okay, first," I announced, holding up my hand and raising a finger into the air, "Yes, I am a girl. You don't need to sound unsure about the fact." I delivered that to the guy who had spoken, before fixing my eyes to the back of Emmy's head. She still hadn't even turned around. I was ignoring the other two guys completely. "And second, how the hell did you know it was me?"

"You're loud," the guy replied, speaking for Emmy.

I flicked my eyes back to him, and then summoned my best glare. He was tall, skinny, and wearing wire-framed glasses that appeared too narrow for his eyes. His shoulders were slightly stooped, but he had a look of quiet capability about him. It annoyed me.

"She also has a somewhat distinctive blunder—it's not quite a walk, but it does seem to propel her forward," another of the guys added.

I cut my glare to him and found him just as unimpressive as the first. He was the same height, but a little stockier, with shockingly blonde hair and a thoughtful frown. The third guy remained quiet, a little darker in appearance, with sooty hair and dusky skin. I didn't need to examine him, because I knew exactly who he was. That was *Fred*, the idiot who apparently wasn't an idiot at all, because his father had a chance at becoming the next Vice-Chancellor.

And he was a sol.

And Emmy was still brushing arms with him.

"That's enough," Emmy said quietly, just as Fred opened his mouth to say something—probably to add an insult to those I had already received. She turned around, then, and I could see that her expression was tired, her shoulders dropping forward. "I guess we're done here for the sun-cycle. Let's go, Willa."

She didn't wait for any of the guys to say anything, and they didn't seem inclined to speak of their own accord, so I planted my feet against the ground and resisted when Emmy reached me and attempted to drag me away.

I knew something was going on, and I knew that it was something I wouldn't approve of. Considering I broke more rules than even the Abcurse brothers—and that was not a feat to be underestimated—I was assuming that Emmy was hiding something very *big*, and very *bad*. The only problem was, I had no idea how to force it out of her. She was in a fragile state. I didn't want to push her away on top of everything else.

"Introduce me to your friends," I ground out, attempting to sound polite as I continued to stick my feet to the ground.

Emmy was staring too hard at the side of my face, apparently trying to convey some kind of secret message. She really needed to stop trying to do that. I sucked at secret messages.

"Yes," Fred called out, taking a few steps toward us. "Why don't you introduce us, Emmanuelle?"

"Emmy," I quickly snapped, before I could stop myself. "Her name is—"

"Willa," Emmy cut across me, making my head spin a little bit with all the names being thrown about the room. "As I said before," I realised that she wasn't talking to me, when she turned to the others, "this is Willa, my sister."

"That's only half an introduction," Fred replied, clicking his tongue in admonishment.

I fought off the urge to break out of Emmy's grip and slap him clean across the face.

"Willa …" Emmy continued obediently, taking a calming breath that had me at least partly convinced that she was fighting the same violent urge as me. "Willa ... this is Frederique, Bradford, and Morgan. Their fathers will be competing against a panel of high-ranking Minateur guards in a few sun-cycles, in Dvadel."

"Competing for what?" I asked, my eyes still locked onto Fred.

I knew exactly what they were competing for, but my tone of voice managed to turn it into some sort of scathing remark. I shouldn't have been pushing them. Of all the sols in Blesswood, these would have been the worst ones to pick a fight with, but they were messing around with my Emmy, and all the secrecy was making my skin crawl.

"Competing over who will get to be in charge of unruly little dweller sluts like *you*, actually," Fred replied, a stony smile suddenly etched onto his face.

There was a crash in the storage room that sounded suspiciously like one of the shelves being slammed up against a wall, and I knew that Rome was a moment away from breaking free and having a *crusher* moment with Fred, so I only smiled in response and hurried toward the exit of the room. I could feel Emmy following behind me, so I didn't bother looking back.

"I almost wish you'd stayed and let whichever Abcurse is hiding around here somewhere start breaking faces," Emmy muttered beneath her breath, as soon as we were in the hallway.

"They killed the Chancellor. They had a single rule: if they killed one more person in Minatsol, they'd have their sentence extended—and being the idiots that they are, that's exactly what they did. So they're in enough trouble as it is. I don't want to add to it by upping the body count."

"Makes sense."

"So I take it you're not actually attempting to manoeuvre into sexual positions with those three dicks?" I questioned as casually as I could, while I pulled open the storage door.

Rome was halfway through the wall, shelves bent and pushed aside all around him. He'd basically built himself a twisted, metal cage, and was now stuck in the mess he'd made, breathing through his frustration.

"Manoeuvre into sexual positions?" she asked, cocking her head at Rome. "Is that what you guys do? Because I don't think this one is very good at the manoeuvring part."

I blinked, turning away from the image of Rome pulling himself back through the wall and leaping over a fallen shelf to reach the doorway we stood inside of.

"I can't believe you just insulted Two while he's in angry crusher mode. Are you crazy?"

I wasn't being serious, obviously, because Rome couldn't have cared less what Emmy had said. His face was red and his breathing was heavy for another reason, and I could tell that he was just about to push past me and take the more direct approach into the secret meeting room, so I quickly stepped right into his path, taking up the whole doorway.

"Willa ..." he started to warn, but it was Emmy who cut across him.

"Why don't we take this somewhere else?" She seemed to be requesting, instead of demanding, which meant that she had at least *some* sense of self-preservation still inside her. "These halls are about to fill up with dwellers collecting their supplies for the sun-cycle and you probably don't want the whole academy talking about how you mushed three really important sols into a stone wall during peace-talk time."

She had a really good point, and Rome seemed to think so too, because he didn't attempt to walk through me or toss me over his shoulder. He only stared at me, taking deep breaths until the redness subsided from his face.

"We need to leave," he eventually spat. "Now. Before I change my mind."

That was enough for me. I quickly grabbed his hand, pulling him back toward the way we had entered the temple. Emmy attempted to trail along behind us, but it was making me too nervous that I would lose track of her, so I forced her to walk in front of us instead. Getting Rome away from the damage he would cause if we left him alone down there was my main priority, but it didn't mean that I had given up on getting answers out of Emmy. As soon as we were clear of danger, I was going to find out everything that she had been hiding from me, even if I had to use Rome to squeeze it out of her.

What I didn't count on was the rush of people that collided with us as soon as we passed back into the main halls of the academy. It was finally lunch time, and everyone was heading toward the dining hall. It shouldn't have surprised me that my new rule-breaker of a sister would use the crowd to slip away from me, but it still shocked me enough that I came to a standstill, people battering at me from each side until Rome planted himself behind me, forming a wall.

"What is it?" he asked. "Where did the dweller-Emmy go?"

"She gave me the slip." My voice sounded hollow, disbelieving. "Again."

He made a grunting sound, and it felt as if more of the anger bled out of him. It seemed that he was almost fully over the need to kill the three sols, which was both a relief and a disappointment. A few less dick-sols—as they would be henceforth referred to—would do our worlds some good.

What the hell is Emmy up to? Rome's anger was dissipating, just in time for mine to rear its head again.

"I'm probably almost definitely going to kill my sister when I get my hands on her again," I snarled, as we finally made our way into the dining hall.

The crowds were thinning a little, and I barely noticed the looks shooting our way. At this time, the dwellers and sols were going about their normal routines: the dwellers were serving, and the sols were … being blessed. There was an air of change about the place: a dash more attitude from those forced to serve.

A few dwellers exited the kitchen, and I recognised a bushy head of hair. *Evie.* Our eyes locked as if she'd heard my thoughts, and I tensed, wondering how she would react. I expected a sneer, because the dwellers still thought I was a traitor; instead, she gave me a half-smile and a slight nod, before she turned to deliver her tray to a nearby table.

That was weird. Even weirder than normal, which was definitely saying something since Evie was one of the instigators of the dweller uprising. Evie and Emmy were both instigators, along with Atti. And now Evie and Emmy were both acting strange.

Emmy ... my slippery, sneaky sister.

Rome kept one hand firmly planted on my shoulder, weaving me through the tables. I should have made him hold on to Emmy like this. No one was slipping out from under that firm grip.

"She'll tell you when she's ready." He seemed to be reading my thoughts again. "Knowing what I do about her—meaning the little I have bothered to learn—your Emmy-dweller isn't completely reckless. There's a reason to her weirdness."

A cold fear clenched inside my chest, and breathing became painful for a few beats. "She lost her ... guy. Her love-partner-person." I got choked up, swallowing hard and continuing. "Lost is a stupid way to put it. It's not like Atti is just wandering around with an upside-down map asking for directions. He isn't really lost ... he's gone. He's dead and now lives in Topia as a server named Judy. Emmy isn't acting rationally, and I can't wait for her to be ready to tell me!"

Rome let out an exaggerated breath, which I pretended not to hear, because I already knew that I was being a pain in the ass.

"He's not a server in Topia," Rome explained patiently. "We already checked for you."

I wanted to believe him, but I knew they would lie to me to protect my feelings. Especially since there was nothing they could do even if Atti-Judy had been taken to Topia as a server. We were at the table now, and some of the pain in my body lessened as four sets of eyes locked onto me.

"What's going on?" Siret leaned forward in his chair.

The deep, midnight purple of his shirt was fitted across his broad chest, and even though I was upset, I couldn't help but stare at him as I answered.

"Emmy is hiding something. We just found her in a clandestine meeting with three sols—and not just *any* sols," I continued on in a rush. "Sols whose fathers are in the running to be the next Vice-Chancellor of Blesswood. This can't be a coincidence."

Not a single expression at the table changed; the politics of Minatsol registered at about a minus five on their give-a-shit-meter.

"Why would a dweller be secretly meeting with sols!" I almost shrieked, sick of no one taking me seriously.

Coen leaned back in his chair, his arms stretched behind his head as he regarded me solemnly. "If you want us to track her down, I can make sure she doesn't move until she tells you everything."

I was almost desperate enough to take him up on his offer, but I felt there was less of a chance that she would openly talk with the Abcurses around. Which meant that I needed to get her alone.

I'd keep that as plan B. "I might eventually take you up on that, but not yet."

He shrugged, his lips tilting up lazily as he continued to stare at me. I found myself fighting the urge to crawl across the table and launch myself at him. Ever since Coen and Aros had unlocked my Beta side, I couldn't stop thinking about the way they'd touched me and the way my power had exploded.

It was driving me crazy.

Between those thoughts and the Emmy stresses, I was shocked that they hadn't carted me off to a healer for a mental evaluation.

Yael snorted from my right side. "I'm sure that your mother had something like that tested many life-cycles ago."

No doubt I should be offended by that, but instead I was blindsided by a mental image of my mum. Her blonde curls haywire, which they always were after a big night out. Washed-out blue eyes intersected with red veins. Always bloodshot. Most of the time she was passed out, no time to care or notice enough of my behaviour to worry about whether I was crazy or not. Hell, half the time she acted even worse than me.

I think I surprised all of us when I answered quite seriously. "My mother wasn't concerned with anything but herself and alcohol. I frustrated her, but I was also easily shoved aside. If it wasn't for Emmy … it would have been a lonely existence."

The silence felt a little heavy but not uncomfortable. Like we were each processing those words, and then as conclusions were reached, questions were asked.

Aros was first. He leaned forward, a lock of that golden hair falling across his forehead. "What about your father? You never speak of him."

A derisive chuckle built in my chest as I snorted out, "Can't speak about someone you've never met. Either I was a gift from the gods and just appeared on mum's doorstep, or she got knocked up by a passing dweller she met at Cyan's Tavern."

And since I looked exactly like her, and we all knew how the gods felt about me, there was really only one of those options that we could consider plausible.

"You never asked her?" Rome pushed further, and a jolt of frustration had my voice clipped as I answered.

"Of course I asked her. What kid wouldn't want to know if there was a responsible parent out there? One who wasn't going to vomit in their only pair of shoes?" Always look before putting shoes on. It was solid advice. "She just told me that I didn't have a father, and I should focus on the future, not the past."

Focus on the future, Willa, the past is of no use to anyone. She used to say that to me all the time. Then she would get blind drunk and not have to focus on either.

A part of me was used to it, but I also couldn't think too long or hard about her, because I didn't want to be an angry bitter dweller. It wasn't worth it. It changed nothing.

"Do we have anything happy to discuss?" I asked with a sigh, leaning forward and resting my chin on my arms.

The Abcurses somehow exchanged a single glance between the five of them, and I found myself sitting back up, unease rocketing through me. I didn't like that look. It wasn't a happy look. They were totally not bringing me any happy.

"What?" I finally burst out, my eyes running across their faces. "Don't tell me you're having another sex talk with me?"

A sol nearby gave a gasping cough and I realised how loud I was. *Whoops.* Maybe this wasn't the best place for this sort of discussion, but the guys didn't seem upset. If anything they now looked amused, which I preferred to that serious look from before—a look which unfortunately returned as all five of them leaned in. Siret spoke just loud enough for me to hear.

"Staviti has called us to Topia. We might have to face a trial."

I swallowed roughly. "Because of the Chancellor? They found out you killed him?"

A single nod from each of them confirmed my fears.

"When do we go?" I tried to keep the worry from my voice, but as usual, I failed miserably.

"In four sun-cycles we need to cross into Topia," Yael answered. "We'll have an informal meeting with Staviti, and then he decides if it goes to trial." He didn't seem worried, his words so relaxed and calm.

Meanwhile, I was about to pee myself because I had a very bad feeling about this.

"It'll be fine, Soldier." Siret wrapped an arm around me, pulling me closer. "Staviti is used to us, we might have our time on Minatsol extended, but I doubt anything else will happen."

Usually I would have sunk into his heat, into the comfort of touch, the soul-link no longer strained, but the worry just wouldn't leave.

"What will Staviti say when you bring me along? Does he know you're linked to a dweller? Does he know I might be a Chaos Beta? Is it a good idea to clue him into those things?"

Coen and Rome moved closer together, their broad shoulders blocking out the entire room.

Coen was the one who answered. "You can't come with us, Willa. For those very reasons, and a few more. Staviti won't kill you, but he could make your life very difficult. And we won't let that happen."

I knew my brow was furrowed, I could feel my forehead wrinkling right up as I processed those words. "The soul-link will kill me if we're that far apart."

Which worried me even less than the fact that every time the six of us were split up, something really terrible happened. Like Cyrus ... *wait a freaking click!*

"You guys better not be thinking about transferring the soul-link to Cyrus again. Because I would rather take my chances with Staviti and Rau."

Rome's low growl rumbled through the table to me and I was pretty sure the wood actually vibrated.

Aros spoke up when it didn't seem as if Rome was going to do more than curse and growl. "We won't be transferring the link to anyone. Yael had an idea a while ago, and we finally managed to find the right god to help out. There is a way to temporarily extend our link—you'll be able to be quite a distance from us and not suffer. It would only be temporary, of course. Eventually Rau's curse would eat through the energy, but it would last long enough for us to get through this meeting, and even long enough for the trial, should it come to that."

I was slumping into my chair again when dwellers appeared at our table. They carried laden trays of food, all of which were deposited down in front of us. The guys had to move back to make room for the many selections. For once I really didn't care about the cheesy toast, or the little swimmer puffs.

Before I could stop my hands, they were reaching out and scooping a bunch of both foods onto my plate. Okay, I might have cared a little. Really though, it is important to keep your energy up when you need to argue with five hulking gods.

"You don't have to argue with us," Rome said, reaching for a bowl of pasta. "We will do what is necessary to keep you safe."

"Who keeps you safe? I should be there!" I argued back, before shoving a bite of crunchy bread into my mouth.

Stupid gods and their stupid rules.

"Willa-toy," Yael's voice was surprisingly gentle, for him, and I was astonished enough that the bread halted halfway to my mouth as I focused on him and his next words. "We'll be fine. Staviti would never piss off Abil by trying anything underhanded. He likes to keep the Originals happy."

Siret then brushed his hand across my hair, ruffling it slightly, and I turned to him. "We'll be back before you know it."

My eyes narrowed on him, then with a grunt, I resumed eating. This conversation was definitely not over. I had four sun-cycles to figure out what was going on with Emmy, and to convince the guys that it was much safer for me in Topia with them. Which meant that it was time for another scheme, only this time I wouldn't have Siret to help me. This time I was on my own.

CHAPTER THREE

"So how exactly is this plan going to work? How can we hold off the pain from the soul link?" I asked, toying with the bread still in my hand. "I think Rau did it once before, but it didn't last long. Only long enough to get me to Topia."

Aros pushed back his chair, tugging a timepiece from his pocket and checking it, before settling his eyes on my face. "We have about thirty clicks before classes start up again. Grab some more of that bread—since it's the only damn thing you eat anyway—and we'll go for a walk. This isn't the place for these conversations."

I glanced around at the sols that stared and the dwellers that skirted past him, giving him and the rest of the Abcurse table a wide berth. It was easy to think that they were invincible—that they couldn't be held accountable for anything in Minatsol because they weren't *from* Minatsol, they were from Topia. Unfortunately, that wasn't true. People still had ears, and dwellers *especially* still liked to gossip. I was sure that the gods would have spies within the halls, watching every movement the Abcurses made. They clearly didn't care that they were being watched, but there was always a line. Apparently, discussing the secrets of the gods out in the open was one of those lines.

"Okay." I nodded, dropping a few slices of the cheesy bread into a napkin and wrapping them up.

I jumped out of my seat, waiting to see who would follow us. When none of the other guys stood, I found my eyebrows inching up in surprise. It wasn't like them to let me have alone time with the Seduction god. Usually, it caused me to misbehave.

There had to be something else going on.

"Well ... bye, then," I said awkwardly, looking around the table.

"See you in class." Siret winked at me, before shooting a look to Aros, who ignored it.

"See you, Willa-toy." Yael only glanced up momentarily before returning to his food.

"Don't be late for class," Rome grunted.

I looked to Coen, and he grinned back, his eyes flicking to Aros the same way Siret's had. I had no idea what that was supposed to mean, so I only shrugged and moved to follow Aros out of the hall. Once we were clear of the doors, I pulled out one of the cheesy bread slices and began to eat, strolling quietly by his side until we were out of the building altogether and walking toward one of the gardens.

"Are you bringing me out here to murder me?" I asked casually, finishing off one slice and moving onto the next.

Aros snorted. "Why would I take you to a rose garden in the middle of the sun-cycle to kill you? Give me a little credit. I'd do it in the dark at *least*, and at *most*, I'd pick a more interesting location. Always do a job properly, even if it's murder."

I followed him to a bench and plonked myself down, taking more care not to drop the cheesy bread than I took to make sure I plonked myself onto the actual *seat*. Fortunately, Aros was paying attention, and he caught my arm right before I missed the bench completely, moved me a few inches to the right, and then released me. I resumed plonking, and then resumed eating, all without blinking an eye. I was getting used to our routine of me almost making a fool of myself and of them only just catching me in time.

"Thanks," I muttered. "But I still think this is weird. I'm only ever alone in the garden with you guys when you're giving me mind-shielding lessons, and I thought we'd given up on those."

"You were pretty useless at them," Aros agreed, stretching his legs out and crossing them at the ankle, his posture turned to the side as he watched me devour the final slice of cheesy bread.

"Oh, hey," I frowned, crumpling up the napkin, "with encouragement like that, it's a wonder I didn't succeed sooner."

"I'm about as good at coddling as you are at doing what you're told, sweetheart."

I rolled my eyes, stuffing the napkin into the pocket of the pants that had become my staple daytime wear.

They were some kind of heavy linen blend that moulded perfectly to my skin, since Siret had been the one to create them. There were leather patches at the knee, and hips—because apparently I needed the extra protection. My shirt was simple: a deep red that I knew now to be the colour of Chaos. Siret had started turning some of my clothes red, and I kind of liked the colour, so I didn't say anything about the sudden change.

"Are you going to tell me why we're here?" I prompted. "Because it isn't to talk about how to escape the pain of the soul-link. I know we could have done that at the table—or if not the table, back in the rooms."

"I needed to talk to you, Willa." Aros was suddenly serious, his golden eyes tracking over my face, his hands resting limply in his lap, all of his attention on my reaction.

It was unnerving.

"What about?" I started to fidget, pulling the napkin back out of my pocket and channelling all of my focus into tearing it into very even strips. I paused halfway through my task, after Aros remained silent in answer to my question, and my head snapped up again. "This *is* another sex talk. Oh my gods. You five are ridiculous and I'm going to punch every single—"

"It's not a sex talk." He chuckled, but it sounded strained.

"You're lying!" I tossed the half-shredded napkin at him and buried my face in my hands. "How many times does this need to happen?"

His laugh was warmer this time, and he captured my wrists, pulling my hands away from my face. "It's not like that, okay? They just wanted me to … check in with you. After what happened with me and Coen. The way we unlocked your Chaos …"

I stilled, my body going into temporary shock. The last thing I needed was to be reminded of that whole incident in the middle of the sun-cycle, out in the open, where I couldn't do anything about it.

"Wait just a freaking click," I demanded, pulling my wrists free and jumping to my feet so that I could look down on him—a move which worked on dwellers and sols, but apparently not Aros. He was still level with me, even with me standing and him sitting.

"It's not what you think!" he held up his hands, attempting to pacify me.

I hadn't actually formed any thoughts about why we were in the garden; I'd jumped into action before the thought had a chance to solidify in my mind. Maybe this was my chance to get some more information.

"Oh, really?" I planted my hands against his chest and quickly stepped either side of his legs before he could stop me. I pulled my legs together, trapping his thighs between mine, and quickly pushed my hands along his shoulders, linking my fingers together behind his neck so that he wouldn't be able to feel them shaking. "You didn't bring me here to have this talk so that we wouldn't have to have it back in the room? Where I'd do something … like this?"

The gold in his eyes was flashing to dark bronze, and his hands had moved to the bench, curling around the edges, his knuckles turning white. He wasn't allowed to touch me. That was interesting. The others must have made him promise.

"Please don't push this right now, Willa. I know you're not a damn baby. I know you don't need this talk. The others fucking insisted."

"They think you and Coen … tricked me into it?" I asked, not budging in my stance, though my eyes were now narrowed on his in suspicion.

He smiled, but the tension was back in his expression, and rapidly spreading to the rest of his body.

"They didn't use that word," he answered, and the hook in the corner of his mouth deepened, his teeth flashing at me. "Pushed, maybe. We *did* push you."

"You did," I echoed, getting a little lost in his eyes.

His hands moved from the bench then, like he couldn't resist any longer. They slipped around my back, up over the curve of my spine and to my shoulders. He rested them there, his thumbs slipping down over my collarbones.

"Did you want it, Willa?"

"Want it," I repeated.

Maybe he was hypnotising me, because all I could seem to do was repeat key words back to him. Push. Want. Push. Want. They were on repeat inside my head.

Push. "Yes." I nodded. *Want.*

His fingers tightened in their grip, and he drew me closer, making a sound in the back of his throat.

"Well, now that we've sorted that out," a voice announced from behind me, "why don't we get to class?"

I attempted to pull away from Aros, but his hands tightened further, his expression going tight.

"What the hell are you doing here, Persuasion?" he growled, his eyes never leaving mine.

"We waited. You didn't bring her back. They sent me out," Yael replied. He sounded casual, but I knew better.

Yael *always* sounded casual, until the moment he decided to demand something. That moment would be as soon as Aros walked away. Which put me in a very awkward position. It put me in a position that made me want to fling Chaos at the both of them and run in the other direction.

So that's exactly what I did.

I could feel my newly unlocked energy swirling aimlessly inside of me, and it was easy to draw on with my emotions already riled from Aros—but I had no idea where to aim it or *how* to aim it, and I also had no idea how it would manifest. My only choice was to hope for the best as I closed my eyes, broke quickly out of Aros's grip, and muttered, "Chaos—"

Aros was up from the bench and before me in a fraction of a click, his hand wrapping around my mouth. He was too late. All around us, people were screaming.

"What the hell did you do?" he asked, his eyes wide.

I tried to reply, but only a muffled sound came out, because he was still trying to silence me. I tugged on his arm until he reluctantly drew it away, and then opened my mouth to reply—until another sound distracted me.

Laughter. *Yael was losing it*.

I glanced over Aros's shoulder, and stillness stole through me. Yael was standing there with his book bag held over his midsection, bent over with deep, gasping laughter. He was also completely naked. I flicked my eyes back to Aros, and we both looked down at the same time.

"GODS!" I shouted, as he casually stepped back, grabbed his book bag, and covered himself.

He looked torn between laughter and shock, but I wasn't finding *anything* about the current situation funny. I barely had the foresight to clutch at myself and make sure I was still clothed—which surprisingly, I was—before I was left to stand there numbly, staring at Aros's book bag.

I had seen it all.

It was burned into my mind.

Him covering it wasn't doing anything to combat the image that had just become tattooed on the inside of my brain.

Aros was laughing right alongside Yael, now, and my stunned eyes were distracted from them by the sight of nude-coloured streaks flying past the garden. Sols.

Dwellers. *Teachers*. Oh my gods … I had made everyone naked with my Chaos.

Everyone except myself.

Well that was new.

I wanted to run out of the garden and see the spectacle, but Yael went out first, took a single look, and declared, "No. Not happening."

He and Aros made me sit on the bench between them until everyone was inside, and by the time we made it back into the academy, there was already an announcement echoing through the halls that classes would be cancelled for the rest of the sun-cycle while they 'investigated' the incident. Based on my past records, I would have thought it obvious that I was the one behind Operation Bare Ass. It was pretty much what I was known for—but nobody came looking for me.

As for the Abcurses, they were so distracted by my latest bout of Chaos that they didn't even question me when I announced that I needed to find Emmy—Siret simply told the others that he would go with me, and then he waited above the dweller-dungeons while I went in.

The dweller quarters were surprisingly full by the time I got to Emmy's room. It seemed that the sols weren't the only people in Blesswood relieved of their tasks for the sun-cycle; the entire school—including the dwellers—had been given the afternoon off. Maybe dweller-sol relations were improving already … or maybe the sols were too embarrassed to have their blessed genitals on show for all the dwellers.

When I finally tracked down Emmy and told her what had happened, she didn't even seem bothered by the fact that I had caused her to lose her clothes along with the rest of the academy.

"How did you do it?" she asked, nothing more than curious.

I was beginning to wonder if I had rubbed off on her over the life-cycles. Nudity wasn't a big deal to me, not dweller-nudity or sol-nudity. Maybe the Aros nudity that I had caught a glimpse of … that was a very, *very* big … *Ugh!*

Trying to supress the image was more difficult than I had expected, but I somehow managed to focus back on my best friend. A best friend whose eyes were so washed-out in colour they seemed to be reflecting the crappiness of her dweller room right back at me. I noticed how dark the circles were beneath them, and all of my worry for her piled back in again.

"I have no idea," I finally said. "This Chaos power is random and dangerous. I just lost control of it."

That was mostly a lie. I had deliberately intended to Chaos the shit out of Aros and Yael so that they would stop fighting—but I was honest about the control thing, at least.

I sat down on the bed beside her, leaning my shoulder and shifting around a bit to try and get comfortable, before finally giving up with a huff. My fingers were brushing rhythmically at the rough covers of her nicely-made bed when the next words burst out of me.

"It's growing stronger." It was a rushed whisper, but I was relieved to be able to express my fears to someone.

I loved the Abcurses—they fit with me as though we had all been meant to find each other and keep each other, and I knew that they would never judge me. But they were also gods—*born gods* at that—and they didn't understand the frailties and vulnerabilities of sols and dwellers. Which meant that I wasn't going to get any sage advice, sympathy, or chocolate. Three things that Emmy was very good at … minus the chocolate, which was a delicacy we had never really been able to afford as dirt-dwellers. But if we *had* been able to afford it, Emmy would have been great at it. Hell, even *I* would have been great at it. I would have excelled at it. I would have specialised in it. I would have gone on to make a name for myself. I would have been an upstanding and outstanding pioneer in the field of Chocolate. I would have started a dynasty.

I would have changed the world.

I hadn't even realised that my head was dropping until I was suddenly staring at her hand now on top of mine. She was patting me.

"Will," she murmured sympathetically. "I can't even imagine what you are going through right now. This power has come out of nowhere and you don't have anyone to teach you how to use it properly."

My head shot up then, and I almost kicked myself when I realised that I had reached out and piled my problems onto the one person who needed me more than I needed anything else. I opened my mouth, ready to apologise, to tell her that I shouldn't have given her all of my problems on top of the problems she already had, but she cut me off before I could voice the words.

"The only being who might be able to clue you in on turning from dweller to sol, or whatever you are now, is the Creator. And I wouldn't think it wise to present yourself to him carrying a Beta Chaos power."

Emmy was so smart. She deduced things that I only knew because I was living in this world and had the knowledge of five god-brothers. She was also clearly using my lesser problem to distract me from bringing up Atti again—which, admittedly, was exactly what I wanted to do.

"Rau is going to use me, Em," I sighed, falling back against the wall again. If Emmy wanted to talk about Chaos, I'd talk about Chaos. "He's going to take this power and try and overthrow everything, and I have no damn idea how to stop him because I can't even stop myself from tripping over my own feet. Or being naked. Or making the entire school naked."

Emmy let out a bark of laughter, loud and harsh. "Willa Knight, I did not just hear you say that. You have more control and strength then any dweller or sol I know. You were born of Chaos. You've always controlled it, right from the sun-cycle you stumbled into this world—your mum wouldn't stop telling that story of how she birthed you and you almost came out backwards. I never used to think it was true, but now I'm convinced."

I laughed along with her, but my mind was starting to spin. *Born of Chaos.* It was an odd way to phrase it, but I guess in a way she was right. Unknown father. Absent, mess of a mother. My life had never been calm, it had always been chaos. Emmy had joined that chaos because her perfectly normal life had been pulled apart by death, but she was not *born* of chaos like me—for her, it was simply a by-product of being close to me.

Neither of us spoke again for some time, each of us lost in our own thoughts, each of us battling our own demons. It wasn't until she let out a small sigh that the spell was broken, and I found myself reaching out to the side and snagging her around the shoulders, pulling her to me. She resisted for a bit, but I wouldn't let her escape this time. I just held on tight, wrapping both of my arms around her, and hugged her as tightly as I could without crushing her ribs.

She was stiff, unresponsive, and it had almost reached the point of awkward—where I was about to chalk this up to another failure, and hope to try again later—when a much heavier sigh escaped from her. It whooshed past my ear, blowing my curls back, and then she collapsed against me. She felt so frail in my arms, her thin frame shaking; the intensity of it rattled me. Her chest was heaving with sobs, her breath wheezing in and out as she tried to draw in air and cry at the same time. It was like an avalanche trying to fit through a tiny hole in the side of a mountain, there was so much pain rushing from her with no way to easily escape.

The sudden ache in my chest was so intense that I wondered for a moment if I was having a heart attack. Eventually I realised that my own cheeks were wet, and that my arms were trembling almost as much as Emmy's as I tried to wrap myself even tighter around her. I felt like I could put her back together just by holding her—all of the broken pieces and the jagged edges that she had been locking away since she lost Atti.

I didn't know how long we cried for, but eventually the anguished gasps and sobs died off from Emmy, and I started to gently rub her back while whispering nonsensical words of comfort. I told her that we would go back to our village one sun-cycle; that we would explore all over Minatsol, and that I would never let anyone hurt her again. That Atti loved her and would want her to be happy, and that we would all be together again, when the time was right. I had no idea if any of it was true, but they were secret dreams and wishes I held in my own heart, and it felt better to wish them out loud.

She finally fell asleep against me, and I was only slightly disappointed that there had been no revelations about what she was up to with those sols. But we had made progress, and I would have to accept that.

For now.

Untangling myself from Emmy, I tucked her into the bed and spun around to leave the room. I barely managed to cut off my shriek at the shadow there, my feet tangling up as I reached for one of Emmy's shoes and tossed it blindly. Siret lazily batted it away, sending it into the wall with a muted *thud*. All five of the Abcurses were standing beyond the doorway to Emmy's room. All five of them, leaned back against the wall, arms crossed over their chests, expressions sombre.

"How long have you guys been standing there?" I whispered low enough that it might not wake up Emmy. I hadn't heard or noticed them outside. I hadn't felt them in our soul-link, or even felt the twinges of pain from their absence while they *hadn't* been there. "You were here the entire time?"

Siret shook his head, before holding his arms out to me. Without hesitation, I walked into them, and he wrapped me up as tightly as I had wrapped up Emmy. That ache in my chest increased, and I fought against the emotions that wanted to swamp me.

"Your pain …" Siret's low murmur drifted to me, and I remembered how they had told me long ago that they could feel my pain.

Another set of arms replaced Siret's and the burnt sweetness was the only hint I needed to know that it was Aros.

"Felt like your heart was breaking," he grunted softly, before picking me up off my feet and moving us further away from the room. I heard Emmy's door click shut, and then his voice rose again to a normal level. "We don't know if it's the soul-link, or just because we've all spent so much time together, but we can't ignore it …"

He trailed off as I was passed to another Abcurse. Yael's strong arms swept around my lower back and hauled me up higher so that we were practically face to face. I blinked a few times, mesmerised by the strange intensity shining from him. It was the glow of god-energy: I had seen it on some of the beings when we went to Topia, but my boys rarely displayed it. It was possibly because Minatsol drained them of their powers gradually, but it was also possible that they were deliberately toning it down to blend in.

We stared for some time, before he set me on my feet and ushered me across to Coen, who was patiently waiting. It was unlike Yael to have nothing to say, but in all truth, that look had held a lot, if you read between the lines of silence. Possession. Reluctance. Relief.

Frustration.

I waited for Coen to hug me, anticipating his strength and those tendrils of pain that he liked to lace across my skin, and I wasn't disappointed. Just as I was relaxing against his body, Rome joined us. The twins held me. I couldn't properly describe the sensation of being surrounded like that. Heat and strength and power. It thrummed across my skin and I stopped thinking, letting myself enjoy the moment.

Over the top of my head I heard Rome say something, but it took a few clicks before my ears and brain registered what it was.

Tell Staviti to go screw himself.

I stiffened, before pulling back. They parted slightly, letting me see the other three again.

"What are you talking about?" I demanded. "You can't tell that ... *guy* ... to go screw himself! He will ... un-create you—or whatever he does!" The words burst from me in an angry whisper.

Each of them seemed to be staring directly at me with no unease in their expressions whatsoever, but I knew that they had something to tell me. It was obvious. They didn't just go around muttering that the Creator could go screw himself all the time.

A thought occurred to me, then. "You were all close enough to Emmy's room to come as soon as you felt my pain. You were already up there waiting for me with Five? Which means ... you all came to find me?"

Aros lifted a hand in a placating gesture, which only had my worry spiralling out of control further. "You're right," he said, "we were all waiting for you. Staviti has called us for the trial tonight. We just got a message from D.O.D."

My stomach clenched, and probably everyone in the dweller-dungeon could hear the rapid pulse thrumming through me. "Is that normal? For him to make a date and then change his mind just as quickly?"

Why was I the only one who seemed worried or upset by that? Couldn't they feel the ominous clouds on the horizon? It felt like we were teetering on the precipice of something terrible, and as soon as the storm hit, the winds would push us right over the edge.

"It's going to be fine, Willa-toy." Yael's voice was low and rumbly, his Persuasion trickling across my mind, calming the rush of adrenaline that had been trying to kick me into action. "Staviti almost always does this; we were expecting it."

I wanted to growl at them, and I could have fought against Yael. He wasn't hitting me with too much energy, but another part of me needed to take the edge off my worry. It was too much. So I let him continue to influence me.

"We'll have to leave soon, which means that we need to try and see if we can lengthen the link between us now." Rome started ushering me toward the door.

Yael's Persuasion stayed with me all the way back to Coen's room, which was also where my little hidey hole still was. I might have a schedule where I slept in a different room and bed each night, and had my clothes and things scattered between all five, but I always felt like Coen's space was a little bit more mine than the others.

As soon as we were fully inside with the door closed behind us, a figure stepped out from my little area and I couldn't stop the small snarl that escaped from me.

What the hell was he *doing here?*

CHAPTER FOUR

CYRUS had his long white hair pulled back from his face, his pale eyes flicking right over me, as though he refused to acknowledge me at all. The severity of his hair only highlighted the unnatural beauty he possessed. And by beauty, I really meant that he was clearly still a gorgeous, arrogant bastard.

"Is she sleeping in there?" he asked, motioning to the little room with a nudge of his head.

"No." Coen was the one to answer, while the rest of them stood around, watching Cyrus.

Nobody seemed surprised to see him, but maybe they had been expecting him to appear at some point. He *was* the Neutral God—the one who enforced Topian law and handled the disputes of the gods. I supposed it made sense that he would be there, seeing as the Abcurses had been called in to trial. He arched a brow at Coen's response, but nobody said anything further.

After a moment, his eyes settled on me, and he brought up his hand, his fingers flicking in a 'come here' gesture.

"Bring her here," he ordered. "I'll do what I can, but you five need to be back in Topia within the next five clicks, or Staviti will rule a sentence in your absence, and it won't be a favourable one."

"Whoa." I planted my feet before any of them could 'bring' me anywhere, a frown suddenly tugging down my lips. "What's going on? I thought you said we weren't going to transfer the link back to Cyrus?"

This time, my glare was on the five Abcurses. They didn't wither under my panic-fuelled anger the way I had hoped that they would, but Siret grimaced, so at least it did something.

"We're not." Aros's voice was a little deeper than usual, the rough tone carrying a hint of how he felt about that particular memory. "Cyrus is going to bind you to a temporary object. The magic will wear on it over time, and soul-link magic is extremely draining, so it won't last long. But it should be enough to last the trial."

"And if it isn't?" My fierceness had melted away at the explanation, and I was now left with mostly fear. Fear for my guys, and a deep-rooted unease at the thought of being disconnected from them once again.

"Cyrus will be back to check on you tomorrow," Rome answered, looking as though he had swallowed something distasteful. "If the trial isn't over before then."

"It could go that long?" I refused to turn and acknowledge Cyrus.

I was grateful that he had agreed to help, but I didn't really believe that he was the *helping* sort. He was powerful and cold. I couldn't help but think that he had an agenda, but I also couldn't figure out what he could possibly want from me. He had kidnapped me once, determined to hand me over to Rau in exchange for a server—which was somehow both endearing and insulting at the same time. *Maybe Rau had found another way to blackmail him?*

"We don't have any other options," Yael cut into my thoughts, his eyes tracking hesitantly over my face.

None of them liked this idea.

"We need you to stay here," Coen added. "And Neutral is aware of what will happen if we return and you're not safe and whole."

At those words, the Abcurses all shifted, their postures changing, their expressions shuttering. They had turned their attention back to Cyrus, effectively ending the negotiation part of our discussion.

"Actually, I'm not aware." Cyrus was smiling, but there wasn't any humour in it. It was the smile of a person who thought that he was untouchable.

Okay, fair enough. According to Topian law, Cyrus was ... untouchable—*but when had the Abcurse brothers ever followed the rules?*

I turned back to the guys and witnessed the ripple of change that passed over them. Siret was trying not to smile and the hard look in Coen's eyes had eased a little.

"Why don't you fill me in before we start?" Cyrus prodded, sounding closer than he had a click ago.

I jumped at the touch on my shoulder, spinning around and brushing his hand off, but once again—his attention was on the guys.

"We might not be able to kill you," Rome growled, as another hand landed on my shoulder, golden skin peeking into the corner of my eye.

Aros pulled me back, bringing me into his chest and away from Cyrus, as Rome stepped forward and slid in front of me, his voice lowering.

"But there are so many ways to hurt a person without touching them. There are so many ways to get to you, Cyrus. You know who our father is—you think he taught us *nothing*?"

"This is getting us nowhere." Siret was suddenly beside Rome, reaching back to me, his hand on my arm, dragging me out of Aros's grip. "This isn't ideal for any of us—we all know why Cyrus agreed to this. He's built of secrets, full of them—and Willa is an unknown in this world. The only way he can get close enough to observe her is to strike a deal with us—"

"And it just so happens you need something from me," Cyrus cut in, smiling that same humourless smile. "And you had better hand her over before you run out of time. There's every chance that Staviti will decide to pull you from exile and jail you for a period in Topia. What will you do with your little Beta-hybrid then?"

Jailed?

I quickly untangled myself from all the hands currently gripping me. Aros was still holding onto one arm, while Siret had the other, and Rome looked as though he was a fraction of a click from grabbing onto something, too. Only I had run out of limbs, which would mean that he would have to grab a leg or wrestle one of his brothers, and I didn't want to waste any more time.

"Where's the object?" I demanded quickly, managing to break free and squeeze between Rome and Siret. I squared my shoulders and tilted my head back, looking Cyrus square in the face and forcing him to meet my eyes properly for the first time.

There was no expression there as he stared at me, but he reached into his pocket and pulled out a leather string, dangling it from his fingers so that the smooth, pale-gold rock attached to the end was visible. It swung gently before my face, and I reached out to touch it, surprised by the way it hummed beneath the pads of my fingers. It was warm—almost warm enough to be uncomfortable, and the room dropped into a heavy sort of silence.

"How did you get that?" Yael finally asked, sounding shocked.

"What is—" I started to ask, before Cyrus answered the both of us.

"A semanight stone," he said, stretching out my fingers and dropping the warm rock into my palm. "And it was traded to me in exchange for the use of my … services. The soul-link will not drain this stone." He watched as I brought it up before my face, allowing the light from the window to hit the back of the stone, turning it almost transparent.

"Doesn't magic drain everything?" I asked.

"Not semanight stone," Coen answered quietly. "This is a type of rock native to Topia. It *produces* magic, instead of surviving from it, but it can't be mined in the occupied pockets of Topia."

"Which brings us back to the question of how you got it," Yael added, a little more forcefully.

"It was given to me by an envoy of the panteras." Cyrus's voice turned sharp, his pale eyes icing over. "And that is not something that concerns you. Any of you."

He cut his eyes to me, and I closed my fist around the semanight stone. "Don't look at me like that. I was just standing here looking at the rock. I didn't ask you any personal questions. I don't even want to *know* anything personal about you. You go ahead and have your secret pantera business and stay as far away from me as possible."

"Feeling hostile, are we?" He ignored most of what I'd said, reaching out to take my hand again, this time curling my fingers tighter around the rock. It hummed warmly in my grip. "Very well. Let's not waste any more time. I'm going to need a little more *room*."

The press of bodies all around me eased off immediately, and I could feel the changing tension in the air. They were shifting around restlessly, somehow reassured by the appearance of the stone, as though they needed to see with their own eyes that Cyrus had not intended to transfer the link back to himself and drag me off to Rau again. They had turned their minds toward the trial already.

"You should all go," I said, as the warmth began to spread down to my wrist. "I'll be fine. I have my super special rock and this idio—"

"Careful," Cyrus muttered, sounding distracted. "You don't want to insult me while I'm working a spell over you."

"He has a point," Siret said, shaking his head at me—though he was starting to smile again.

"I have this *upstanding Topian gentleman* making sure my little cannibal soul won't start feeding on itself as soon as you all leave, so you should go. I'll be fine. I can take care of myself."

"You can't even walk down a hallway by yourself." Aros smirked at me, but Coen was now ushering them all toward the door.

"Fine." I wrinkled my nose at him, shifting uncomfortably on my feet—the warmth had reached my shoulder now, and it was starting to burn. "But I really don't want anyone to be jailed. Being jailed sucks—although I'm sure it's not so bad in Topia. The cells are probably made out of gold, and you probably get served seventeen meals a sun-cycle."

"Marble," Siret corrected, a laugh in his voice. "You better be here when we get back, Rocks. Don't lose the stone."

"And it's five meals a sun-cycle," Rome grumbled, sounding offended. "We're not bullsen. We have *some* civility. Don't lose the stone, don't get angry at the stone and throw it anywhere, and don't try to eat the damn thing."

"Okay, that's going overboard," I argued. "You make me sound completely useless."

"He wants you to be completely useless," Coen told me, pushing Rome out the door after Siret. "He wants you to be so useless that you can't possibly last all this time without us. He wants you sobbing and running into his arms when he gets back. He's old-fashioned like that."

"That's weird!" I shouted out, loud enough for Rome to hear me.

"I don't want her to sob, you dick," I heard Rome snapping, his voice carrying back into the room.

"This is all very touching." Cyrus's voice brought my attention back to him, and the feeling of fire now burning up through my veins, dripping down into my chest. "But I need to concentrate here."

Aros and Yael both shared a look with each other, and then with me, before exiting the room after their brothers.

"You better not be up to anything," I said to Cyrus, as soon as we were alone. "Those guys might not be able to kill you because of whatever laws you have on Topia, but I bet there aren't any laws about *dwellers* killing gods. You all probably thought you were too good for that law."

"Are you threatening to kill me, doll?" His eyes were closed, his attention clearly divided, but the scathing way that he had flung out his nickname for me was enough to have my fist tightening further around the stone.

"Yeah," I gritted out from between my teeth. "I guess I am. So you better watch out."

He started to smile, just as the fire in my chest turned to pain, ripping through me with sharp agony.

"Consider me warned," he said, his words floating away as blackness descended over my vision.

♡♡♡♡♡♡

I had been at Blesswood for no more than a few moon-cycles, which was strange when I thought of all the things that had happened to me during my time there. There had been so much strangeness that it would have been hard for me to actually choose a single incident to rise above all the other incidents in strangeness.

Until this sun cycle.

I opened my eyes to find myself sitting up in a cart.

What the hell?

As my rapid blinking slowed down, I found my brain catching up to my eyes, and I jerked properly upright in a rush of motion. Multiple eyes locked onto me as my right hand slammed against my chest, trying to quell the rapid beating of my heart. I attempted to think back to my last memory, because I had no recollection of getting on a cart, and while it was somewhat of a relief that Emmy was also there, it was still mostly just …

bizarre. One click I had been standing ... in Coen's room? And then the next click I was ... rolling down a bumpy road?

What happened?

A face flashed into my mind: pale hair, pale eyes, a sharp smirk.

"That fuc—"

"Will!" Emmy interrupted my burst of anger, her hand wrapping around my right bicep as she pulled me closer. "Is everything okay? The journey is almost over."

Disorientation pressed in on me again and I struggled to sort through the jumbled mess of my mind. "Journey," I mumbled, hoping that a memory would be triggered if I mentioned the word.

The other sols were still watching me, all of their shininess directed toward us. Emmy and I were the only dwellers in the cart, and I really wished that they would just turn away so that I could pull myself together. Leaning in closer to my sister, I murmured as low as I could, "What's going on? Why aren't we in Blesswood any longer?"

Emmy tilted her head back, the oddest expression crossing her face as she spoke right into my ear. "Don't tell me you've forgotten already? We have to visit Soldel for the first meeting of the council. The Chancellor will be hearing from all of those applying to be Vice-Chancellor. The sols here are all members of high-ranking families. It's the vote this sun-cycle."

I took a really good look at the sols surrounding us. I had been trying to avoid looking at them because they were close enough to hear us if we hadn't been whispering, but the three familiar, sneering faces now caught my attention. Fred, Dipshit, and Numbnuts. *Great.* Emmy's three ... whatever they were.

"If the sols are voting then ... why are we here?" I didn't bother to lower my voice this time.

"We're the dweller reps." A low voice from my left had me jumping, and I twisted my head to find Evie there. I was taken aback, realising I hadn't noticed her at my side until that very moment. That was quite a feat, considering that her bushy hair had suddenly developed a very real personality of its own—apparently reacting to the weather. I was more out of it than I had even thought.

Wait a click ... what had she said? Suddenly, everything made sense.

"This is what you two idiots have been doing?" I asked. "Seducing sols to try and get a foot in the door for the votes and meetings?" My words were loud again, and both girls shushed me. Most of the sols had lost interest in us by then, but at the loud shushing they were once again staring.

Sinking down lower, I averted my eyes, all the while muttering beneath my breath. "No one told me about a freaking meeting. How the hell did I get in this cart?"

I ran a hand over my face to try and clear the fuzziness in my head. I was so confused, and yet at the same time I felt as though I should have known something more.

Pale eyes flashed across my mind again, and I stilled. *That asshole!*

Whatever Cyrus had done to me, it had messed with me big time. I didn't remember much of anything he had said to me, and I sure as hell didn't remember getting into this cart.

As more of my brain clicked back into gear, painful clarity followed it. I reached to my throat, patting along my collar bone, before releasing a sigh of relief at the small lump there. My fingers delved beneath the collar to double check, but I was right with my first guess. The amazing, special, non-magic-eating stone hung from a leather tie around my neck. Which meant that I shouldn't die or almost die any time soon, which would be a nice change.

"I've been doing this for you as well, Willa." Emmy drew my attention again. "You're practically in a six-way-love-fest with … sols." She stumbled a little before continuing. "Wouldn't you like to see more of what we're trying to do? More rights for the dwellers? More dweller and sol relationships? More representation for us on the councils? It's time we took a stand, and the only way to achieve that is with some inside help. Dwellers were never going to get representation, but if we have the ear of the Vice-chancellor, maybe we can … adjust some thinking."

It was my turn to snort out laughter now. "Those shweeds are never going to help us. They're using you two, plain and simple."

A part of me was instantly pissed with myself and my attitude to what they were doing. I should have been supportive. I *did* want all of the things that Emmy and Evie had been fighting for, but I didn't think they were going about it the right way. And I was upset that Emmy had been hiding it from me.

Liar. All of the breath I had inside of me exited in one huge exhalation. My bad mood was more than just annoyance at Emmy ... it was the Abcurses. The moment my memory of Cyrus clicked in, so did my memory of them. The trial. The soul-link being transferred to the semanight stone.

The worst part was that I still felt the soul-link to them, but at the same time, I didn't. It was messing with my mind; with my emotions. It was as though something was still being drained from me in their absence.

Gone. Another heavy exhalation. *All gone.*

The word echoed around my mind until I felt like I would go crazy.

"Are you even listening to me, Willa Knight?" Emmy had her shrill, school teacher voice on. I had been conditioned for many life-cycles to respond to that tone, and it helped snap me out of my weird, depressive state.

"No," I said, quickly.

Emmy froze momentarily, before she tilted her head to the side and asked, "What?"

"No, I wasn't listening. But … I am now. So, tell me everything."

What I really wanted to say was *turn this damn cart around and take me back to Blesswood.* I wanted to be there when the Abcurses returned. I wanted to know that they were okay and that none of them had caused a god-war or ended up in jail. Instead I somehow ended up in the slowest cart known to Minatsol, trundling along to what would probably be the most boring meeting known to Minatsol.

I didn't demand they turn around, for a multitude of reasons, but mostly because it felt slightly too co-dependent, and I was not that. No way. I could totally survive without those five gods.

"For the love of Topia, Will, you're even more scatterbrained than normal. What is going on?"

Emmy had been talking again, but I hadn't been listening. *Again*. Something snapped inside of me. "They're gone, Em, and now I'm gone. Which means no one is there if something happens. I. Am. Going. To. Kill. Cyrus!"

She was silent for a beat, before shaking her head. "That was probably the least understandable sentence you've ever uttered, and considering your track record …"

She trailed off because there was really no need to finish. Before I could snap something back at her, a jar was pressed into my hands. I glanced down to find water, which I immediately chugged. I hadn't even had time to process what I was doing before the cool liquid was sliding down my throat.

"Is she okay?" I heard Evie whisper. She had been the one to hand me the drink. I swallowed the last of the water down as Emmy replied with, "I don't think so."

Before another word could be said, a loud shout came from the head of the cart, and the momentum started to slow, before coming to a grinding halt. The sols were up then, excitement across their faces. Most of them had to duck their heads low to not hit the roof of the cart, and then they were exiting on the left side.

Emmy hauled me up, apparently expecting that I would be unsteady on my feet, but I managed to remain upright, so the pair moved toward the door. I followed, but my shoe got caught in a rope that had been coiled up beneath the seat. My arms flailed about as I plunged headfirst onto the floor of the cart. Well, almost. A strong set of hands caught me just before my skull crashed against the hard timber. My knees and hip still smarted from where they had clipped the wood, but I was at least glad that I wasn't about to black out for the second time that sun-cycle. My head was already a big old mess, it didn't need a concussion to add to it.

Rocking back onto my knees, I tilted my head up to find Dru crouched before me, his massive hands still wedged in under my arm pits.

"Careful there, dweller. Your boyfriends wouldn't like it if you messed up that pretty face."

Everything inside of me seized up; he filled the space completely and I was immediately wary. He hadn't been in the cart with us. I knew that for certain. There was no way to miss a mountain-sized sol. My breathing got rapid as I asked, "Are you stalking me? Why are you always around?"

I was mostly steady on my feet now; Dru had to bend himself almost in half to fit in the small back section. "I was riding up the front of the cart, so I was just checking that everyone was off before I went in."

Swallowing hard, I fought against the rising tide of red that was creeping through my cheeks. I knew it was happening because my face felt like it was on fire.

"Well, great ... then. Good work and stuff. See you later."

I dashed out, catching my foot on the door before practically tumbling down the small steps that had been lowered off the side. Emmy caught me with ease, and before I could do more than mumble out a thank you, she had her hand around my elbow and was yanking me across a small courtyard. The pincer grip was strong with this one.

"You need to stay away from him," she said firmly. "He's bad news."

No shit. "Do I need to remind you of the three sols you've been hanging around?"

She visibly shuddered, and that made me feel instantly better. At least she found them as repulsive as I did. Sols were generally shiny and blessed, but those three made my skin crawl.

As my eyes adjusted to being out in the light, I took stock of what was going on. We were somewhere I recognised: the Minateurs' council chambers and training facility.

Small pockets of people were gathered around the entrance, conversing in loud booming voices. I recognised the sols on account of their general shininess and the confident way they commanded their own space. There was a dweller or two scattered in there also: they were the ones holding bags and folders, standing in the shadows of the blessed ones.

"There's no way they're going to let us into this meeting." I tried to keep my voice neutral, but my annoyance at being there just kept seeping out in everything I said. "Can one of you tell me how I got into that cart when I was passed out?" I had no idea why I hadn't asked that earlier. For some reason, I kept waiting for one of them to mention how I got there, but they kept acting like I should already know.

Which I really didn't.

Case in point: Emmy and Evie both stared at me, their eyebrows bunching in close as they gawked as though I had suddenly grown a second head. "What are you talking about, Will?" Emmy finally asked, her hand flying out and resting against my forehead.

I let out a little growl. "I'm not sick. Stop looking at me like that."

"You were a little out of it when we found you in the sol's room," Evie chimed in. "But you were definitely not passed out. We told you that we were headed to the meeting, and you said that you'd received a message naming you the third dweller representative, and that you were supposed to come with us. Emmy didn't believe you, but you followed us right into the cart."

Emmy nodded her own head then, as if to reiterate the point. "You're the worst liar I've ever met, Will, but I didn't want to cause a scene in front of the sols—and then you fell asleep before I could get any answers out of you, and we couldn't wake you up."

Flashes of images drilled into my brain, Cyrus's face was so clear for a moment, and then it was gone again. *What did he do to me?* How long had it been since he switched the soul-link? And were the Abcurses okay?

CHAPTER FIVE

DRU approached before we could continue our conversation, dropping an arm over my shoulders and nudging Evie out of the way so that he could stand between us. He also dropped an arm over her shoulder, but she was so tiny that she basically started to get sucked into the space between his arm and his meaty torso.

"Evie?" I called out, perhaps louder than was really necessary.

I heard a muffled reply, before Dru announced, "She's fine. The important question here is what are *you* doing here?"

I knew that he was talking to me, because he was staring at me, but I wasn't quite ready to answer his question yet. Mostly because … I had no idea what I was actually doing there. Apparently, I had blacked out and then returned to consciousness without being aware of what I was doing, whilst actively plotting to join in on a very important meeting for the future of Blesswood—acting as a fake official dweller representative. Either Cyrus had somehow manipulated me into doing something while I wasn't entirely aware of it, or else I had finally gone insane.

"She was invited," I finally answered Dru, spurred into saying something simply to escape my thoughts. "She's an official dweller representative." I was motioning to Emmy, who was frowning at me.

"I was talking about you," Dru clarified.

He sounded genial enough, as though we were old buddies and he was pleasantly surprised by my sudden, unwarranted appearance … but there was something more in his eyes. Something that glimmered. Something that didn't belong there—and I couldn't place what it was. Anger, maybe? Suspicion. *Yes, probably suspicion.*

It *was* suspicious, after all. I wasn't an official representative, I hadn't been invited—I shouldn't have even known about the meeting—and yet there I was, standing right outside a building with stone columns lining a front courtyard and giant oak doors leading into a huge hall teeming with sols. It seemed as though the most important sols of Blesswood had not been the only people fortunate enough to be invited to the meeting.

"I'm here because …" I fumbled for an answer as I stared past the doors, following the robes of the people as they passed into the crowd and began to clump into little groups, conversing with each other in hushed little whispers. "Someone put an enchanted necklace on me, because my soul was trying to eat me, and then I passed out. Because it *hurt*, you know? Anyway, when I woke up, I wasn't really aware of waking up. I don't remember it at all, but apparently that version of me really wanted to come to this meeting, so I just walked into the cart. I don't think the other sols cared enough to count how many dirt-dwellers were in the other seat. We were probably just one big, dirty blur to them."

Dru chuckled. "I never know what's going to come out of your mouth—but I have to admit, it's almost worth it to never get a direct or honest answer from you."

"I just told you everything," I deadpanned.

"Right." He chuckled again, before allowing me to escape from beneath his arm.

I reached around for Evie's arm, and pulled her out too, almost expecting her to have suffocated at some point—though she looked more or less the same, with only a few extra inches of frizz added to her hair.

"So are you going to let me go to the meeting?" I asked Dru, since Emmy and Evie were standing there and staring at him instead of moving toward the building like the others.

I couldn't actually see any other dwellers standing around, so I assumed that we were waiting for Dru's approval. There was every chance that the other sols present in the hall would object to our appearance, so we would need everyone from Blesswood, at least, to support our attendance. I supposed that was why Emmy and Evie had spent so much time sucking up to Dipshit, Numbnuts, and Fred.

Dru was sizing me up, his small eyes flicking from my head to my feet, as though trying to visualise what the other sols would see when they looked at me. I also looked down, and then sideways at Emmy, and then at Evie.

"We're all dressed," I stated dryly. "We have all the same parts you have. The head. The arms. The legs. The lack of ball—"

"We *were* assigned to be present at this meeting," Emmy cut in quickly, "by the new Chancellor himself."

"Then you'd better get the hell in there," Dru said, his smile stretching into a grin. "It's about to start."

Emmy and Evie didn't waste another click, and they each grabbed one of my arms and started dragging me toward the hall, as though I would cause irreparable damage if left alone with a single sol for any period of time. They were probably right. I was already craning my neck to look suspiciously over my shoulder as Dru followed us. *What was his deal*? He gave up that fight way too easily. He was a terrible sol. Sols were supposed to make it hard for the dwellers to feel special. It was basically written into their genetic makeup.

"It's starting," Evie whispered to Emmy—speaking right across me.

"Is it?" I said in a normal tone, forcing her to acknowledge me. "That's nice. And why are we here, again? I mean *you guys*, not me. I know why I'm here—or not, actually—but why is Blesswood sending dweller reps to a sol meeting?"

"Because the Abcurses demanded two dweller seats on the dweller-relations committee," Evie replied. "And the entire committee is expected to be present, as well as all other Blesswood committees, and all relevant people from the other academies across Minatsol."

I opened my mouth to answer, but nothing came out, and I stumbled, fighting off a sudden, disorientating wave of nausea. Evie and Emmy only tightened their grip on me, half-carrying me all the way across the polished wooden floor, toward the back row of seats. The entire hall was set up with folding wooden chairs, all facing a raised dais at the front.

"You weren't exaggerating at all," Evie muttered with a huff. "She really can't walk on her own."

You said that about me? I attempted to chastise Emmy, but again, the words wouldn't surface, and another wave of dizziness hit me. I quickly wrestled out of their grip and took a step back, holding a finger up to Emmy when she tried to reach for me again.

I need a click.

I tried to plead with my eyes, hoping that she got the message. She nodded, and I huffed out a short breath of relief, before quickly running to the back of the hall again and passing through the door we had entered through. I made it around to the side before the next wave of dizziness hit me, and then I was on my knees in the grass, my hands on the outside wall, my head pounding with sudden pressure. There was a blackness edging into the corners of my vision, and panic clawing up to the back of my throat. I suddenly wanted to run back inside and grab Emmy, but as soon as I tried to stand, the blackness reared its head and flooded through me, claiming me completely.

♡♡♡♡♡♡

"We have to get her to a healer; she's never going to make it otherwise."

Emmy's voice floated to me through the ringing sound in my ears, and I cracked one of my eyes open. I was back inside the same cart in which I had woken up only what felt like ten or so clicks ago.

"What happened?" I croaked out, searching for Emmy.

I had been crammed into the corner of a seat, and there was a massive arm crossed over my front, clasping the windowsill, as though it had been needed to keep me from slumping to the ground. I didn't bother identifying who the arm belonged to—I only knew one sol with limbs that huge—but looked past it to the sight of Emmy on the seat opposite me. Evie was stretched across most of the seat with her head in Emmy's lap, and her arm dangling limply off the side, fingers touching the floor of the cart. Most of her dress was singed black, and there was a cloth covering half of her face, but I could still smell the stench of burnt flesh in the air.

I clenched my teeth against the sickening scent and forced the words out again. "What. Happened."

Emmy looked up then, her expression shocked, her eyes wide. "We have no idea. The meeting was about to start ... and then, suddenly ... there was fire everywhere. We couldn't stop it. The flames were completely surrounding the building. Only a sol could have made fire that quickly, but no sol would have been powerful enough to produce so much of it."

"It must have been the work of several," Dru muttered, his voice rumbling out beside me.

"But ..." I frowned, fighting against the lingering pain inside my head. "I don't understand. Why would anyone attack the hall? It was just a meeting."

"Someone who wanted to stir up the community," Emmy whispered, her eyes returning to Evie's covered face. "Someone who wanted to take advantage of the current state of Blesswood to spread the chaos further."

I stared at the two of them, feeling my body freeze and go hot with panic, all at once.

"How did I get in here?" I finally asked, my tone quiet enough that I almost thought I needed to repeat myself, before Emmy answered.

"You ran right up to us when we were carrying Evie out." She didn't seem to be paying any attention to me, which I was grateful for—but I could feel Dru's stare pricking against the side of my face.

"Right," I forced myself to say. "I ... yeah. I think I inhaled too much smoke, it's messing with my head." I had no idea whether smoke had the ability to do that, but I didn't have any better excuses.

I had no idea what was going on, but I had a very bad feeling that whatever it was, it had something to do with me. I needed to get off that cart, and get myself far away from the people I might hurt, before it was too late. I also needed to find Cyrus, because if this *did* have something to do with me, then it definitely also had something to do with him.

CHAPTER SIX

I already knew that the plan was to get Evie to a healer, and I assumed that it would be easy enough for me to separate myself from them in the chaos of the moment, but I had no idea what I was going to do after that. Cyrus had said that he would check on me, which meant that he was somehow already keeping an eye on me. I just needed to get somewhere private before I could test that theory, and I couldn't do that with Dru breathing down my neck.

"Shouldn't you be carrying her?" I asked pointedly, as Emmy struggled to get Evie out of the cart.

Dru glanced at them, and then shrugged. "I suppose." He managed to squeeze himself out of the cart through the other door, before pulling Evie free and lifting her into his arms. "You," he narrowed his eyes at me, sticking his head back in through the door, "you need to follow us—you can't wait here."

"Sure," I lied. "I'm right behind you!"

We were in a densely populated area of Soldel, lots of small hut-like dwellings bunched close together. Dru seemed to know where he was going: he moved with purpose, which gave me a surge of confidence that he was really going to get her help. I moved with them for a few clicks, wanting to make sure that they were almost inside before they noticed me gone. Relief hit me as I saw that one of the huts we were moving toward had a small healer symbol above the door. It was a simple emblem: the crossed arms with clenched fists on the end to show the power of a healer.

I turned to bail, but my feet froze. There was one thing I needed to check first. "Are you sure this healer is going to help a dweller?" I called out to Dru. "Sols don't usually care that much about whether or not we die."

Evie was most probably injured because of me, and I needed to make sure that she would be taken care of before I disappeared. Dru paused, before turning back slightly to see me better. Some of the sheet had fallen off Evie and I couldn't stop my gasp. She looked terrible, hanging limply, her pale skin red and splotchy. There were angry weeping sores scattered over every inch of skin that I could see, and it looked as if half of her bushy hair was gone. I had to swallow hard multiple times to keep the contents of my stomach from erupting. At my side Emmy had her hand pressed against her mouth, her face a chalky white as she stared.

Had I actually done that?

"I know this healer." Dru looked semi-serious, his usual joking façade fading. "She will help if I tell her to." I must not have looked convinced, because he hurried on. "She's going to be fine. Right now I'm keeping the dweller unconscious, which will help with the shock and pain. She shouldn't remember any of this when she wakes."

"Is that your gift?" I realised that I had never even wondered what Dru was capable of as a sol. They were almost always gifted in something. I would have guessed that his was weight-lifting, or dweller-shot-put. You know, something which required biceps as big as thigh muscles.

He was turning away again, and I was glad to see that he did not take lightly the urgency of healing Evie. I was sure he wouldn't answer my question, but to my surprise he did call back to me, "Yes, I am gifted with Psyon. I can dull the senses. Cloud the mind. Manipulate the brain waves."

Something creepy would have been my second guess ... so that sounded about right.

Emmy dropped her hand then, her breathing heavy and ragged. "She's going to die. Those burns, they're ... they're so bad, Will."

I took a step toward her, my arms wrapping around her shoulders, as I pulled her into a tight hug. "Dru said she would be fine. We have to believe that he knows the capability of this healer. I need you to go in there and make sure that they don't treat her like a dweller. Lie if you have to. Tell them she's sleeping with the chancellor's grandson and he would be pissed if she died."

Emmy let out a strangled laugh. "Not even a lie, so should be easy to sell."

Not a li ... Oh, gross. Nobody needed to be *that* dedicated to a cause, even a good cause.

Emmy started walking then, only to suddenly realise what I had said. "Why will I have to make sure Dru and this healer don't slack off on Evie? Where are you going, Willa?"

She had her school teacher voice on again. I was obligated to answer. "I need to track down a god." My voice lowered on the last word. "I think he knows something about what is going on with my blackouts, and the fire, and a tonne of other things. He won't visit when others are around though, so I need a moment alone."

She stared me down for a few tense micro-clicks, and I tried not to squirm like I was lying. Because for once, I really wasn't.

"Is this god an Abcurse?" she finally asked.

I shook my head. "No, they're all in Topia. For ... reasons."

Emmy brushed that away like she really didn't give a shit. "If there wasn't so much going on I would have realised earlier how weird it was that they let you out of their sight." Her eyes got really huge then. "You're out of their sight, Will! The link ... how are you not dying in pain right now?"

She lurched toward me, hands held out in front of her as though she could stop the pain just by touching me. I was the one now to wave her concerns aside. "That's why I have to find this god. He did something to temporarily transfer the link, but I don't think it worked. Or it didn't work very *well*, anyway. So now I have a god to find, and a pair of balls to kick."

Some of the worry and fear eased on her face then as she shook her head at me. "Never change." As she turned away to head into the healer hut, I heard her call back over her shoulder. "And please try not to get yourself killed."

Where was the faith?

As soon as they were out of sight, I turned and hurried along the path, searching for a secluded place. The streets were fairly empty, but there were still plenty of doors and windows—all of which could easily be looked out of. Cyrus was a monster, taller than the Abcurses, with an ego to match. He would draw attention easily. The last thing I needed right now was more trouble or attention.

A darkened, stone-lined alleyway caught my eye, and I hurried toward it. It seemed to grow gradually darker the further back it went, which would hopefully mean that there were no sols living within. It also turned cooler as I ran along, and I felt that pang in my chest at being there alone. If Siret had been there he would have made a joke and woven me into the tightest sweater ever. My boobs would have been popping out, but my nipples would have been hidden. They really liked me to keep my nipples under wraps.

When I felt like I was about halfway along the alley, I stopped and leaned back against the cold wall, mentally shouting out for Cyrus. I had no idea if he would still be able to hear me in this way, or if there was any connection between us, but I had to try.

Cyrus, you bastard of the gods, get your ass here now! You've really fucked up this time, buddy! You have no idea. No idea what I'm going to do to you. I don't know either, yet, but it's going to be bad. Really bad! It'll be the worst you've been in trouble since you were a damn kid and your damn mother caught you looking up the skirts of the other gods, or whatever you did to get in trouble. Never mind, I just realised you were never a kid. That explains the lack of child-like innocence in your eyes. Eyes which I'm going to repeatedly stab just as soon as you get your ass over here!

My rant went on and on, and I kicked out at the wall while calling him every curse name I could think of.

Bullsen tit.

Shweed.

Tosspot—that was a personal favourite of my mother's.

Ballbag—another favourite. It's what she called our town leader when she was sober enough to realise how useless he was. "He's just a walking ballbag, Willa. No brains." She wasn't wrong either: he was the reason I ended up with the Abcurses, when he reassigned my gender and named me Will Knight.

I owe you one, Leader Graham, you ballbag.

Cyrus still hadn't appeared by this time, so I decided to abandon the mental shouting and try some *actual* shouting. Maybe he was powerful enough to hear his name on the breeze or something. *They could do that, right?*

"Cyrus!" It was a tense whisper-shout. "Get down here right now! You need to fix whatever it was you broke!"

I didn't see the shadow creeping up behind me until it was too late. A low shriek burst from me as a heavy hand landed on my shoulder, and for the third time in as many rotations, I found myself fighting against a darkness that wanted to eat away at my mind.

♡♡♡♡♡

I came to in a cart. *You've got to be fucking kidding me?* This was beyond a joke now. If I woke up in one more cart, I was going to hack the stupid wooden transport into a million pieces. The disorientation was worse this time; my head was fuzzy and my mouth was dry as though I had been walking through the desert without water for too many sun-cycles.

As I tried to roll over and sit up, my head slammed into the side of the cart, and the pounding behind my eyes increased. As some of the fuzzy cleared, I realised why I'd hit my head in the first place. It looked like I had been tossed into the corner, my back to whomever was controlling the cart.

Hating the vulnerability of not seeing, I rolled away from the side of the cart and clumsily launched myself into a sitting position, spinning around at the same time.

A pair of familiar faces were sitting across from me, staring, and as anger built within me, a tinge of red started to flicker on the edge of my vision.

"Don't you be trying any of that," Dru said, with a smirk. "Keep whatever messed up freak-show power you have to yourself. I have no problem knocking you out again, but just be aware that you've been down for two and a bit sun-cycles, and if you go down for another, you'll probably die of thirst."

Over two sun-cycles? Was he for-freaking-real? "Emmy? Evie?" I managed to croak out, understanding why my mouth was dry as the desert.

He shrugged. "Left them with the healer—your friend seemed to have it under control."

I tried to squelch some of my worry. There was nothing I could do about it right now. I needed to deal with these new pair of ballbags across from me. Even though only one of them had balls.

Karyn grinned as I turned slitted eyes in her direction, trying to kill her with a single look. "Bet you thought you'd seen the last of me when I didn't show up again."

I tried to play dumb. "You mean that time I knocked you out and stashed your bleeding body in a laundry cart? With the dirty, old, used up, pee-sheets?"

Gods, it would have been so awesome if they had been peed on.

Karyn's psycho-nice face disappeared, and she launched herself at me. Dru caught her when she was half-way across the cart, hauling her into his lap.

"Baby, you know we can't anger the gods. You've been trying for a long time to get rid of her, this is our best chance. Blesswood is chaos. Her protectors are missing. She keeps blacking out and burning shit down. It's perfect."

I chose to focus on the fact that I had been right: I was the one causing all the chaos. Which made sense considering what I was—but I had been learning to control it while I had been with the Abcurses. Now I couldn't control shit.

I missed them.

The thought hit me so hard and I pushed it deep down. Into the place where my mother's neglect was. Where my loneliness was. Where my isolation due to a curse which I did not ask for was. I locked the crushing emotions away, striving to keep a clear head.

"So you two have been working together?" I should have known. Dru had beady eyes, definitely evil.

Karyn, who was still melded to Dru like they were the same person, nodded. "Yep, Dru was Plan B, if Elowin and I couldn't end you." She tilted her head back and her face softened as she gazed into his eyes. She seemed to be showing her appreciation for him stepping up to the challenge of killing me. After I cleared my throat, she turned back to me with what looked like great reluctance. "He was going to take one for the team and pretend he had an iota of interest in a dirt-dweller like you," she told me. "He would earn your trust, and then you would follow him wherever he wanted."

Dru let out a frustrated sigh. "It took much longer than usual because you never do what I think. And you always had those five dumbasses around."

Dumbasses? He was one to talk. Speaking of, I'd actually been surprised he could talk when we first met. The stringing of words together in coherent sentences seemed beyond him. It felt good to insult him, even if it was only in my head.

"Where are you taking me?"

Karyn's creepy grin was back again, and I wished there was more space between us. "To a place where you can't bother us ever again. We won't have directly killed you. I'll even let Dru help you out of the cart. All gentlemanly-like, if the gods are watching." Her laughter was high-pitched and grating. "How are we to know if you can make it back on your own. Maybe someone has before."

My eyes darted around the cart, trying to determine if I could jump out. The back was fully enclosed, so I had no idea where we were, but I would take my chances. I was faster and stronger, now that I was a beta-sol-dweller, so as I dived toward one of the zippered side panels, I managed to get my hand up under it, wrenching the opening free before either of the sols even moved.

I had half of my body through, wiggling in the small gap, when I felt hands on my legs. Thrusting myself forward, I kicked out with all of my strength. Connecting solidly, I felt the thump and heard the curse, which I ignored to continue freeing myself.

The cart came to a screeching halt. Bullsen could be heard pawing at the ground and making loud snuffing noises. I had just hit the ground and was scrambling to my feet, when three sols appeared.

Dru was very red-faced, his nose already looking swollen. Karyn was standing beside him, and next to her was a girl that I recognised as one of her friends back in Blesswood—she must have been the one who had been driving the cart. I was tensed, crouched low, waiting for them to attack me. Instead, they all exchanged a single happy look, tossed a bag at my feet, and then climbed back into the cart.

With a shout of laughter, the clicking on the ropes could be heard, and then the cart and bullsen were moving. I stood there frozen, watching them disappear into the distance, wondering why they had let me escape.

It wasn't until I turned and looked around, taking in my surroundings, that the true horror and realisation hit me. They hadn't cared about me escaping because this was where they had been planning on leaving me all along. The dirt beneath me was dried and cracked, a stale, arid taste to the air. There was barely any vegetation, and absolutely no civilisation in sight.

We were in a place so dead and desolate, that it could only be one area.

The abandoned rings. The dead zone.

I stared at the plume of red dust that was slowly settling back down to the ground, and then walked over to the cart tracks, nudging at the indentations with my boot. There were no other tracks around—there was *nothing* else around. Just dirt, and sun. A sun that was about to set … and I had no food, no water, and no map. Not that there were any landmarks to reference on the map.

"Cyrus!" I shouted again, turning my face up to the sky even though I knew that Topia wasn't actually *in* the sky.

He didn't answer, of course, so I ended up screaming out an incomprehensible sound of frustration instead, before marching off down the tracks left behind by the cart. I had no idea where I was going, but at least I was following some kind of direction.

I picked up the pace a little as the sun began to sink lower and lower. My legs were aching and there was dust in my eyes, but I couldn't just stop and sit down under a tree. There weren't any trees, and there were probably wild packs of animals that came out at night to snack on the bones of abandoned dweller-sol-betas. That was probably why nobody ever came back from the dead zone—other than Dru and Karyn, apparently.

I was almost running by the time something finally came into view. I pulled a hand up over my eyes, squinting against the horizon. It was only a blurry outline, backed by the sun, but it seemed to be moving. I halted, watching as what seemed like another cart approached me from the horizon. The cloud of dust rose behind it, gently obscuring the sun in a hazy red glow, and for a moment, I was reminded of my Chaos. Of the damage I had done to Evie's face. It seemed as though my soul-link to the Abcurses had been keeping me from blacking out and leaking Chaos up until this point, but now I was on my own. Well … on my own with whatever version of me took over whenever I blacked out and leaked Chaos everywhere. So … not really on my own at all. I also still had the semanight stone, if that counted for anything.

I waited while the cart approached, unable to see the person steering it properly through the haze of dust. When it finally skidded to a halt, veering off to the side of me, I realised that it had been following on the exact same track as Dru and Karyn had left. Maybe they had changed their minds, and were back to kill me.

"The hell are you doing out here in the middle of nowhere?" The blunt question drew my eyes up to the front of the cart, where a guy was standing from the driver's seat, looping the reins for the bullsen over a handle in front of him.

He was easily several life-cycles older than me, but there was something experienced about him that denied his still-handsome appearance. A roughness that came from hard work and cynicism, instead of age. I knew that he was a dweller immediately.

"A couple of sols knocked me out, threw me into the back of a cart and dropped me here," I announced plainly.

I even gestured in the general vicinity of my head, to indicate where the 'knocking out' had occurred. He arched a dark brow and jumped down from his seat, causing me to glance toward the cart to see if anyone else would come out.

"So," he brought my attention back to him as he approached, "what'd they knock you out for? Did you steal something? Polish the wrong shoe? Accidently sneeze in front of someone important?"

I couldn't help the smile that tugged at the corners of my mouth, and I examined the guy a little more closely: he had sooty hair, dark eyes, and darkly tanned skin, as though he spent a lot of time in the sun. Probably driving carts. Through the dead zone ...

"Wait a click." I shook my head, frowning, and gestured back to the cart, checking again to see if anyone was poking their heads out to see what was going on. "What are *you* doing out here in the middle of nowhere?"

"It's my job," he replied, like it was obvious. "I take the deceased out to the ruins, and ... er ... put them to rest." He was rubbing his hand over the back of his neck, watching the look on my face.

The look that was probably full of disgust and horror. Which would explain why he was suddenly acting uncomfortable.

"What kind of deceased?" I eventually asked. "And who the hell *pays* you to do this?"

"My father pays me." He almost looked like he was blushing now, and he started to glance back toward the cart. "It's the family business, you see. One of the gods asked my great-grandfather to take the bodies to the cave behind the temple, where the guardians live—"

"Guardians?" I interrupted. "I thought nothing lived out here?"

"Well if the guardians catch it out here … it probably won't live for long." He cut his eyes back to me, trying to convey the seriousness of that statement, but I was still stuck on all the horror and disgust over the fact that he carted dead things around.

"You still haven't answered me," I prompted. "What bodies?"

"The bodies of the dwellers." He watched the alarm chase away my disgust, and then he was shaking his head, seeming torn between amusement and annoyance. "They're already dead. I don't *kill* them or anything. I just take them from one place to another."

"*Who the hell is killing dwellers then?*" I demanded, my voice becoming shrill.

"Nobody! Or … well, I guess sometimes … listen, I really need to get this load to the temple before nightfall, otherwise the guardians get pissed. And you really don't want to know what happens when the guardians get pissed. You can come with me, and I'll hide you in the cart. Or you can stay out here and wait for them to find you. If you decide to come with me, I'll explain everything to you on the way back home, and then we can discuss what the hell to do with you."

He walked over to the cart, pulled back the canvas wrap, and motioned me inside. I stayed right the hell where I was.

He groaned. "Look … what's your name?"

"Willa." I wasn't even looking at him. I was still staring at the cart. "What's yours?"

"Zac. And I kind of want to keep it that way. If I'm late tonight—or if they catch you out here—we'll become Patricia and Kenneth. I know this probably doesn't make any sense to you, but they do things with the bodies. Change them. Give them new names, and then send them to Topia to serve the gods."

"Actually that makes perfect sense." I took a shaky step toward the cart, bracing myself for what I'd find inside.

Zac seemed to relax as soon as I made it clear that I was going to go with him, and he pulled the canvas back further for me. Laid out across the benches were several wrapped bodies, shapeless white figures, all stacked up on top of each other. The smell was awful, now that my nose wasn't full of dust.

"Just ... try not to make any sounds, okay?" Zac seemed almost embarrassed that he was forcing me to hide in a cart full of dead people, even though he was technically saving my life, and probably putting himself in danger to do it.

It made me realise that I should probably be a little more grateful, so I quickly pushed into the opening and then reached out and caught his hand before he could close the canvas on me.

"Thanks." I tried to sound sincere, instead of sick-to-my-stomach. "I won't blow your cover, I promise. And as soon as we reach the ninth ring, you can get rid of me. I'll find my own way back to Blesswood."

His dark eyes widened for a moment. "You're from there? You were serving in Blesswood? That's a long way to travel, just to dump a dweller. It would have been easier if they'd killed you and waited for someone to come and collect the body. I don't do the Blesswood pickup myself, but my brother works the sol-cities. There's another guardian temple right in the middle of Tridel. So why didn't they just kill you?"

"Well," I shook my head, a laugh bubbling out, "turns out I'm not so easy to kill. By the way, you're a weird guy, Zac."

"Says the dweller walking around the abandoned lands all on her own before sunset," he replied dryly, quickly securing the canvas and disappearing.

I looked around, trying to find somewhere to sit before the cart started moving—but I was too late, and one of the wrapped bodies was jostled off the seat before I could move, landing right at my feet with a sickening *thud*. I tried not to scream, or anything pathetic and girly like that, but a sound might still have slipped out, because the little wooden window facing toward the front of the cart slid back.

"Did you just squeal?" Zac asked.

"No," I snapped back. "Do I look like the kind of girl that squeals?"

"Little bit, actually."

I reached forward and slammed the little wooden window closed again. "Asshole."

"This asshole saved your life," he sang back to me, apparently all cheerful and friendly, now that we were moving again.

"You don't really have many friends, do you?" I shouted back, stepping over the body and crouching into the only unoccupied corner of the bench it had fallen off.

"It's a lonely profession, this." He slid the window back again, so that he could talk to me.

"That's because you drive dead people around. I don't know if you've noticed, but dead people aren't that responsive. They're not fun to show affection to."

"Especially the ones that died of flame-rash."

I jumped clean off the bench again, accidently landing on the chest of the body that had rolled off earlier. I edged away, backing myself against the canvas lining. I was three clicks away from jumping out of the damn cart and taking my chances with the *guardians*.

"You squealed again," Zac decided to inform me, laughing. "I was only kidding about the flame-rash. The guardians only want the dwellers that they can turn into pleasing little puppets for the gods. There's nothing pleasing about a flame-rash death."

"You want to make more friends?" I spoke through gritted teeth. "Then here's a tip: quit talking about gods-dammed flame-rash. That stuff is nasty."

"Noted." He suddenly sobered up, and I saw one of his eyes peeking through the window at me, before turning away. "You can sit down. None of the bodies are contaminated. If you pull the panel off the front of the seat, you'll be able to crawl into the storage space beneath. We'll be there in two clicks."

"We haven't gone very far," I said aloud, while internally I was cursing Dru and Karyn for dropping me so close to the secret guardian-hideout.

"Who's Dru?" Zac asked.

Okay, maybe not that internally.

"Some ballbag," I replied.

"*Aww*. Is he your boyfriend? Did you guys get into a fight? Is it because you were being a bad dweller and pissing off the sols?"

"Seriously?" I groaned, crouching back onto the bench seat. "Who taught you manners? Please tell me it was one of the dead people. That would make so much sense."

He didn't reply, and I realised why a moment later, when the movement of the cart started to slow. I pulled my legs up to the bench, curling my arms around and trying to turn myself into a little ball of invisibility. I could hear muted voices, and then louder conversation as we approached.

"Zachary," a man spoke up, his voice so raspy it made my skin scrawl, "you're late."

CHAPTER SEVEN

"ONE of the wheels broke, I had to fix it." I could hear Zac speaking as he jumped down. I expected him to come to the opening of the cart immediately, but his voice was travelling further away the more he spoke. "I brought seven from the ninth ring. All clean deaths. Only one over the age of thirty-five—"

"Take it back," the husky-toned man replied. "The Sacred Ones don't like wrinkles. You know that."

I wrapped a hand over my mouth, catching the derisive snort before it erupted out of me, and then eased up toward the still-open window, trying to peek out without being seen.

"I told them that," Zac was replying. "His family. They insisted. These people think that I'm transporting the bodies to the cemetery caretaker, but someone started a rumour that *my* cart takes the bodies of the people that the gods have favoured, while the *other* cart from the cemetery takes the bodies that the gods have frowned upon."

"They think the gods care about whether they are *good*?" The raspy voice sounded angry.

I could see him now, walking beside Zac. He was cloaked in heavy black cloth, the sleeves pushed up to the elbows, displaying long, pale arms. The hood was drawn over his face, but I wouldn't have been able to make out his features anyway, because he was facing away from me, approaching another group of hooded people. They all stood gathered at the entrance to a worn-down temple, the stones cracked beneath the sweep of their dark robes. There were only three torches lit, set into brackets against the pillars out the front of the temple, so there wasn't enough light to make out their features. I could only decipher the pale blur of their faces beneath the hoods.

Zac and the guardian were too far away for me to hear anymore, so I drew back from the window, staring down at the body on the floor of the cart. It was almost annoying, that these bodies were about to go exactly where I needed to go, whereas I would have to find my way back through all the rings to Emmy, before taking the cave entrance to Topia. Which would probably kill me, because I wasn't attached to a god while entering.

Could I even be close to Emmy?

I had no idea what was happening with my Chaos, but it seemed to have an agenda. It had brought me to the meeting of Vice-Chancellors—probably because I hated the vice-chancellors—and then it had proceeded to burn down the building. Probably because there was some small part of me that wanted to burn down the vice-chancellors. Even though I now knew the real reason that Emmy was hanging around with the creepy sols, my Chaos had still taken matters into its own hands, intent on ending whatever was going on, once and for all.

Bad move, Chaos. Bad move.

I glanced out the window again, and then quickly slipped to the floor beside the body. I had no idea what they did with these bodies before taking them into Topia, but I was about to find out.

I was about to go and get my Abcurses back.

Unless they had already returned, and were currently scouring Blesswood for my whereabouts. In which case, I was going to find Cyrus and force him to fix this whole mess, because even if it wasn't his fault, I still liked blaming him.

I started to unwrap the body on the floor, scrunching up my nose the whole time. There was another under-wrapping beneath the outer-wrapping, which was just fine by me, because that *really* wasn't something I needed to see. I rolled the body away from the bench seat and felt around for a little handle, since Zac had told me to hide in there. There were two latches on either side of the front panel, and the panel fell outwards when I released them, revealing a small, dark storage space. I rolled the body into the space, accidently hitting the head once or twice—not that it mattered. The person was already dead.

When the body was nicely squished into the storage space, I quickly re-latched the panel and rolled myself up into the top sheet that I had taken off. It wasn't a very precise job, and I was just laying there on the floor of the cart, one of my feet still poking out of the sheet ... but I doubted that anyone really cared about how well-wrapped the bodies were. They were about to be turned into Topian serving robots anyway.

"Another four sun-cycles before I get back from the eighth ring," I heard Zac saying, his voice becoming clearer again. "Do you have any you want me to take back this time?"

"No," the raspy voice replied. "We have disposed of them already."

Well that's not creepy at all.

I tried to be as stiff as possible, playing dead. I heard the canvas being pulled apart, and then there was a hand on my ankle, right on the exposed foot. Whoever-it-was hauled me out of the cart and dumped me onto another hard surface—something that smelled like musty wood. The sheet slipped off my face, and since my eyes were still wide open, I ended up taking in the entire scene of one of the guardians standing at the opening to the cart and reaching in, while another guardian stood off to the side, watching. I could see his face clearly, and it was deathly pale. It had the same waxy quality as the Topian servers, though somehow less refined. Uglier. I was laying on another cart—open-topped, and considerably smaller. A common cart used to transport fruits and vegetables ... and dead people, apparently. That didn't seem hygienic. I quickly flipped the sheet back over my face and braced myself as a body landed beside me half a click later. The cart thumped several more times, with one of the bodies landing directly on top of me, and then it was moving.

I felt bad for Zac. He was going to discover the body stuffed in the storage space at some point, and probably freak out—but as bad as I felt, I knew it needed to be done. I had to get into Topia. I *had* to find either Cyrus or the Abcurses, and I had to figure out what the hell was happening to me.

As soon as the thought entered my head, I started to feel dizzy again; the same kind of dizziness as before. My hands were tingling and dark spots were starting to flash behind my eyelids as I screwed them shut. The heat inside of me flamed to scorching levels. I could feel bile rising to the back of my throat, and I curled my hands into fists, my nails cutting into my palms.

This cannot be happening right now!

♡♡♡♡♡

When I opened my eyes again, the white sheet over my face had disappeared, along with the smell of musty wood and the feel of bodies stacked around me. Instead, I was staring at a rough, stone ceiling, and the surface beneath me was cool and hard.

"Have all the bodies been collected?" a voice asked, sounding close-by.

I turned my head, taking in the rest of the room. There was a row of cupboards beneath a work bench of some kind—one of the cupboards hanging half open.

Other than a wash-basin in the corner and the steel bench that I was lying on, the room was bare. A curtain over the doorway was the only thing hiding me from discovery. I started to slip off the bench when the other voice answered.

"One of the bodies is missing. Summon each of the guardians tasked with transforming a server tonight, and figure out who hasn't submitted yet. Staviti will not want to be kept waiting any longer."

"I will summon them immediately."

I froze, halfway off the table, and glanced around again.

What the hell had I done with my guardian? No— scrap that. What had my evil, Chaos alter-ego done with my guardian?

The guardian on the other side of the curtain was still referring to the dead people as *bodies*, and not servers, so I assumed that Staviti would be needed to put life back into the them. That was an important thing to know, because it meant that I couldn't just get off the table and start walking around. I would need to figure something else out.

I shivered when my bare feet hit the stone floor, glancing down to find that I had been stripped to my underwear. My guardian had definitely been here. He had started the process—but he hadn't gotten as far as putting one of those creepy bodysuits on me, so that was a plus. Reaching up, I brushed my hand across my hair, relieved that it was still there. I skirted around the room, trying to find something that I could maybe use as a weapon, just in case I would need to fight my way out of the temple. Not that I'd be any use in a fight, but I could always practise positive thinking.

I grabbed the top of the cupboard door that had been hanging open and pulled it out further, bending down to peer inside.

"Holy gods in hell," I gasped, falling back onto my ass.

There was a pale face staring back at me, eyes closed, a small trickle of blood leaking from a gash in his forehead. A bloodied object had been stuffed into the cupboard with him—it looked like a small, stone bowl, and the unconscious guardian had been made to look as though he was cuddling it to sleep, like a stuffed toy. I didn't even pause to think about the fact that *evil* Willa had gone ahead and stuffed another body into another tiny storage space, as though taking cues from me. The *good* Willa. I simply reached in and wrangled the hooded cloak right off his back, standing and pulling it around my shoulders before re-arranging him and closing the cupboard door.

I'd feel bad about that later, but for now, I had to sneak into the land of the gods. *Again*.

I had taken two steps away from the cupboard when those voices floated in through the sheeted door again. "The guardian must have fled. We have no time to hunt him down now, we need to catch the next transport to Topia. But he will be disposed of as soon as we find him."

Disposed of? They were definitely taking their employment termination advice from Staviti. Speaking of … I needed to be on that transport. I had to get to Topia. Who knew what would be left of Minatsol if my Chaos was left to its own devices for much longer. That was the *real* reason I was in such a panicked rush: I was worried about the good of the worlds. *Yeah*, that's right. I wasn't needy and pathetic and missing my Abcurses.

I was a heroine.

I needed to save the worlds.

Both of them.

Sneaking to the door with as much stealth as I could muster, I managed to not make a single noise. To be fair, it wasn't hard to avoid the single, steel-topped table that I'd been lying on after somehow beating my guardian senseless. Maybe this Chaos thing wasn't so bad; it had already kept me from one of those skin suits, and I still had my hair.

Making it unscathed to the curtain, I quickly peered around one of the edges to find at least a dozen cloaked individuals. They were busy carting the dead out of a large doorway. Red dirt was visible in the distance. No one noticed me, and since most of them kept their cloaks right up over their heads, I hopefully wouldn't stand out.

With a deep, fortifying breath, I slipped out from the curtain and hunched myself over as I walked purposefully to the door.

I noticed a body stretched out across a slab of timber as I passed. It was a female: she was dressed in a skin suit, her head shaved, her eyes wide open and glassy. I tried to breathe through my mouth as I hauled her into my arms, since the scent of some sort of embalming fluid was strongly emanating from her. I grunted as the solid weight fell against me. Of course I would pick the dweller who lifted weights and broke in wild bullsen with pure muscle and strength of will. Her will was so strong it was almost sinking us both into the ground.

Staggering slightly, I hurried with a few others to the doorway.

"Where is my body?" I heard a low, confused-sounding man ask from somewhere behind me. "Did someone else move her?"

There was no answer and I didn't bother to look back. Stepping outside, there were still a few rays of sun left in the sky, so I could see everything clearly. I looked around for the cart, because random carts seemed to be the story of my life lately, but there was nothing like that in the area. Instead, the plain housed a dozen pantera, all kicking up the red dirt in a restless, irritated manner. I should have guessed; nothing but the best for Staviti and his creepy little server-creations.

The Jeffrey concept was starting to make me ill. Dwellers were treated like shit in life, and now I find out that in death they got an even worse lot. They were wiped of all free thought, relegated to slaves, and then, when they displeased a god, they were dropped in the banishment cave to waste away as trapped spirits.

Wow. Put so succinctly, it was horrendous. How could Staviti do something like that? I thought he was supposed to be a wonderful, benevolent, creator-type god. *Nope*. He was an asshole, just like the rest of the gods. He was the king of the assholes, actually. Just a stupid creator asshole who had made some asshole minions to serve him and his asshole imaginary friends in their asshole floating platforms.

A shove from behind cut off my internal ire, and I started shuffling along again. I bumped into more than one guardian, but when they glared at me, I only mustered up a raspy voice and snarled, "Learn how to carry a dead body! What is this, apprentice-sun-cycle?"

I was sure that I was getting a few confused glares beneath those hoods, but they were too busy to stop and question if something was amiss—which was lucky, because I was ready to bring out all my skills. I had clumsy and Chaos on my side. Ten tokens said I could take them all out in one well-timed blackout.

From the few hood-free faces I could see, it didn't seem as if any of the guardians were nervous as they approached the panteras, despite the truly intimidating aura of the creatures. I remembered the way I'd had to meet and be accepted by Jara before I could ride her, and yet the guardians were almost dismissive of them. It struck me as wrong on so many levels. I focussed on a black and white pantera, about five yards away. I could see that it was yet to have a body placed in the roped harness across its back. It was smaller than the others, which was why I was heading right for it. Smaller seemed safer.

When I was at her side—braced for a kick to the gut, because that's what I would have done if someone was trying to put a stinky dead body over me—I finally noticed the collar around her neck, standing out starkly against her white. It was a thin piece of wire, silver and slightly barbed, twirling and twisting around. I could see old scars where she had clearly rubbed against it, along with a few fresh marks.

"What the hell?" I murmured under my breath. The pantera turned and faced me, intelligent eyes locking onto me.

I waited for a voice in my head, but none came.

"I'm so sorry," I whispered, leaning forward and draping the heavy weight across her. She was still staring at me with eyes far too wise. "Why are you helping these guardians?" I murmured, as I adjusted the ropes. I had to take a few sneaky peeks at how the guardians around me were securing their corpses, but I eventually figured out what I was doing.

The pantera started making a low humming sound, from deep in its throat.

"You can't talk to me with that collar on, can you?" I let my hand brush just over the top of her throat, not quite touching it, as a terrible thought struck me. "You're a prisoner?"

The Abcurses had spoken with such reverence about the panteras, as though they were old and magical, and should be respected above all others—and yet here they were, collared and stripped of their voices. I was really starting to hate the fucking gods.

As my anger rose up in a blinding force, I felt the dizziness creep across my mind.

No, not now. I don't have time for you now.

I tried everything I possessed to shut it down, even reaching up and clutching my stone necklace which had not been removed, thankfully. But nothing was stopping Chaos when it was ready, and apparently it had something to say.

I came back to myself at the sound of a shout; my eyes snapped open as I was awkwardly crouched behind a pantera, my legs aching only a little, which meant that I must not have been there for long. As my head cleared further, I realised that the pantera before me was the black and white one I had been placing the body on.

She adjusted her position as I moved, like she was protecting me from sight. I straightened from my crouched position, shook off the dust, and tried to get my bearings. When I felt more stable, I peered around my new friend.

Chaos had struck again.

The main building was on fire: it was clearly a specialty of mine. I was trying to figure out what else I had done when I noticed a glint on the ground. I quickly dropped back down to examine the object, and then shot back to my feet to examine the pantera's neck, because the collar looked exactly like the collar that I had seen just before blacking out again.

The pantera's neck was now bare—the collar having been flung carelessly into the dirt, and I could see how the two ends joined. There was a small clip that could be flicked across to release the contraption.

You saved me.

I jumped at the voice, before my head darted widely around.

My name is Lucille.

Common sense returned, and I realised that it was the pantera, finally able to speak with me. *If you want me to take you to freedom, you need to get on my back. I can take you to Topia.*

My heart sprang in a hopeful way. *Thank you,* I tried to project back. *But shouldn't we free your friends too?*

Lucille just shook her head, pawing a hoof through the dirt, stirring up dust. *You have done all you can, now it is time to find freedom.*

I was figuring out how my Chaos worked. Sometimes it was for me, sometimes against me. But it seemed that in a roundabout way, it was almost always working in my best interests. The building being on fire was a distraction for the guardians, during which I had managed to unlock the collar. Without it killing me.

I'd been afraid to touch it earlier, but Chaos apparently didn't have the same worry.

"I know you have no idea who I am, but I have some powerful friends. I'm not allowed to make promises on their behalf anymore, but just know … I will do everything in my power to save the rest of your kind." My whisper was made against her side, as I got into position to pull myself up.

The body was gone from her back. The harness was still there, but no body. I didn't even want to think about what Chaos Willa had done with her—no doubt it involved a tight space and squishy body parts. Luckily, this one had already been dead, because it didn't seem to matter to Chaos. Dead or alive, if it could squish, it could fit.

Being as gentle as I could, I lifted my leg and hooked my foot into one of the side ropes, using it as leverage to clumsily sprawl across Lucille's back. Thankfully, I didn't kick her wings. They stood out in strong, wide fans on either side of her back, and were patterned in black and white to match her pinto colouring. No doubt she wouldn't appreciate me crushing those feathers.

The fire was just starting to die down when I finally got seated on the back of my second ever pantera transport. *Hold on,* was my only warning before her wings beat against the ground, and her powerful legs launched us upward.

Wind gushed around us, forming giant clouds of red dirt. I heard shouts, but couldn't see anything. I imagined that the guardians were scurrying around like shweeds, prepared to bring the panteras back into line.

"Good luck with that, assholes!" I called out, not even bothering to contain my gloating, even though it would have been the smarter move ... just in case Lucille had a flight malfunction and sent me crashing back to the ground.

That would be embarrassing.

I might have even fist-pumped when the dust cleared and I noticed that we were already ten feet above them and still rising.

"Oh my gods!" I exclaimed, as the other panteras also started flapping, each of them shaking their heads and flinging the collars free. Guardians pulled little boxes from their cloaks, aiming them at the creatures. One or two, who hadn't managed to shake their collars free, let out a high-pitched shriek before they collapsed on the ground in convulsing spasms.

Those bastards.

I must have projected my angry thoughts, because the pantera answered me. *They just have to shake the binding free; you unclipped all of them already.*

Panteras rose around us, the sound of flapping filling the air. Guardians were converging on the few who they'd managed to zap with their collar buttons, but before they could do anything to contain them, bodies started falling from the sky.

Literally.

The dwellers, who had been strapped across the panteras, were being dropped onto the guardians below, each one landing with a thump, and eliciting a muffled groan from beneath a cloak.

"Ten points!" I chuckled as a pure black pantera managed to knock down two in one shot. "Bonus points for you," I added, pointing at him.

As the guardians started to run around like crazy people below, the few panteras on the ground were given time to shake their collars free and launch into the sky. Soon, the guardians were forgotten as the entire herd rose. I couldn't do anything but hold on for the ride and hope that I wouldn't get dumped somewhere even worse than the dead zone. The harness was still across Lucille's back, so I quickly looped a few of the straps around my legs, just for extra protection against the possibility of falling to my death. I then slumped forward and let the soothing rhythm of her wings calm the erratic tic in my mind. The Chaos was growing stronger, I could feel it roaring inside of me … trying to get free.

I didn't want to fall asleep, since I couldn't be sure I was out of danger yet, but it was hard to keep my eyes open. Despite the numerous amount of times I had lost consciousness over the past few sun-cycles, it felt as if I had not had any decent rest.

I was exhausted.

CHAPTER EIGHT

"I don't care what Cyrus says, I won't leave her out there for one more click on her own. She needs us. I'm going to fucking kill him." Yael's face was a little fuzzy, which was when I realised that I had somehow slipped into one of their heads. I must have fallen asleep after all.

Wait a click ... I was in one of their heads!

An overwhelming amount of emotion rocked through me as I drank in the sight of my Abcurses. Well, *one* of my Abcurses, and then a few Abcurse-shaped-blurs in my peripheral vision. Whoever I was currently hijacking was staring straight at Yael.

He was furious, his voice laced with more venom then I'd ever heard from him. "She has been missing for almost four sun-cycles now. Willa can get into trouble in a fraction of a click, and she's been running around on her own now for *four sun-cycles*."

The head I was in started shaking left to right, before speaking. "We need to get around Staviti's order. We're grounded to this platform until the next arena battle, and if Siret hadn't stolen D.O.D's mortal glass, we wouldn't have even been able to see into Blesswood and we wouldn't even know that Willa was missing."

Rome. I was seeing through Rome's eyes, which I should have known from the fact that I was actually looking over Yael's head. Only one god was that tall.

"Maybe we can just call his bluff. Disobey him again and deal with the consequences when they happen." Obviously, that had been spoken in Siret's voice.

You're going to get yourselves killed! I wanted to shout at them, but I had no control over Rome, I was just a silent stowaway.

Right?

There couldn't be a way for me to speak through Rome, surely? I would have figured it out by now. The concept wouldn't leave me alone, though, so I decided to give it a shot.

Scratch your nose.

I thought the command with all the concentration I could muster, and there was a brief pause in conversation as disappointment rocked through me ... until suddenly, a huge hand appeared right in my line of sight and started rubbing the bridge of Rome's nose.

It worked? Something I tried actually worked? *Hell yeah!* I started silently congratulating myself, only to find Rome shouting, "Hell yeah," at the same time as my mental thought.

Yael briefly paused from where he had been explaining his plan to take down Staviti, and looked up to eye his brother. "Did you just have a seizure? What the hell is wrong with you?"

Ugh, Yael was so mean. Dick.

"Ugh, Yael. You're such a dick."

Rome's voice was far higher pitched than usual, his big body jumping in surprise as he spoke. Four sets of eyes were turned on him, each with a look of disbelief clouding their faces.

"If you don't get yourself together, I'm going to put you through a wall." Aros wasn't normally the violent type, but this sun-cycle, apparently, he was channelling it hard.

Rome lifted both hands up then, as if to say *I have no idea what is going on*. To be fair, he really didn't. I could just imagine the look on his face. He would be so confused—and for someone as contained as Rome, I could only imagine how much he must be freaking out. It almost made me want to try something else, just for the fun of it. Peals of laughter burst from me, echoed by Rome. The longer I tried to control him, the more natural it became ... but I needed to stop before I did something he would kill me for later.

Siret took a step closer to his brother, peering right into his eyes as though he could see deep inside. "Soldier, you in there?"

Hesitancy and confusion were prominent in those words, but also a sliver of hope. *How the hell did he know it was me?* Actually, who cared about that part, I needed to let him know I was there. I nodded my head, and Rome's head followed suit.

"How is she doing that?" Aros asked, looking a little freaked-out.

I didn't blame him. If I thought that one of them had the ability to slip into my head and control me without my knowledge …

Wait just a click.

Holy.

Fuck.

"I think Cyrus lied," I spluttered out, Rome struggling to talk as fast as I needed him to. "I think he linked himself to me again, and he's somehow controlling me. I thought it was the Chaos, because every time I black out, something really chaotic happens … but if the soul-link has been manipulated so that something like this can happen, then that would explain everything. Rau still has something on Cyrus—otherwise he wouldn't have set the building on fire back in Soldel. And then I thought the Chaos was *helping* me by knocking out that guardian and shoving him into a closet, but actually it was probably Cyrus, trying to stop me from sneaking into Topia. And when I unlocked the collars on the panteras, it was probably Cyrus trying to stop me a second time … oh wow, he really underestimates how often I need to use bad situations to my advantage."

The four guys were just staring at me—or Rome—their mouths a little unhinged.

"Did she say that she set a building on fire?" Yael rasped.

"And knocked someone out and stuffed them into a cupboard?" Aros, this time.

"And set a bunch of panteras free." Coen was scratching his head.

"That's my girl." Siret was the only one who seemed pleased by my overload of information.

"Rome is messing with us." Yael was shaking his head. "This is too fucked-up."

"I'm not." I tried to sound as convincing as possible, but Yael only shook his head and stepped closer to Rome, his fists clenched.

"Cut this shit out right now," he seethed, "or I'll hit you so hard she'll have to start calling you *Crushed*."

"That's not very nice—" I started to say, but apparently Yael wasn't in the mood for pacifications.

He pulled his arm back and slammed it into the side of Rome's face. I couldn't feel the actual blow, but my vision swam to the side, and then suddenly I was staring at the sky—I hadn't paid much attention to where we were, but the sky was bluer than blue, the clouds all happy and perfect. They were still in Topia.

"You *hit* me!" I yelled at the sky, and it was almost humorous to hear Rome's deep voice so full of feminine outrage.

"Oh." Yael sounded genuinely shocked. "It really is her. Rome just dropped like a bag of rocks."

"He's still not moving," Coen noted, his head appearing in my field of vision. "You okay in there, dweller-baby?"

"He hit me!" I repeated.

"I think she's fine." Yael's head appeared beside Coen's. "Rome's head is too damn thick for any of the pain to reach her—right, Willa-toy?"

"You still hit me!" This time, it was a growl, and Siret's head popped up beside Yael's.

"You should get revenge," he suggested helpfully. "You have so many muscles right now. You're the God of Strength right now. The possibilities are endless."

"No they aren't," I said, "Rome is going to wake up soon. I don't always black out for long. But you have a point."

I struggled to get back to my feet, but controlling Rome wasn't so easy. His limbs were bigger than expected, and I accidently knocked over a low wooden table, up-ending a bowl of fruit and sending apples and oranges scattering over the marble floor. When I was finally standing, I focussed on Yael, and tried to swing a punch at him. Unfortunately, I miscalculated the distance to his face, and Rome's fist connected with the pillar just to the right of Yael's head. I watched in fascination as the stone cracked beneath Rome's fist, caving in around his hand. I was so fascinated that I didn't even realise I was stuck until I tried to pull his fist back again and it wouldn't budge.

"Well ... this is awkward." Yael was smirking, turned to the side so that he could see the fist I had embedded into the pillar.

"Can we stay on track?" Coen snapped, throwing Yael a dark look, and then turning it on me. "The way you're controlling Strength right now—you think Cyrus is doing that to you?"

"Yes."

"I'm going to kill him," Coen growled, and even Yael looked pissed, now that he believed me.

"And he's been causing chaos?" Aros appeared beside me, taking Rome's wrist in his hand and yanking it out of the pillar.

"Yes," I repeated, a little exasperated. I wished that they had listened the first time around, but they were probably preoccupied with the fact that I had managed to take control of their brother's body and mind.

"Why would he be causing chaos?" Siret sounded both angry and thoughtful, and he was pacing back and forth, his eyes snapping back to Rome every few moments. "That's not in his interests at all."

"Have you seen him since he gave me the semanight stone?" I asked.

"No." Yael was the one to answer me, a deep frown taking over his striking features. "But we can't leave this platform. They assigned us a server, Phineas, and he's the only one we're allowed to have contact with."

"Can you send him to Cyrus's cave?"

"You can be sure that Cyrus has fortified his defences since we were there last," Siret answered. "So there's a good chance that Phin will die trying to get in there. If we lose the server, we lose *all* contact with the people outside of this platform. Until they decide to pay us a visit, of course."

"Don't worry." Coen's voice had gone cold. Hard, almost. "We will find a way to connect with Cyrus. You need to tell us exactly where you are and exactly what's happening before Rome gets control of himself again."

"I'm with a flock of panteras, and I'm currently in Rome's head, so I have no idea where they are."

"She's ... with a flock of panteras," Siret repeated numbly. "Because why not?"

"It's a long story," I started, but Rome wasn't saying the words.

I tried again, but this time the faces before me began to blur, and I realised that I was losing my grip on whatever mind-link I had managed to form. Darkness swam into my head, and I slipped into sleep, as though the whole scene had been just a colourful dream.

♡♡♡♡♡

Wake up. Lucille's voice flooded my nerves, jolting my eyes open and kick-starting my body into action. *We have arrived.*

I tried to sit up, but my back was stiff and cold, so it took me a few moments. The cloak that I had stolen from my guardian-victim had blown up around my shoulders, tangling about my neck. I pushed it away and winced against the feeling of the blood rushing back into my limbs, as though I had been crushed under a weight for a long period of time, and it had only just lifted.

I began to try and swing my leg around Lucille to jump to the ground when something had me pausing.

I was surrounded by pantera—not just the pantera that had escaped from the abandoned lands, but many, many more. We must have been somewhere in Topia, because even the *air* tasted better than it did on Minatsol. We were in a clearing with a high mountain on one side, and a small brook twisting through the trees on our other, forming a little island of sorts. I slipped carefully off Lucille's back, my feet landing in the soft grass, and I quickly untied the guardian's cloak, dropping it onto the ground. I was still barefoot and dressed only in my underwear, but I doubted that they would care. They weren't wearing any clothes either.

The panteras were surrounding me, all staring with their too-intelligent eyes. There didn't seem to be any hierarchy amongst them, that I could see—not one of them had stepped forward from the others to examine or address me. They were simply watching.

Waiting.

"I'm sorry about what was being done—" I began, but one of them cut me off.

You set us free.

It was a voice different to Lucille's, but just as calming. I didn't know what to say to that ... because technically, Cyrus had set them free. So I said nothing.

How can we repay you? This time, it was Lucille's voice, and I turned sideways to look at her.

"My friends are somewhere here, in Topia. I need to get to them."

Not yet, Lucille answered, *but soon. When you are ready, we will take you to them.*

"Ready for what?" I glanced around at the other panteras nervously.

You need to be taught the beauty in Chaos, Lucille answered. *The gifts of the gods are not good or bad—they are only gifts, shaped from the very forces of the world. It is the* person *who makes them good or bad.*

I paused once again, my eyes scanning the numerous sets of eyes all trained unflinchingly on me. *It is the person who makes them good or bad.* I repeated the words inside my head.

What did that say about me?

I had set a building on fire—no. *Cyrus* had set a building on fire. But I *had* set the room on fire when Coen and Aros had kissed me. In fact, so far my Chaos only seemed to be manifesting as fire, which wasn't a great sign. Of all the ways that it could manifest, fire was probably the worst. Lucille was right. I needed to learn about this power before it destroyed me, or someone else.

Come with us, we will show you.

Another pantera this time, I didn't know which one, it was just a lower toned trilling of words in my head. But there was a small group of four dark-furred males that broke away from the main group and started walking toward the stream. I followed, since it seemed I wasn't getting out of there until they decided I was ready.

The four paused at the edge, staring down into the water that trickled past, almost lazily.

Drink from the stream.

Those words were not a request. They held a note of command, which immediately had me on the offensive.

"Why?"

Large, soulful brown eyes met my gaze, and I found myself almost uncomfortable under that penetrating stare. *You need to understand.*

I needed to … *seriously*? Riddles were so not my thing. Emmy, on the other hand, was great at reading between the lines. It was probably easier for me to just obey.

Dropping to my knees, I leaned forward and placed my hands in the crystal-clear water. It was shallow here: I could see all the way to the stone and sand-lined bottom. My hands were covered in red dust from the guardians' lands still, so I let them trail through the sparkling water until they were clean enough to drink from. Cupping up some of the water, I brought it to my lips, and as the first trickle slid down my throat, I let out a breathy sigh.

Firstly, I had not realised how thirsty I was; and secondly, the water tasted nothing like the water in Minatsol. It was sweet almost, with a hint of fizz that danced across my tongue. I let the rest spill into my mouth, needing to taste more of it, and immediately my head went a little fuzzy.

I stumbled to my feet, my wet hands falling to my sides, and I tried to glare at the twelve dark-furred panteras. *Twelve* ... when did the others come across? The one closest to me shifted, before coming back into focus. *Oh crap.* I had been seeing three copies of the original four that led me to the water.

"You drugged me," I slurred, before swiping out with both arms, in an attempt to keep them away from me.

Your mind is now opening to the magic. You need to stop fighting it.

One of my flailing fists hit a small trunk that had been rooted close to the edge of the creek. I let out a shriek, hopping away. That hurt so much more than when I was in Rome's head.

As my mind focussed on the pain, it seemed to forget about my previous disorientation, and that seemed to give the water just enough time to do the job it had been trying to do all along.

Clarity hit me with the force of a cart colliding into a brick wall, and as the fuzziness in my brain vanished, something rather strange took its place. *Knowledge.* Flashes of images started to crash through my mind. Over and over. One after another. At first I had no idea what I was seeing, but then I recognised some of the landmarks that I had seen in Topia before.

This is our Topia. A pantera told me. *Before the gods. Before the gifts.*

My history lesson continued, and I finally got my first glimpse of a human-like figure. It must have been Staviti. He stood in a blank landscape of Topia, staring around in confusion. Water ran in rivulets down his face, and along the ragged shorts he wore. He was smaller than I had expected, lithe and striking with his golden hair and flashing dark eyes, but not as massive as I'd begun to think all gods were.

I was no-doubt spending too much time with the Abcurses.

The next image was Staviti drinking from a stream, a stream which appeared to be very similar to the one I stood before, and then he lifted his hands to the sky and marble platforms began to form. Elements were ripped from the ground. Panteras and creatures fled from the being who was destroying their world.

The water of Topia is unique. It carries within it all of the magic that keeps this land alive. This water flows into Minatsol also, for our two worlds are connected. The water there is not as strong as it is here. It is tainted, in a way.

"Why doesn't everyone in Minatsol have gifts then?" I couldn't see past the images in my head, it was frozen on Staviti, his hands held aloft.

It runs deep within the earth. Not accessible by many. Staviti was sick as a child, growing worse as he aged. His father was a miner, and had heard about a magical water. He searched for many life-cycles, somehow finding a small reservoir of it.

"He gave it to his son?" I guessed.

Yes, and it changed him.

The origin story of the gods was a little wrong, then. This sort of made more sense, though, than the thought that he had just been struck by a random gift.

"What happened to his father? Did he try and get more water when he found out it had healed Staviti?"

There was no more. The rest runs deeper than any can access.

So the water changed Staviti, and then he became a cocky shweed, using his ballbags way more than he should have, and all of his offspring ended up with the same magical gifts as he had. Then, when they had bred with other dwellers, this gifted thing had continued on until there were suddenly two very distinct beings on Minatsol. Dweller and sol.

"I just drank the water ..." I said each word slowly as I tried to figure out what that meant for me.

This is not the first time you have tasted the water. You, too, were saved.

"By who?" I demanded, slightly panicking that I was about to learn something about myself that I couldn't handle.

Maybe I was Staviti's sister. No, wait. I would have to be centuries old. Maybe I was Staviti's ... great great great great—

Your father.

"But there was no more water. That's what you said, right?"

They didn't reply, and I felt that this was the end of the knowledge they were imparting. Or maybe they simply didn't know.

"That's why you called me Divine One?" I knew it wasn't this pantera specifically, but it had been one of them.

Yes.

None of this made sense. Not a single freaking thing they had said. I needed to speak with my mother. I would demand that she tell me exactly who my father was this time, and what had happened when I was a baby. Why was she such a mess? There had to be some sort of traumatic event. What if it was about me all along?

The world of Topia was back in my eyesight, and I blinked a few times to clear the last of Staviti from my mind. Only a single pantera remained before me, the others had re-joined the herd.

"How did Staviti capture you?" I asked. "You're stronger than the gods, right?"

He lowered his head, in what seemed like a nod. *Stronger in many ways, but the water does not work for us the same way it does for you. If you control the water, you control all of the world.*

"Those collars were made of this water, somehow?"

It runs within the chain, and we are bound to the one who controls the magic.

Staviti was moving right to the top of my shit list. "Have I learned all I need? Can I go back to the Abcurses now?"

He let out a weird snorting noise, which I was choosing to believe was him clearing his throat. *You have learned almost nothing,* he told me. *Surely there is more you want to know.*

Uh, not really. Gods-dammit. Time to pretend I was smart. "So, my Chaos … I should be able to control it better now, thanks to the water?"

The pantera made another snorting sound.

I pointed to a tree just behind us. "Chaos!"

That's not how it works.

"Yeah, so I've heard," I muttered.

An explosion rocked through the picturesque valley, shooting me back a few feet to land on my ass. Pushing back long tangles of my hair, I blinked a few times to make sure I was seeing things correctly.

The tree was completely engulfed in flames. Nothing else around it was touched. The pantera appeared to be doing a similar wide-eyed stare with me. I climbed to my feet and stood at his side.

"Not how it works, hey?" My voice had a touch of smug to it, which died off when he turned narrowed eyes on me.

The word does not create Chaos. It is the mental intention. Clearly your words and brain have no barrier.

It was like he had known me my entire life. "Yeah, I tend to react rather than think. Thought and words happen at the same time."

If you intend to control Chaos, that has to change.

Well, in that case … *we're all screwed*. "I did at least hit the target I intended." My voice was meek as I searched for the silver lining.

Controlled subtly will get you what you want much faster than brute force.

"Don't tell Rome that, he can't even open a door without taking out half the building. I mean, don't get me wrong, he always gets the job done, it's just never very pretty."

The pantera didn't reply, which forced my mind back to the task at hand. I was starting to understand what he meant. All of my bursts of Cyrus-Chaos had been … messy, and hadn't really achieved much outside of a distraction. If I wanted to instil real change, then I needed to figure out how to make the randomness of my gift work in a more refined way.

For the next few rotations, I practiced attempting to control Chaos. It required a mental strength that was frankly beyond me, and I could sense the frustration of the few panteras who were working to help me.

"Maybe I need more water." I stared hopefully at the stream, which was a few hundred yards away.

You need to focus. The water has already done all it can.

I almost stomped my foot. "It's faulty. The water is broken, we should all go and check the water right now and make sure it's still working."

The water is fine.

I had long ago given up trying to figure out which of them was talking in my head, there were too many. They surrounded me on the ground, not to mention the many flying through the air, frolicking across the meadow, drinking from the stupid water.

"I'm never going to get this." My words were a warning and a statement. "I have never been able to control my gift-that-feels-a-lot-like-a-curse."

Chaos is not a curse. If the person wielding the Chaos only uses it for evil, it becomes a curse—but that is only by the fault of the person and not the gift. Chaos can be a beautiful thing, if you know where to look for it. If you learn to see it properly and wield it properly.

I thought about the panteras' words, scanning their ethereal eyes while I mulled over the shifting of everything I thought I had known. Maybe they were right. Maybe the only reason my Chaos had been manifesting as fire was because I kept associating it with Rau.

"Okay," I finally sighed out. "Will you show me?"

CHAPTER NINE

My name is Leden, the pantera told me. Her voice was softer than the others, almost a whisper, and her coat was a glistening, snowy white. She was beautiful.

I climbed onto her cautiously, hesitant to put dirt all over her lovely white fur, but she only made a small, snorting sound and reared up a little, forcing me to fall forward and cling.

Hold on, her soft voice cautioned me, sounding amused.

She launched up from the ground, and four other pantera followed, two spanning out either side of her as she took to the sky.

"Where are we going?" I shouted, pressing my face into her soft neck.

She was *fast*. Faster than any other pantera I had ridden—and she knew it, too, because there was a small hum of appreciation that vibrated through her body as soon as the thought flitted through my head.

We are taking you to the mortal glass. The eyes of the world.

"The what?" I shouted back. "Did you say *eyes*? You're taking me to see some eyes?"

Leden didn't answer, which wasn't a good sign. I groaned, shaking my head and cursing internally. That was the gamble you made with magical objects: sometimes they were pretty and they tasted good, like the stream; and sometimes they were ... *eyes*.

They didn't fly far before they began to dip toward the mountains, swooping into a cave and landing in a spray of pebbles and dust. Leden wobbled a little before she managed to straighten herself, and I quickly jumped off her back and took a few steps away before I turned and grinned at her.

"The speed is excellent, but you need to work on the landing."

She made a grunting sound in the back of her throat that was more animalistic than the graceful noises I had become used to from the pantera, and then she flicked her hoof into the gravel and kicked it up, sending a cloud of dirt and rocks right at me. I quickly covered my face with my arms and laughed. I liked her.

It seems the girl is forming a bond, one of the other panteras noted, causing my head to peek out from between my arms.

"A what?" I asked the cave in general, since I wasn't sure which of the four, massive, black-furred pantera had spoken.

A bond, this time from Leden, *it happens on occasion, between the gods and the pantera. They are children of the same magic, children of the same land.*

"I thought you were here long before the gods?" I asked, turning to peer into the cave. It was dark—

almost too dark to see anything, though I could still distinguish a faint, black glimmer.

And the land was here long before us, Leden replied, pushing her snout between my shoulder blades and urging me forward, further into the cave. *It is not uncommon for the gods to bond to the animals of Topia.*

"But I'm not a god," I whispered, trying to resist the insistent pushes I was receiving, "and I also can't see in the dark!"

We will bring light, one of the other panteras announced, and then only a moment later, tiny little balls of light began to flicker on, beating against the wings of miniscule creatures that flittered sleepily about the cave.

I stopped moving altogether, my mouth falling open and my eyes going wide. The walls of the cave were lined with a glittery black rock, so smooth in some places and so jagged in others—it almost appeared like glass. The little lights moved around, illuminating further into the cave, and I followed them without the nudging of Leden this time. I could see my own reflection in the rock, walking alongside me with so much awe painted over her face ... but then the reflection began to change. Suddenly, I could see five broad backs, their owners all facing the edge of a marble platform.

"What's happening?" I whispered, as one of the reflections spoke.

"We could just jump. I mean we can't die or anything." It was Siret's voice.

"You know Staviti would have stationed people below," Yael replied, sounding downright depressed. "Maybe even Crowe himself. Staviti is serious this time—if D.O.D hadn't insisted that we should be used to test the sols in the arena fights, he might have attempted a way to strip us of our gifts by now."

"This is bullshit," Rome growled. "Staviti loves it when sols die—that's the whole point of the arena fights isn't it? He doesn't want them to *prove* themselves. He just wants them to die."

"It isn't about sols dying." Aros seemed to be offering the voice of reason, judging by his tone. "Staviti doesn't like us not obeying his commands because it shows the other gods that he can be disobeyed."

They are not like the other gods, Leden told me, her breath warm against the back of my neck. *They are the only beings born of a union between the gods.*

"How is that possible?" I asked, reaching out to touch the broad back of Coen against the rock. "So many hundreds and thousands of life-cycles and no children born?"

The voices of the Abcurses were fading away, barely audible to me anymore as the reflection gradually shifted back into my own face.

There were other children. Leden's soft voice grew even softer, her tone only a gentle hum inside my mind. The sorrow emanating from her was suddenly so acute that I had to wrap my arms around myself.

"What happened to them?" I asked, my voice a rasp.

Staviti did not allow them to live. The reply was short—simple—and yet it dripped with the kind of loss that made my heart ache. The panteras had been born in Topia, just like the Abcurses. It would make sense that they felt connected to the other children born in Topia.

"Why did I see the Abcurses?" I turned from my own reflection, finding the four black panteras lit up by hundreds of little illuminated bugs, while Leden waited directly behind me.

You see who you want to see, Leden answered. *Every shard of glass in this cave is a part of Topia. It is how the world is seen. How every being on this world is seen. It is as sacred as the water, and just as protected—*

And just like the water, one of the black panteras cut in, *it has not escaped the urge of the people to steal and defile.*

Suddenly, all of the little light-bugs converged into one small section of the cave, illuminating a part of the rock wall that had been hacked at in several places. Silvery liquid had spilled out and over the cuts like blood, drying and congealing only halfway down the wall.

I flinched, but Leden only nudged me around to face the same part of the wall that I had been facing before, and the bugs dispersed around the cave again.

Let's begin, she whispered inside my head.

"Begin what?" I replied aloud, probably killing her dramatic vibe a little bit, but I really wasn't great with riddles and secret caves and magical rock-glass and water that was apparently alive. Those things weren't inside of my comfort zone.

Leden didn't answer me, but she didn't need to, because the glassy surface before me had begun to shift again, my reflection dissolving away. The shape of a woman began to form, almost as if through a screen of smoke; small wisps of colour licked over skirts and limbs, swirling around an upturned face. Suddenly she was clear, and it felt as though I could see her more distinctly here—in the rock—than I might have been able to if I had been there in person. She had ice-blue eyes, melding to green around the pupil; her hair a dusky, golden blonde. She was beautiful—but there was something else about her that drew me in. I couldn't figure out what it was until she reached out, her hand on the rock that separated us—as though she wanted to reach right through and comfort me in some way.

Pica. Leden's soft voice sounded inside my head. *The goddess of Love.* And then I watched, in a series of rapid images, as Pica touched the lives of people who couldn't see her. Some, she gifted, and some, she cursed. There was a kind of irrational beauty to what she did, as sols courted each other and dweller children ran around each other in the dirt, flirting playfully. All the while, there were two men standing behind her, watching the things she did. I recognised them as Rau, the Asshole of Chaos, and Staviti. Both of them reached out to her, but she only ever turned to Rau. There didn't seem to be a reason behind her love. It was chaotic.

As soon as that realisation hit me, her image dissolved away, to be replaced by another. The stream from the pantera camp was suddenly flowing along the wall before me: a glittering thing full of life. It seemed so calm and peaceful, little currents visible through the transparent depths. I watched as silver-skinned swimmers wriggled their way through the water—although I realised after a click that they were swimming the wrong way. They were going against the current—*upstream*. I frowned, watching them wriggle and wriggle and wriggle, until suddenly I could see the entire course of their lives. They struggled to the top of the river, and laid their eggs, before dying. That was the course of their existence. I then watched as their eggs hatched, as the swimmers matured and travelled downstream, and then as the whole process repeated itself.

"It makes no sense," I found myself saying to the wall.

The things that we are driven to do that go against all sense—those are the things you will find Chaos in, Leden replied. *It is not a force of evil, simply a force of nature.*

"I think I understand now." I turned away from the wall, to face the panteras. Mostly, I was lying. I *did* understand what they wanted me to see, but I had no idea how to apply it. More than anything—I just wanted to see the Abcurses again.

Without thought, I turned back to the wall. "Will you show me again?" I asked the rock, touching it lightly with my fingers.

The panteras didn't seem to be controlling it anymore, because it was only showing me my own reflection again. I watched in relief as the image rippled, and the five faces came into view. I was seeing them almost from above this time, as they sat around a circle of benches. There was a familiar glint of midnight black stone set on a table directly in the center of their circle, and I gasped when I saw it. It had been melted down into a gilded frame, almost like a mirror, and I remembered Rome saying something about Siret having stolen D.O.D's mortal glass before they were banished to their platform.

"Is she in another cave?" Coen grumbled.

"Are those fire-bugs?" Siret added.

"And panteras?" Yael, this time.

"Hey guys!" I replied.

I watched as they all froze, glancing at each other, and then back to the mirror.

"Who's she talking to?" Siret jumped up from his seat and leaned over the mirror.

"Hey, Five!" I said this time, just to clear up any confusion.

"Me?" Siret sounded dumbfounded, and then the others were all jumping up from their seats, too.

You do not have time for this. Leden broke into my reunion moment, her voice carrying a hint of urgency. *Your escort will be arriving soon.*

"I can't be here for long," I told the guys, keeping the 'escort' thing to myself, since I had no idea what that was supposed to mean. "But I'm coming. Stay there. I'll be there soon."

"You're in *Topia?*" Coen's question was stuck between surprise and anger. "You snuck into *Topia*? Do you have a death-wish, Willa-damned-Knight?"

A truly excellent, loaded question. My simple answer was no, I really didn't. I had always been about living as fully as I could, mostly because death was always one step away. Now, though, death meant something a little different. Would I end up out with the guardians? Or would I become a god, like the Abcurses?

The thought of what might happen when I died stirred up a deep and painful emotion within my chest, cracking little fissures across the protective layer that had been in place for as long as I could remember. A layer that shielded me from the constant rejection and loneliness of my life. Emmy had slipped through: her persistence in loving me had broken the shielding long enough for her to become family. But there had been no one else, until now.

Of course, all of that information remained in my head as I said simply, "Where you guys go, I go."

Five sets of eyes were locked on the framed stone, and each of their expressions were so different from the other. But each reflected a single quality. *Need.* In differing ways, the six of us needed each other, and being apart like this had taken a toll. It was deeper and more cutting than I had expected, as though our separation should have been a graze. A little irritating, but easy enough to live with. Instead it felt almost like a fatal wound. Or a poison, where the longer it remained in my system, the more damage it began to cause.

"You need to come back to us now, Willa." Those solemn words, almost gruffly spoken, came from Aros.

My golden Abcurse didn't look his usual ethereal, shining beam of light. There was a heaviness in his broad, tense shoulders; a darkness shadowing his furrowed brow and rigid jawline. He was unhappy in a way I had never seen before.

I reached out and brushed my fingers across his image, and his eyes began to glow.

"Come home to us," was the last demand I heard before their images flickered and disappeared.

A small whimper escaped before I could stop it, my body slumping into the rocks. The pain was almost too much, but I knew I could deal with it. They weren't dead, even though it felt like all the worlds were working to keep us apart now.

Straightening, I smoothed my expression as best as I could, tucking the pain away as I turned to the panteras. Except only Leden remained now, the others had disappeared.

You are stronger than we expected, for one so young. As hard as it is to believe, your sufferings were gifts, in a way. They formed a being far more exceptional than simple genetics ever could.

"Can you tell me more about how I have tasted the water before this sun-cycle?" Couldn't hurt to ask, on the off-chance that my mother had fried the brain cells that remembered my childhood.

All I can tell you is that you did not absorb the water in the same way as Staviti. You are unique.

Like the Abcurses. For some reason that made me happy, and I didn't feel a need to push for more information.

"Can't leave you anywhere, doll. You really should just stick by my side."

The deep, rich voice echoed through the cave, and I immediately dropped into a semblance of a fighting position, a curse falling from my lips. *He* was my escort?

Cyrus was propped against the wall nearby, looking smug and amused. "Are you going to hit me?" His grin grew even broader as he straightened and strode gracefully toward me. "After everything I've done for you."

A red haze started to edge across my side vision, and I was fighting hard to keep myself from charging him. "What you've done for me? You mean besides the part where you broke my soul-link to the Abcurses? Twice! Then you pretended this necklace could take the curse." I reached down and yanked it up, just in case he had forgotten. "Or when you started controlling me and causing Chaos and fires and squished bodies!"

The last part left me in a shriek and I couldn't stop myself any longer. I let out a war-like cry and sprinted as fast as my clumsy little legs could take me, somehow avoiding two large rocks, which would have tripped me up before I started.

Cyrus didn't even move, he just threw his head back and laughed so loudly the entire cave seemed to shake around us. He wasn't even remotely taking me seriously. Focussing on his chin, hoping I could reach it, my fists were already lifting when my right foot hit a particularly loose patch of rocks and I started to slide out. I tried to straighten, my arms going out to the sides in a steadying motion. My right foot tangled in my left then and I was plunging forward. And since my arms had been way up above me, there was no chance I was going to get them down in time to stop my face breaking the fall.

Cyrus was a beat too slow to catch me, since he'd had his head back laughing when I tripped, but he noticed just in time to step into me. Which meant that instead of my head slamming into the hard rocks, it crashed right into his crotch. He let out a bit of a yelping groan, before both of us went down in a heap.

I was stunned for a click, darkness dancing across my vision. *What the hell was in his pants? Steel ballbags?*

Another chuckling groan from above, and I realised I'd said that out loud when he replied. "If you don't get your face off my dick, Willa, you're going to find out."

I gasped when I realised I was still fully face down, on an area that seemed to be enjoying the attention. With another gasp, I rolled over, and lay on my back, breathing in and out quickly. I knew that my face would be bright red. Or whatever colour was even redder than red because *holy shit*.

Why did these things keep happening to me? A shadow washed over my face, but my hand was firmly over my eyes, hiding me from the world. After a click, knowing there was no way to delay any longer, I removed my palm from my burning face, and looked up at Cyrus. He was still wearing that stupid grin.

"Stop looking at me like that!" I hissed at him, trying to bring some normalcy back to the situation.

Before I could say another thing, a second shadow appeared and Cyrus went flying through the air. I jumped to my feet far quicker than I should have been able to from flat on my back, my head swivelling left and right rapidly as I tried to figure out who was attacking us.

The only being standing close by was Leden. And even though it was very difficult to tell on the pantera's face, she sort of looked like she was grinning.

Whoops, she said. *Slipped.*

Cyrus let out a snort as he peeled himself off the wall and crossed back to us. I noticed that he had two distinct-looking hoof marks on his chest, just visible above the line of his shirt.

Leden had kicked him for me? I let out an internal cheer, before reaching out and giving her a one-armed hug around the neck. "I owe you one," I whispered into her throat.

He's not a bad god. But all of the gods, at varying times, need to be taught a lesson in respect.

Cyrus's expression was back to a more neutral style as he stopped near me, looking almost unharmed except for the fading marks. I knew they'd be completely gone in a click.

"Maybe we should start again," he tried, sounding just a tad less arrogant. "I think you might have the wrong idea about my involvement in your life dramas."

I crossed my arms over my chest, finally realising how little I was wearing. Sure, underwear was actually better than my usual bouts of nudity, but I was still pretty skimpily dressed. Alone. With the Neutral God whose Neutral Dick had been briefly having non-neutral feelings.

Lucky I had my new friend.

"You already know why I helped Rau initially. I didn't know you then. I cared nothing for the problems of a dweller, and Rau had something I needed."

I nodded, telling him to continue. I definitely remembered all of that clearly.

"I called you doll because you were so weak, fragile … nothing of substance."

My eyes were narrowing, fists clenching beneath my crossed arms. "You better be getting to the point where I don't want to punch you again."

A half-smirk. "Well, if you remember correctly, you didn't punch me, you dropped your face into my di—"

"Not the point!" I interrupted quickly, feeling the heat climbing into my cheeks again.

He gave me a break then, continuing with his story. "I was wrong. You're not exactly the doll I expected," he finally admitted. "You have substance, Willa Knight. I see now why the Abcurses have threatened more gods in the past few moon-cycles, than they have in their many life-cycles before that."

Oh, was I actually going to find out how old they were?

Before I could push, he changed direction. "They are feared by many. Loved by very few," he added, probably noticing the interest in my gaze. "The fact that you made it to their inner circle. You're no ordinary being."

Leden nudged against me, as if to say *I told you so*.

"But you do need a lot of looking after." Cyrus was back to being an asshole, though for some reason it didn't seem as mean as usual. "Which is why I have been trying to help you through the soul-link."

It's true, Leden said. *When we gave him the stone, we made him promise that you were the only being to have it, and that he would protect you.*

Cyrus nodded, which told me he had heard her words also. "I'm not great at Chaos either." I could tell that not being good at something was unusual, and he looked mighty pissed about it, his ethereally beautiful face going hard. "But you were alive, so I didn't complain too much."

I shook my head, much of my fury at him fading away. "You just used a little too much anger and oomph, I think."

He was very close to me now, and despite the lighting being only provided from the tiny bugs, I could still see every facet of blue in his very pale eyes. "That sol, Dru … he needed to die. I tried to ensure that he would not have a chance to follow up on whatever he was planning."

I gasped, having forgotten about Dru and his side-bitch. "You knew? How did you know? I mean it was weird how he was always around, always showing up, flirting. Never even caring that the Abcurses could break him like a twig. Despite his mountainous size." My words tumbled over each other, punctuated by the rage I was still holding onto.

Cyrus just shook his head. "You're trying to tell me something, I just know it."

I smacked him in the shoulder, before shaking my head. "You understood me."

His expression turned lethal, iciness pouring from him as he looked at his shoulder. I quickly withdrew my hand. Scary Cyrus was back.

His next words were clipped. "Whoever you've been soul-linked to will always have a connection with you. An eternal bond."

I wasn't sure exactly what he was saying, but his closeness was confusing me. Along with his hot and cold behaviour. When I just continued staring unblinkingly at him, he shook his head and took a step back. I finally felt like I could breathe again.

It's time for you to return to your gods. Leden's distraction was a welcome relief. As her words registered, I couldn't stop from throwing my arms around her.

"Will I see you again?" I felt a little bereft at leaving.

She nodded, large dark eyes blinking a few times. *We will meet again very soon. When the water calls, you listen.*

Then with that, she turned and walked out of the cave. The lights were fading around us now, so with a ragged breath I turned to Cyrus. "I believe you weren't trying to use me to cause Chaos." Another deep breath as I struggled with the next words. "Thank you." It sounded a little grudging, but I got there in the end.

He just shook his head before reaching out to me, he paused before touching me, his gaze seemed to be asking for permission. I waited a few beats, before finally nodding.

I was scooped up against his chest, my legs dangling from the ground as though I was a child. "Do you ever wear clothes, doll?"

I shrugged. "Siret always makes them so tight that it's much more comfortable this way."

"Clever Siret." I heard him murmur, but before I could say anything else, he did his flashing thing and everything went dark.

CHAPTER TEN

I knew where I was the moment my bare feet hit the cold marble, because the arm around my back slipped away and the god who had been holding me lurched back with a *thud* and a grunt that hinted at possible injury. I opened my eyes to find myself surrounded by Siret, Yael, Aros, and Coen. Rome must have been behind me, because I could hear the sound of him trying not to use his *crusher* ability on Cyrus. It sounded like an excessive amount of heavy breathing.

"Give. Me. One. Good. Reason." He seemed to be forcing the angry words out through clenched teeth.

"I *could* give you one good reason." Cyrus spoke normally, apparently unfazed. "Or Willa could give you several. If you attack me, I might have to tell Staviti about all the *other* rules you and your brothers have broken, and then you'll definitely have your powers stripped away."

"Well?" Yael asked me, his eyes drilling into mine with a scary amount of force. "Do you have several good reasons?"

Aros and Siret were pressing in, moving until their body heat warmed along both of my sides—but they weren't touching me. They weren't dragging me into their arms in relief. They were waiting for my reply; waiting to find out whether they needed to attack Cyrus or not. Someone really needed to teach them that attacking every person who wronged them wasn't the best way to deal with conflict. Unfortunately, I wasn't in a position to teach them anything, because I seemed to be adopting a similar approach. Hard surfaces wronged me all the time, and I still attacked them at least once every sun-cycle.

"As tempting as it is to have everyone fight over me for a few clicks," I started sarcastically—interrupted by Siret's soft snort beside me. "He helped to get me here. And *tried* to help keep me alive."

"Harder than it sounds," Cyrus muttered from behind me.

"Don't talk like you know her," Coen snapped, his eyes growing cold and flicking over my shoulder.

"I know she's a pain in the ass," Cyrus snapped back, his tone growing impatient. "And now I've delivered her safe and sound. Mostly dressed. I would say that I have fulfilled my end of the deal."

I knew that he had disappeared again because Rome stopped his heavy-breathing exercises and started swearing instead, while Yael and Coen exchanged suspicious glances.

"What deal?" Aros asked me, his arm snaking around my middle.

He pulled me into his chest just as Siret reached over, his hand grabbing onto my other side, forming a cross over my stomach as he started to pull me away from Aros. Yael stepped in closer, and I felt the air brush across the back of my neck. Rome.

They were all starting to close in, but there was only one of me, and the fingers gripping either side of my waist were already starting to dig in stubbornly. I would be a mess of bruises if I managed to survive the mess of a hug that was threatening to happen. I twisted my body to the right, dislodging the hold that Siret had of me, before ducking out of Aros's arms and quickly skipping off to the side.

"One at a time?" I suggested lamely, holding my hands out as though I could caution them all to stay back with the force of my bare palms. "It took a lot of effort to get here in one piece. I'd like to *stay* in one piece."

Coen rolled his eyes up to the sky, and Siret laughed. The others wore blank expressions, though there was a twitch in Rome's—a twitch that bordered on frustration.

"We separate for a few sun-cycles and she's already back to being scared of us," Rome noted, the words grunted out.

I glared at him and stopped backing away, my hands falling back to my sides. His bright green eyes seemed to have lightened, the sunlight slashing over his features. For half a moment, the breath fled my body, and I turned away from him in a bid to get it back. Aros was beside him, so I focussed there, until his golden eyes began to narrow in challenge, and my heart started to beat too fast. I diverted my attention to Siret, who seemed to have forgotten that he was finding me funny, because all the humour had been wiped out of him. His hair was a mess, and he pushed the mess of golden-black strands from his forehead, watching me so intently that my reaction to them grew even worse. My palms started to sweat. I turned to Yael almost desperately, but he had taken on the amusement that Siret had lost: his mouth was turned up at the corners, his eyes darkening as he watched me. It was almost lazy, the *knowing* in his expression. I could have sworn that he *knew* about the breath that rattled in the back of my throat, and he liked it that way.

"That's enough," Coen said calmly, drawing my eyes to him.

His chest was suddenly right in front of my face, and his hands were at my hips, his fingers tightening around me until I could feel the bite of his grip as he pulled me up and into his body. My feet couldn't reach the ground anymore, so I wrapped my legs around his waist and quickly circled my arms around his neck. He smelled clean and warm and not at all like he had been kept as a prisoner in the sky for however many sun-cycles they had been up there. I lowered my head onto his shoulder, breathing him in, and I could have sworn that he took a deep breath as well. His hand tangled in my hair, bunching it up to where he had tucked his face into the crook of my neck, and I felt the pull of his breath all through his body. He released it on a soft groan, his other hand tightening where it still gripped my hip, and then I was being pulled away.

The disentanglement of limbs was a confused, hazy process. It almost seemed to happen in slow-motion, with Coen's eyes opening and connecting with mine just as I was turned and pressed to another body. I knew from the smell that it was Aros, and while it shouldn't have been so easy to turn my attention from one of them to the other, as soon as he pulled me in, my head was full of him, and only him. His hands were so warm I could feel the burn of him against my skin, making me suddenly painfully aware that I was half-naked, once again. He also seemed to be painfully aware, because he made a sound as soon as I was flush against him, and he captured my hands before I could return his hug. He passed me off to Yael by the wrists, his jaw clenched as he watched me go, and suddenly I was crushed in a fierce, breath-stealing hug.

"I'm so happy you're safe and back with us again, Willa-toy." The words were murmured into my shoulder, his arms banded right across my back, almost bending my body into him. "Right where you belong."

"Share," Siret demanded.

Yael released me reluctantly, but Rome stepped in before Siret could grab me.

"I'm not fucking going last," he declared, looping one arm around me and hauling me up into his chest. "Hi Willa. Glad you're safe."

"Hi, Two," I laughed. "Glad you're safe as well."

His mouth twitched, but he didn't entirely lose his grumpy expression, so I brought my hands up to his face and tried to push his mouth into a smile with my two index fingers. He scowled, shook his head to dislodge me, and then he jostled me further up and pressed his mouth firmly to mine. The kiss was short, hard, and hot.

He pulled back too quickly, his eyes flicking between mine, almost surprised, and then he was putting me down and Siret was spinning me around.

"Lucky last," he said, his hands on my shoulders.

He didn't pull me in, or squeeze my limbs in possession the way the others had. He just stared at me, waiting. *Waiting for what?* I reached out, unsure, and touched his chest. Apparently, that was all he needed. His eyes flashed and one of his hands slipped from my shoulder to the back of my head, and he was tugging me in. His other hand moved down my spine, bringing me flush, and I couldn't help the shiver that ran the length of my body. He must have felt it because he pressed harder against the curve of my spine, forcing me so close that the pressure of his chest against mine was actually making it hard to breathe.

"That semanight stone doesn't mean that we're letting you out of our sights ever again," he whispered. "I think you've proven that you're far more dangerous when left alone, than any other situation you could be dragged into by us."

"We leave her behind so that she can be kept safe from Topia and all the gods here that might find her *interesting*, and what does she do?" Coen seemed to be talking to his brothers.

"It was a very involved story," Aros answered. "Something to do with fire."

"She brought herself here anyway," Siret added, his words still mumbled against my skin. "Like the stubborn little soldier that she is."

"As much as I'd love to claim all the credit," I began, pulling away from Siret reluctantly so that I could address them all, "I was technically being controlled through Cyrus's hold on the soul-link. He's even worse at keeping me safe than *I* am. He thought he'd get me out of Blesswood, and that I'd be safer with Emmy—but that didn't work out so well. Then he thought he'd set a whole building of sols on fire, just to get rid of the couple of idiots that wanted to hurt me—again, not the best plan, but he tried. Eventually, I just ended up in the outer rings where they turn the dead dwellers into Jeffries. Dru dumped me out there because he thought it would be a fun way for me to die."

"Of course." Rome rolled his eyes. "She couldn't possibly have just been murdered like a normal person."

I immediately started looking around for something to throw at him. There were a few marbled squares set off to the sides of the platform, cleverly disguised by garden beds and creeping vines. I could spot doors in some places, so I assumed that they were rooms, or even entire residences. There wasn't a single loose object in sight, unless the stone bench a few feet away counted. It probably didn't, because I doubted I could pick it up and throw it at Rome.

Or could I? I was some kind of dweller-sol-beta hybrid, and I could do things like create fire and cause nakedness, so why couldn't I throw a stone bench? I quickly side-stepped and grabbed the edge with one hand, attempting to lift it up.

"What's she doing?" Rome asked, his brow scrunching up in confusion.

"Gods-dammit," I wheezed out, managing to get the bench almost half an inch off the ground.

"I think she's exercising," Siret answered, completely serious if his expression was anything to go by. "I've heard that the dwellers need to do that, otherwise they get ugly."

"Impossible," Aros scoffed. "Willa can't get ugly."

I accidently dropped the bench, and then had to cover my mouth, because I didn't know whether to laugh or not.

"What if I lose all my hair?" I asked him. "Will I be ugly then?"

Aros started to shake his head, and Yael stepped forward, anger marking his face. "Of course not!"

The laugh threatened to bubble out of me again, but I managed to hold it back.

"I'm picturing her as a server now," Coen groused, pressing the heels of his palms against his eyes.

"See!" I pointed at Coen. "He thinks I can be ugly."

"I'm picturing that stupid thing the female servers wear," Coen clarified. "The image is burned into my brain."

"Yeah, even he's not thinking that you can be ugly," Aros told me.

Hot and cold flashes were racing along my skin and I probably looked like I was exercising my jaw now, with the way my mouth was opening and closing. Coen dropped his hands from his face, and suddenly they were all staring at me. It was too much. Too much tension. The heat inside of me flared, and it was followed by a burn licking across my skin. I had a brief thought that I should walk away for a click and cool off, but just when I thought I could tear myself away from them and take a step back, a flash of orange light caught my attention.

"*Argh!*" I let out a shriek and started patting at the flames that had sprung up across my chest.

Heat licked gently over my hands, but there was no burning sensation or pain, so I patted harder. Emmy's fire-safety lecture popped into my head as I patted desperately. *Drop and roll, Willa. Drop and roll!* It had worked the last time I had set my clothes on fire, but this time there were already several sets of hands reaching for me, and there was no way they were going to let me drop to the ground. I shoved out my hands to keep them away from me—not wanting anyone to get burnt, even though the flames hadn't seemed to be burning me—and as soon as I did, the fire spluttered out.

One click, I had been on fire, and the next, I was standing there looking completely normal, as we all stared at my chest.

I ran my hands along my body, blinking rapidly as I tried to work out what had just happened. I was surprised that there were no burns or blisters, or blackened stubs where my limbs should have been. There wasn't even a rash. There wasn't even a *blush*.

"This is part of Staviti's punishment, right?" Rome had one hand against his forehead, before he ran it through his hair. "One far worse than house arrest or losing our gifts."

I had no idea what he was talking about. *A punishment*? They were all staring very intently at me, and all of them wore pained expressions.

"I'm fine, you don't have to stress," I said, still confused, my hands planted against my bare hips. "Just a little Chaos-fire, they happen regularly." As my hands slipped further down my body, the feeling of skin finally registered.

I'm not wearing underwear anymore.
I'm naked again.

With a sigh, I dropped my eyes down to find that my underwear had indeed gone up in flames, and I was actually completely bare, without a single burn or even the Chaos-fire left to cover me up. If this was Cyrus's doing, I was going to kill him through some form of slow and laborious torture.

Time for Plan B. I picked my head up, staring them all dead in the eye and refusing to use my arms to cover myself.

"I totally meant to do that," I said calmly.

Rome's punishment remark made sense now, but he better have said that because he couldn't touch me, and not because he had to look at me naked again. He had his angry face back on and I didn't like it. I felt like we'd made some real progress recently, but in an instant, we were right back to where we'd started from. *Just because I was naked, again? Seriously?* Hating the feeling of judgement—or whatever he was doing—I stepped closer, my finger already lifting to point at him. "What's the problem, Two? I'm sure you've seen more than your fair share of—"

I was snatched up off my feet before I could finish, and then he was turning and striding away with me. I struggled against his hold, but it was like struggling against god-made steel bands. There was no give, no way for me to shift his muscles even an inch. "Put me down. I don't need your … angry pity."

I hated when people felt sorry for me. When they tried to help the stupid girl who couldn't even keep her clothes on.

"Strength …" I heard the warning from Coen, though he wasn't coming after us yet.

Tension slithered across the already tense muscles bunched beneath me as Rome briefly paused. "I'm going to find her some clothes, I'll be right back." His words were gruff, and he started to move again.

Since I was still pressed into a broad chest, I couldn't see anything, but I was done being treated like a doll. Cyrus was right, I had more substance than that.

"Let me down," I demanded. Further mortification pressed in on me as a hot burn started behind my eyes, a thickness blocking up my throat. "Please." My voice wavered more than I would have liked, but it alone seemed to halt Rome.

He peered into my eyes, for what felt like an infinite amount of time before he gently set me on my feet. "Trickery," he called, still not taking his eyes off of me.

Siret was there in an instant and with a graze of his hand across my cheek, Rome left us. I watched him walk away before turning to Siret, who looked a little grim, his eyes on my face.

Siret ... who could have clothed me several clicks ago. Suddenly, Rome's behaviour became even more inexplicable.

"How much longer can we go on like this?" I murmured to Siret, as he placed both hands on my shoulders, his gaze scorching me with its intensity. "I'm a beta-sol-dweller-hybrid now, would your powers really still hurt me?"

His groan came from a place low in his throat—a deep, desperate sound—and instead of answering, he just let his powers free. Clothes wrapped across my body, silky and smooth, the material different to anything I'd felt on Minatsol.

I glanced down to find a tiny, blood-red ... wrap of some kind. Almost a dress, cut off at mid-thigh and hugging my body. I had soft black boots that fitted firmly to my legs, stopping just below my dress. "You have got to stop dressing me like a night walker," I drawled. "Men are going to start asking me how many tokens for a session."

It was the sort of lifestyle I was sure my mom indulged in. She called it survival, but when she spent all the tokens on alcohol, I called it destructive.

"I have a lot of tokens," Siret deadpanned.

I snorted. "You don't need them."

The humour died off his face. "Willa …"

An exaggerated clearing of a throat distracted us all, and I jerked myself back. I hadn't even realised how close I'd been to Siret, practically pressing myself to his body. Peering around him, I couldn't see anything because the rest of the Abcurses were already surrounding the throat-clearer.

My boots were surprisingly silent as I padded across the platform, wiggling my way between Yael and Aros. A Jeffrey stood in the centre: female, looking very wide-eyed as we all stared at her. There was a blankness in her wide eyes and she cleared her throat again, the mechanical sound grating across my nerves. Now that I knew how the Jeffreys got here, I couldn't stop thinking about the guardians.

"I'm here with an official summons from the Great and Humble Creator," the server started.

Coen waved his hand, and let out a low grumble. "We know why you're here, Greg, so can you just get to the point?"

"Greg is Staviti's personal server," Yael murmured close to my ear.

My spine tightened and I let out an exasperated huff of air. I had a few things to say to the *Great and Humble Creator*, and it was very difficult not to let the venomous things spew from my mouth. No doubt Greg would take everything I said straight back to him.

She cleared her throat again and started speaking in her mechanical way, as though she was a recorded message repeating to us. "The six of you will be required to attend a special games event in the Sacred Sand Arena in Blesswood, tomorrow night. You will face a chosen group of challengers. You will not be permitted the use of your powers during this event." Her large eyes turned to look directly at me. "Except for you, Willa Knight: you will still remain armed with whatever vestige of sol-power you possess."

She turned then, as though that was the whole message, and she didn't really need a response.

"Stop." The command in Aros's tone was enough to have all of us pausing.

Greg turned back to face him, waiting expectantly.

"Our punishment did not include Willa," he said. "She won't be fighting in the arena."

The server swayed on her feet, before a low gasp rocked from her mouth. "Staviti gave the order." She didn't look happy at the evidence of another god disobeying Staviti.

Siret crossed his arms and leaned back against a nearby pillar. "He has no control over Willa. She's not a god."

Greg cleared her throat again, and nodded briefly—though the movement was more of a bow. "Staviti would like it known that if he is disobeyed on this order, he will ensure that no sols ascend to godhood ever again."

A harsh curse burst from Rome, followed by multiple curses from the other Abcurses—distracting me from my own horror. I had been thinking about the fact that if no more sols became gods, then I would eventually be ripped away from them when one of my accidents finally hit the mark. But there was something more here. Something bigger than just me.

"What does this mean?" I asked Coen, who was closest.

His jaw was rigid as he tilted his hard stare in my direction. "Staviti can't just *stop* sols from becoming gods. That process isn't something in his control, despite what he wants everyone to think. It is a magic beyond our knowledge—we only influence and strengthen those who carry enough of the magic required to evolve."

Siret added, "It means he plans on locking up the sols, weakening them, draining their gifts, so that none will ever take the place of the current gods."

"He'll eventually kill all the sols," Rome finished.

"I'll do it!" I blurted out, turning to Greg, who had been quietly waiting. "I'll fight in the arena; you can tell Staviti."

Greg nodded, and then with a pop, she disappeared.

My chest was rattling as panic filled me. How could Staviti consider killing off an entire race of people, just because a few gods and a dweller-sol hybrid refused to participate in an arena battle? The sols might have been arrogant, shiny assholes, but they didn't deserve to just be wiped out on the whim of a single god.

I was pulled from my panicked thoughts as the five Abcurses formed a huddle. "Whose turn is it tonight?" Siret asked, his eyes flicking between his brothers.

Turn? What the hell was he talking about?

"It's mine," Yael declared, not an ounce of hesitation in his voice. "But I think it's a bad idea for any of us to be alone with her."

Right, *bed arrangements.* Well, that was as good a distraction as any.

The sun was very dim in the sky, so I supposed it made sense that they would start trying to figure out where to sleep. I still couldn't stop the snort from escaping, though. Yael would never usually admit to a weakness like that, which meant that he was worried. But seriously, did he really think that two Abcurses in my bed tonight would keep things from escalating? *Not freaking likely.*

After they finished quietly discussing who my second babysitter for the night would be, Yael and Rome broke away from the pack and led me into one of the marble rooms. The doorway had been hidden behind rose bushes, and the scent of sweet honeysuckle drifted in as we descended the stairs into the main room. There were no windows, since the residences had been set down into the platform, but it didn't feel small or claustrophobic. The space was spread out and open, a roaring fireplace the only light, it's warmth pleasant as it brushed across my face. The boys stopped on either side of a mammoth bed that was dressed in white linens, with lots of fluffy pillows at the head.

"Would you like to clean up?" Yael asked me, his eyes looking darker than usual in the muted lighting.

I found myself unable to speak. There was an intimacy and tension ricocheting between the three of us, and it had something tightening low in my gut. I knew they were waiting for an answer, so I quickly nodded my head. Not speaking at all seemed like the safest option.

Rome was the one to stride to a darkened wall and open a door I hadn't even seen there. "The bathing room is in here; I'll help you with the controls."

Swallowing hard, my feet were moving before my brain even registered what he'd said. Yael followed close behind me, for once his overly-brash arrogance tucked completely away. Stepping into a large and brightly lit room, I noticed that there were small illumination domes on the walls, and I watched Rome stop beside a huge, rounded shape on the floor as my eyes adjusted to the brightness. My brow furrowed as I crossed to him and stared down into it.

"What is this?" I asked.

He smiled, an actual real smile, and it was so shocking that I stumbled forward and almost fell head-first into the big bowl.

"This is a bather, we can fill it with water and you can relax in there."

I gave the bather another suspicious stare. "Where does the water come from?"

Rome lifted his head and stared at the ceiling: I followed his gaze but couldn't see what he was looking at. Then water started to fall, like rain, sprinkling the bottom of the bather. Glancing back at Rome, I noticed his hand against a panel on the wall.

"It's all controlled from here," he told me. "But you don't have to worry, I'll set you up and then you can call when you're ready to get out."

I nodded with enthusiasm; suddenly, I could think of nothing better than crawling in and letting the water wash over me. "It's like climbing into a well while it's raining, just ... smaller," I decided out loud. *Which was lucky, because I couldn't swim.*

Yael chuckled. "Yes, but this is warm, and the water has natural minerals to help clean and refresh your skin."

"Not drowning is probably the main benefit," Rome concluded.

Shaking my head, I ducked down and grabbed my right shoe as I started to hop around in an attempt to pull it off. "I'll have you know that I haven't drowned even *once*, and I've fallen into at least three wells."

It had been close that last time: Emmy had been forced to loop all of our bed sheets together to get me out—but they didn't need to know that part. "So, you don't have to worry about me," I finished, hopping a few more times before losing my balance and tumbling over.

Yael had me up and off the ground in a fraction of a click. "Why do I not believe you, Willa-toy? Something tells me there will never be a time where we don't have to worry about you." He deposited me on a small chair I hadn't noticed in the corner of the marble room. "Foot!" he demanded, holding his hand out.

I lifted my right leg, the red dress riding up even further so that my new, Siret-fashioned underwear was very clearly on display. Yael's eyes briefly moved up my leg, but he didn't say anything as he caught my ankle in his firm grip. He rested the ball of my foot against his abdominals, before sliding his hands down to the top of my boots. Fingers brushed against the skin which showed between my dress and boots.

I shifted in my chair then, forcing myself not to reach out and pull him to me. With slow movements, he slid the top of my boots down, before lifting my foot completely. My mouth was dry by the time he finished the second boot, and I was starting to think that he had done it to me deliberately.

"Bather is ready," Rome said, and I sprang to my feet.

Somehow, I managed not to trip and slam into Yael, who still stood close by, and I wasn't sure if I was disappointed or relieved by that. I was one big ball of tension by the time I crossed the bathing room. The bowl was about half full, and water still trickled in gentle streams from the ceiling. "Do you need help with the dress too?" Yael grinned darkly. He was still holding my boots in his hands.

I shook my head quickly. "No ... I'm good." I probably wasn't. Siret fitted everything so firmly to my body that it was nearly impossible to get it off without help, but I would be damned if I ended up naked in front of them again this sun-cycle. There was only so much a girl could handle.

CHAPTER ELEVEN

AS it turned out, Siret hadn't just moulded the ridiculous dress to my body—he had finished off the design without a single fastening. No zips. No buttons. He was trying to keep my clothes on by making them impossible to take off. Unfortunately, that also made it impossible for me to clean myself. I considered my options as the sound of slowly-trickling water drew me to the bather. I could call one of the guys in again, but things were already tense enough without me asking them to rip the dress off my body. I might have accidentally flashed them a lot, but I wasn't going to deliberately torture them. Not when they had made the girl-brother pact to keep the dynamics of our group intact. I could feel the lines slipping already, but I could also see how uneasy it was making them. I almost suspected that they were each torn between wanting to act before anyone else did, and wanting to maintain distance so that the others would do the same.

As for *my* feelings ... I didn't even know what they were. I didn't want to mess up the dynamic of our group either, but I completely lost all cognitive function whenever one of them touched me. I wanted them. All of them. Equally.

"I'm aware that's physically impossible," I told the bather, since the water chose that exact moment to stop trickling and it seemed like a sign. "I didn't mean *at the same time*."

The bather didn't respond, which was hardly surprising, and then I was back to my original conundrum.

How to get the dress off.

I started pacing by the side of the bather, but then stopped to try and concentrate, placing my hands against the dress.

"Chaos," I whispered. *Nothing*. "Fire Chaos?" This time it was a question, but still, nothing happened. "Gods-dammit."

I closed my eyes and thought back to what Leden had said about Chaos being in the *intention*, instead of the word.

"I *intend* to set my dress on fire," I muttered, and then I visualised flames crawling over the tight material for good measure.

The tickle of warmth was the only indication that I had succeeded, and I opened my eyes to the image of material flaking away from my body in smouldering pieces. My mouth dropped open as I watched the little embers float around the room. It was strangely beautiful, and not at all what I would categorise as chaotic … until one of the embers landed on a stack of fluffy-looking white towels, and then suddenly there was a *real* fire.

"Shit."

I rushed over to a fancy pearl-toned bowl that was sitting on a little side table—it didn't seem to serve any purpose other than decoration—and quickly knelt down by the side of the bather. I filled it and leapt toward the towels, dumping water onto the flames. Once the small crisis was averted, I returned to the bather and slipped into the water, luxuriating in my small victory. I was so busy luxuriating that it came as a jarring surprise to me when I stepped out half a rotation later and realised that I had nothing to wear.

I also had no towels.

The flames hadn't caught onto all of them, but the pile was a soot-smudged, sopping mess. I walked to the door and opened it a crack.

"Rome?" I called.

He appeared a moment later, his brows lowering in suspicion. "Why are you showing me a single eyeball right now?"

"I was just wondering if I could borrow your shirt."

"Why?" His expression grew dark, his huge arms folding across his chest. He actually looked like he would refuse me on principle. I wasn't sure what the principle would be.

"Did you see that dress?" I faked a light tone. "It was ridiculous."

His mouth twitched. Just a little bit. "Siret likes to abuse his power."

"You all do. You're all regular power-abusers."

The dark expression was back. "There's nothing regular about us."

"Okay yes you're very special. Can I please have your shirt now. Your *special* shirt."

He reached back over his shoulder, grabbed a handful of material and pulled it up and off, holding it out to me. I tried not to stare at all of the bare, golden skin that he had just put on display.

"I don't appreciate the tone." He pointed a finger at my face as I took the shirt. "But it *is* a special shirt, so try not to burn it."

"Liar." My voice was muffled because I had already pulled the shirt through the opening and was tugging it over my head. "You don't think it's special at all, you just don't want to see me naked again."

"Not the words I would have chosen," he mumbled.

I shook out the shirt so that it fell comfortably around my legs, and then I pulled the door fully open, leaning against the door jamb and folding my arms over my chest. Rome's eyes slipped from my face, taking in the sight of his shirt falling to my knees, and then he pulled me from the opening. One hand was planted on my shoulder, steering me back toward the main room. Yael was standing in front of a low table that had two armchairs on either side of it, arranged before the fireplace. The entire surface of the table had been covered in food, and I was too hungry to even question where it had all come from. I rushed over, fell to my knees, and started stuffing grapes into my mouth. There was a lot of fruit on the table ... and wine. I paused, pulling back a little as I finished chewing the grapes. There was some sort of cooked bird on a platter, decorated with spikey herbs.

"This is the most stereotypical meal of the gods that I've ever seen," I stated blandly.

"Didn't know you dwellers had theories on what we eat." Yael was loading a plate and pouring wine at the same time, his eyes focussed on the task.

"The gods are pretty much the only thing that the dwellers talk about," I informed him, accepting the plate that he handed me. "They think about what you're eating while they have hard bread for the seventieth life-cycle in a row. They think about where you're sleeping while they curl up on the floor. They think about what you're wearing while they scrape for enough tokens to mend a shirt."

I started to load my plate up while Rome sat silently in one of the chairs, his eyes flicking between me and Yael. Yael had stopped everything, and was now just kneeling there beside the table, staring at me. Eventually, he reached for the goblet that he had been pouring into, and took a long swig.

"That's depressing as fuck," he finally noted.

"You wouldn't know." I shrugged, sitting back on the floor and attempting to speak between bites of food. "The gods only watch the sols—and the dwellers around the sols. Nobody watches the dwellers in the outer rings; nobody cares about them. They're just a living server-farm for Staviti."

Yael winced, but Rome remained stony-faced, and we finished eating in silence. My thoughts were drifting back to Emmy, wondering where she was and what she was doing. She was tough, and smart—I wasn't too worried about her safety—but I hated that I wasn't there for her. She was still trying to deal with Atti's death and I had disappeared again.

"The Mortal Glass," I said, breaking out of my thoughts and glancing up to find Yael seated in the chair across from Rome. "Can I use it to see Emmy?"

"Was wondering when you'd ask," Rome stated, standing from the chair and walking to a small table beside the bed.

I recognised the gilded frame, and the glittery black stone set into the oval. He handed it to me, and I gripped it tightly, closing my eyes and thinking of Emmy with *intention*, just the same way as I had manifested the fire to burn my dress.

"*What the hell?*" An all-too-familiar feminine shriek filled the marble room, and I jerked back from the mirror.

The guys moved behind me and we all huddled forward again, watching Emmy's image manifest into the glass. She was sitting up in her bed, the sheet clutched to her chest, her hair tousled around her shoulders.

Cyrus was standing in the doorway.

"*What the hell?*" I echoed, only a few decibels quieter than Emmy.

"I didn't realise you would be sleeping." Cyrus sounded too formal, and he looked like he wanted to back out of the room and close the door, but he stood his ground.

"Who … *who are you?*" Emmy was scrambling out of bed, her eyes wide in fright.

She could clearly see that Cyrus—with his striking looks and white robes—wasn't a dweller. She still reached for the lamp beside her bed and held it out before her like a weapon.

"I am Cyrus," he replied, eyeing the lamp in almost-amusement. "The current Neutral God."

"Current?" She hastily set aside the lamp, and then started attempting to straighten up her sleep clothes. "I thought gods couldn't die?"

"A conversation for another time. I am here to inform you that Willa is with Abil's sons in … a secure location."

Emmy dropped all pretences of trying to be presentable and polite in front of the god that had stepped into her bedroom. She slumped down to sit on the side of the bed and let out a groan, her head falling into her hands.

"She snuck back into Topia again, didn't she?"

Behind me, Yael chuckled.

"A secure location," Cyrus repeated.

Emmy recovered some of her poise then, rising again to her feet. For someone who was a proud, card-carrying member of the dweller-club, I don't think she realised how much she acted like a sol at times. She was strong, smart, and capable. If she had been born a sol, she would have made it to Topia. I had no doubt at all of that.

"When will I be able to see her again?"

Cyrus took a step closer, towering above her. "Tomorrow. She'll be at the Sacred Sands arena."

Emmy opened her mouth again, but Cyrus did his disappearing act and she was alone. She blinked a few times in rapid succession, and I could see that her hands were tightly clenched at her sides. In a move I totally did not expect, she turned back, grabbed the lamp again, and threw it with all of her strength at the wall. It shattered, crashing with a racket to the floor.

"Fuck!" she cursed, and I almost jumped. Emmy didn't curse a lot, and I was torn between amusement and worry.

I couldn't tear my eyes from her as she continued to stare at the wall, until finally, with a sigh, the physical anger deflated out of her and she crossed over to the broken lamp. There was no way she would have been able to sleep with that mess on the floor, so it came as no surprise to me when she dropped down and started gathering up the pieces.

Before she could put them into the rubbish bin, though, there was a distinct whirling sound, and she let out a low shout, falling back onto her butt. I practically had my face pressed into the glass now, trying to figure out what just happened.

Emmy reached out again, and lifted the lamp up off the floor.

Holy gods.

It was perfect: not a scratch or mark on it. Considering that it had been in fifty pieces not a click ago …

I'd seen someone repair a lamp like that before. A lamp I had broken. *Cyrus*. It was the only possible explanation. I jerked my head up, clipping the side of Yael's jaw. He'd clearly been closer than I thought.

"Ouch." I rubbed the spot while he just shook his head at me. "What is Cyrus up to?" I asked, thankful that the pain was fading fast. "What does he want with Emmy?"

Yael and Rome exchanged a glance, and I lowered my hand from my head in case I needed to use it for physical violence.

"Calm down, Rocks." Rome shook his head at me. "Cyrus won't hurt your friend. I don't know what he thinks he's doing, though."

I didn't trust the Neutral God, but I also didn't think he planned on hurting Emmy. Not yet, anyway. I'd just have to keep an eye on him … somehow. By the time I turned back to the mortal glass, Emmy was in bed, and the lamp was on the small table. I doubted that she was asleep after all of that weird, but I also didn't need to keep watching her. She was okay for now, and that was the most important thing.

Unsure about how I was feeling, I handed the glass back to Yael. "We should get some sleep," I decided. "Tomorrow we need to fight a bunch of sols."

I was trying really hard not to think about that, because I wasn't sure how I could participate. Given that my only strength was the occasional burst of uncontrollable fire, I was more worried about accidentally burning someone to death than accidently dying myself. I'd have to think of other creative ways to win. Like running. Or hiding. Or discovering the power of invisibility—which would obviously be the ideal scenario.

The two gods stood and I followed, tilting my head back to take them both in. "So, how is the bed situation going to work?"

I figured that there was no point in dancing around the issue. Lines had been drawn by the five of them while I had been listening-in, somewhat uninvited, and now the lines were starting to blur. My near-constant nakedness was probably a significant contributor to the issue, but the rest was entirely their fault. They didn't have to walk around looking all perfect and … *godly*. I was just a poor, lowly dweller. That's what it was. *That's* why I couldn't stop wondering if I was going to be allowed to sleep on top of one of them.

It was hero-worship.

Shadows danced across Yael's face, giving him an air of mystery. "You're going to be in the middle of us, and we're going to make sure that Rau and Staviti don't steal you away in the night."

Right … *in the middle*. I could almost feel the sparks of Chaos wreaking havoc inside my chest, and it felt as though the room had just grown several degrees warmer. I wanted to fan my face, but that would be too obvious, so instead I turned and scurried across to the huge bed. I needed to focus, before the feeling of Chaos turned into *actual* Chaos and I managed to set fire to one of the Abcurses.

The decadent piece of furniture had definitely been created for the gods—probably by Staviti himself, though it was hard to imagine him decorating the interiors of marble rooms. It took me more than one try to scramble up over the side and move up near the pillows. I sprawled out on the cloud-like mattress, revelling in the feel of sheets spun from the softest of silk. Rome's long shirt tangled around my legs as I rolled over, staring up at the marble ceiling. There was a small, open dome right above the bed that I hadn't noticed before. I could spot the stars dotting the sky, and the faint ripple of glass that protected the room from the elements.

When I lifted my head, I realised that Rome and Yael were both still standing at the end of the bed, staring down at me. They seemed uneasy, and the strangeness of our grouping finally hit me in that moment. Rome and Yael were the *least* likely to break the girl-brother pact, at least when they were paired together. Yael was too competitive to share, and Rome was the easiest to rile into an argument. Especially an argument about me.

The others had somehow chosen this grouping with my discomfort firmly in mind, and that annoyed the hell out of me.

"Are you both going to sleep standing up?" I grumbled, propping myself up on my elbows. "Is this some kind of weird, true-god sleeping position? Does it keep your heads upright so that you can easily look down on everyone?"

"What got into her just now?" Rome asked Yael, turning his head to the side to talk to his brother, while his eyes stayed fixed on me. His posture was wary.

"No idea." Yael's voice was low, as though I might not hear him if he tricked me into thinking that the conversation was a private one. "It was very sudden. But mortal women are supposed to have mood swings. Did she not eat enough? Should I put some bread in her mouth before it gets worse?"

"Is that why you all have such good posture?" I pressed on, my voice getting louder—possibly to drown out Yael before he said anything else about what mortal women were like. "Because you sleep standing up like you might wrinkle your powerful reputation by laying down?"

"Too late." Rome's eyebrows shot up a little. "It got worse."

"I think she's nervous about sleeping with both of us." Yael placed his hands on the end of the bed and bent down a little, his eyes catching mine. "Are you nervous, Willa-toy?"

I grabbed one of the pillows and tossed it at his face. "No, I'm not *nervous*. I'm ..." *Upset that I won't be sleeping on top of anyone.* "Hungry."

"You just ate." Yael was smirking now.

"You also just projected your thoughts," Rome added dryly.

I grabbed the other pillow, but Yael shot forward and wrestled it off me, tossing it over the side of the bed and settling his weight onto me, his hands wrapping my wrists and pulling them up beside my head. The gesture was more playful than restraining, but my body didn't really care, because his body was slowly sinking down into mine and I could feel the hardness of his stomach and chest crushing against me, as well as the nudge of his hips as I tried to fight free.

"Guess we're sleeping without pillows tonight." Rome's gruff voice halted my efforts to struggle free for a click. "And she has nothing left to throw at us, so get the fuck off her, Persuasion."

Yael's smile flashed onto his face again, a dark gesture made even darker by the narrowing of his eyes and the tightening of his grip.

"Sweet dreams, Willa-toy," he muttered, rolling off me and settling at my side, one of his arms folded behind his head.

Rome had a stony look on his face. He sank down onto the bed after kicking his shoes off, claiming my other side. I glanced over at Yael's feet as he also kicked his shoes over the side of the bed. He was leaving his shirt on, but Rome's had already been stripped away, and I was starting to tense up, wondering if they were going to undress completely.

Wait—why the hell would they undress completely?

A warm palm landed on my thigh, stilling me. I'd been fidgeting, without even realising it.

"You need to sleep," Yael told me, the gentle tone so unlike him that it gave me further pause. "And we need to feel you safe with us. Worry about the other stuff tomorrow."

He squeezed my leg, and while I knew that it was to emphasise his words, I was struggling to find any moisture in my mouth. All I could think about was pulling my foot up along the bed to bend my knee, and whether it would force his hand to move further up my leg.

That was gravity.

Gravity couldn't get in trouble for breaking the pact. Right?

"That was nice advice and everything," Rome drawled, "but she's not listening."

"Will we restore the soul-link?" I squeaked out, trying to change the subject.

Rome rolled on to his side then, facing me. He propped his head up on one hand, staring down. He didn't seem to be focussing on what Yael was doing, instead he reached over and slowly pulled the hem of his shirt down my body. It had ridden up a lot, and I was minus underwear, so I was about to flash my goods to the world. *Again.* Yael didn't move his hand, though, so half of the shirt was back at knee level, but his half remained high on my thigh.

"We can restore the soul-link as soon as Cyrus comes back," Rome told me, and I was briefly confused until I remembered that I'd asked the question.

I shook my head. "Is it possible to have the link returned between us six, but also keep it with the semanight stone? That way I can still have some distance ... if needed."

Yael's hand clenched tighter around my thigh, and I started to worry that I was going to bruise.

"We'll see," was all he said.

I didn't argue further. There was a time and place, and right now was neither. I was too distracted. I vaguely entertained the idea of burrowing under the blankets and pretending that they weren't there.

Rome's palm landed on my stomach, spanning right across it and causing me to jerk a little. "Go to sleep, Willa."

I squeezed my eyes shut, trying to find some equilibrium. I knew I was fidgeting again, but I couldn't seem to stop myself. Being back with my guys after so long apart had me desperate to wrap myself around them and never let go.

Heat flickered across my face, and I heard Rome mutter, "She's going to set the room on fire again."

Intention.

I needed to sort out my Chaos intentions before I destroyed Topia. The only problem was that I couldn't think of what my intentions were. I just kept picturing the two Abcurses on either side of me, and wondering if they were going to take any more layers off.

"Shit." Yael's curse had my eyelids snapping open.

I scrambled up on the bed as my eyes flicked between the two of them. Over and over. Back and forth. Eventually, I got too dizzy to continue.

Rome and Yael were standing on either side of the bed now and I was standing on the mattress, right in the centre. I still only came to Rome's height.

"You're staring, Willa." Rome lifted one eyebrow, his arms hanging loosely at his sides.

I couldn't breathe. It was getting really hot, and it wasn't because of my little fire accident.

It was because of my ... *other* little incident.

"You ... you two need pants," I finally choked out. My voice sounded a little high and strained.

"We had pants," Yael drawled. "They disappeared."

Fuck. Double, triple ... a million fucks.

They weren't even trying to cover themselves. They were just standing there casually, and I just continued to stare. I'd seen Aros once before: that image was burned into my memories. Now I had two more to add.

"You have no sun-lines." *What the hell is wrong with you, Willa?*

Rome actually laughed. Out loud. "On Topia, clothing is a formality. Most gods don't wear much under their robes."

It was like I had been born to live there.

"I'm going back to bed," I decided. This was too much for my dweller brain. It was going to short out.

"At least you didn't use fire this time," Yael said as I slid back under the covers. "You're learning to control the Chaos."

Rome muttered, "She could have burned something *very* important."

I wanted to be grateful that I hadn't set fire to anything *very* important, and that I seemed to have developed another Chaos trick: the instant nudity trick. Unfortunately, it was hard to think about all the things I was trying to be grateful about. I needed to keep thinking about my new trick so that I didn't have the penis gallery in my head.

Just when my heart rate was almost back to normal, I felt them shifting around on either side of the bed. I had closed my eyes only half a click ago as an act of self-preservation, but now I cracked one of them open again. I had no idea where the clothing had come from, but Yael had a new pair of pants on, and he was tossing a second set over to Rome.

I quickly closed my eyes again and took a deep, shaky breath as they settled back to the bed, their bare arms pressing in against mine. At least they had pants on, and they had left just enough warm, golden skin for me to cuddle up to.

Just as soon as they fell asleep and I was able to do it undetected.

"Don't even think about it." The reprimand was a rough sound, vibrating through the half-bared body to my left. Rome. "You put your hands on me tonight and

I'll break the stupid pact and take every damn consequence they give me."

My eyelids flew open again—both of them this time, and I blinked back up at the dome in the ceiling, my mind spinning too fast to form a reply. The fireplace was still emitting enough light to fill the room, and I wondered if anyone was going to put out the fire—surely three bodies in a bed together would heat up pretty quickly.

Yael released a heavy breath, shifting beside me, and I worked to quieten my mind, to pull a shutter over my thoughts and gain some privacy.

"What are the consequences?" I asked suddenly, because gaining control over my mind apparently meant *losing* control over my mouth.

"A broken face," Rome stated plainly.

"Dick," Yael amended. "A broken dick."

"Yeah, more likely," Rome agreed.

"What?" I continued to blink up at the dome in the ceiling, since it seemed like a perfectly safe place to direct my attention. "They would actually do that?"

"I would." Yael sniffed, sounding almost insulted that I doubted their ability to fight over me. "That's what matters. Strength would, too. Probably twice, just because he likes breaking things."

Rome snorted, but it sounded like an agreement.

"Let me get this straight." I struggled to keep myself from sitting up and looking at them both. "If someone breaks the rules—which, if I remember correctly, were nothing *sexual*—then they get their … ah …"

"Dick," Yael supplied helpfully.

"Dick," I repeated, shifting around uncomfortably. "Yeah. That. They get *that* broken."

"That's correct." Rome let out a sigh. "Is this conversation going anywhere, or did you just want us to know that you have a problem with the word dick?"

"I didn't want to break any pact rules by talking about body parts!" I defended myself, a little louder than was really necessary. "That's too *sexual*."

"Point," Rome groaned. "If there is one, you need to get to it."

I immediately surged up from my spot and scrambled to the edge of the bed, right over Rome's legs. I made a haphazard grab for the pillow on the floor, ready to throw it in his face much harder than I had thrown it the first time—but arms wrapped around my waist and tugged me back.

I landed hard against a bare chest, my hands captured again and bundled up together over my stomach as I tried to get my breath back. I was laying on top of Rome, facing the dome in the ceiling again, the back of my head against his chest and the heat of him burning up through the entire length of my body.

"I can't sleep like this," I croaked out. "I need my hands."

"You don't need your hands to sleep." Rome's voice was in my ear, lower and softer than it had been all night.

"Sorry, Willa-toy," Yael's face was suddenly looming above mine, his hand brushing over the side of my face. "But we're really going to need you to sleep now."

A quick flash of anger spread through me, but it was followed by an even quicker flash of exhaustion. It settled against my senses with a heavy intention, pulling darkness over my eyelids and piling weight into my limbs.

He was using Persuasion to knock me out.

What.

A.

Dic—

CHAPTER TWELVE

THE warmth woke me first. I was surrounded by it, as though I had fallen asleep in the bather and the warm water still licked against my skin. But ... I wasn't in water. My eyes flew open and I tensed. I was still sprawled across Rome's bare chest. He had both arms wrapped around me, and at some point I must have turned so that my face was snuggled in between his shoulder and neck. The warmth was starting to make sense now, and the scent, because all I could smell was spice and god. *Holy fires in hell.* It was really hot in here now, and as sparks of Chaos lit up my chest, I fought against my urge to press myself tighter to him.

"I know you're awake," his deep voice rumbled all around me. He knew I was awake and hadn't loosened his grip on me. *That was a win.*

I still had my nose pressed against his smooth skin. "Did you hold me all night?" Somehow, through no fault of my own, my hand was running up and down his side, gently tracing the hard planes of his body.

His chest rumbled under me. "You talk in your sleep. You fidget in your sleep. This was the only way for me to keep you quiet."

My fingers brushed across the band of his pants, and images flooded my head. Rome and Yael naked … that wasn't something I was going to ever forget. Tilting my head slightly, I could see a wide, unoccupied expanse of bed off to the side, prompting me to think that Yael must have left.

"Where's Four?" I reluctantly lifted my head so that I could see Rome's face.

He looked a little tense, his jaw set in a firm line. "Meeting with the others, talking strategy. I was just waiting for you to wake up, then we can join them."

I was awake, but neither of us moved. Arms were still wrapped around me, and I was still running my hand along his side.

"This pact … I don't want the others to break your … thing." My face flushed as soon as those words fell thoughtlessly from my mouth.

I just couldn't stop thinking about the Abcurses. It had reached the point where I almost couldn't handle this sexually-tense-line we were precariously balancing on. Something had to give. The corner of Rome's lips twitched, and I felt a bubble of laughter fighting to free itself from my chest. We lost it at the same time, and I wasn't sure I'd ever heard him laugh like that. With an unrestrained sort of amusement, his powerful arms tightened, pulling me back into him.

"We're not breaking any pact yet."

A thought struck me then, and I stiffened, before wiggling my arms free and placing both palms onto Rome's chest. I pushed with all my might … and didn't move an inch. He must have noticed that I was trying to get free at some point, though, because he easily released me. Ignoring the waves of cool air, which immediately felt intrusive and annoying, I leveraged myself up so I could glare fully at him.

"I'm done with this pact," I grumbled. He opened his mouth but I cut him off before he could speak. "There's nothing you can say to change my mind. The pact is stupid. It's my life and my body and I will make the choices for it. Not you." I jabbed a finger at him. "And not those other morons!" Second finger jab in the direction of the doorway.

Chaos swirled within me, and I jumped to my feet before I burned the bed down. Rome lifted himself slightly, leveraging his elbows under him. His chest looked even more massive than usual and I had to force myself to stare at the wall behind him so that I wouldn't get distracted.

"You're right."

His words were so unexpected that I swung my head back to stare at him. My eyes widened even further when I saw how serious he looked.

"You're no longer a dweller, you're learning to control the power of Chaos. I think you can handle our powers ... if you want to."

Holy dweller babies.

He lifted himself all the way up, using just abdominal muscles, before he shifted forward onto his knees. I was standing, we were almost eye level. My heart started stuttering in uneven beats as he stared.

Then, in a micro-click, his arms went back around me, and I was hauled up into him.

"It's my turn," he murmured, before his lips landed on mine.

The kiss was surprisingly gentle, considering the fact that his power was Strength. His tongue traced along my lips, and I parted them for him. The most delicious sensation was his lips moving on mine, his tongue caressing mine. But ... was he holding back for fear of hurting me? *Had that been his issue all along?* Suddenly, I needed to see him lose control. Just a little bit. Before he had a chance to counter my actions, I pressed my feet into the mattress and pushed. We tumbled down together. Our lips never parting as he caught me with ease. His back hit the soft mattress. I wiggled across the top of him, every inch of my body pressed to the hardness of his. The warmth was back and I let out a low moan into his mouth. Rome froze for a tiny fraction of a heartbeat.

"Fuck," he muttered, as he sprang into action.

Before my slow brain had time to process what had happened, our positions were flipped and I was the one pressed into the soft mattress. The sensation of skin against skin was almost too overwhelming to process, and it took me a whole click to realise that he had wedged himself between my thighs, and I was still completely without underwear. I could feel the heat of him, the hardness of him, even the *size* of him. His lips weren't kissing any longer, but claiming, his tongue demanding more as it stroked my mouth. My head was spinning, but in the best kind of way. My body was moving against him, needing so much more. I never wanted the kiss to stop, so when he pulled away, I groaned.

"You better not stop, or I won't be held responsible for the Chaos that happens." I was breathless and aroused and annoyed.

His eyes were laughing at me, but his expression remained serious. "You need to tell the others about the pact first. It's the only way to ensure that there isn't a huge fight. Gods don't take lightly to breaking pacts, and our battles are bloodthirsty."

Rome seemed to have gotten himself under control again, which pissed me off more than anything else that had happened that sun-cycle. It had taken me forever to break through his thick outer layer; I didn't want that distance to come between us again.

As if he had read those thoughts on my face, he reached down and cupped my chin and cheek. "Listen, Rocks, I might have fought against you being part of our world, but it was because I didn't want you to get hurt. We're gods, our world is no place for a dweller. Especially one so breakable." His hand slowly lowered, before pressing against my chest, just above my heart. "I know you're ten times more resilient than I gave you credit for. You're worth a hundred gods, and I'm going to embrace every inch of crazy and naked you bring into our world."

My eyes were leaking; I had no freaking idea how that happened. Maybe my brain had malfunctioned.

"We need to talk to the others," I choked out.

I was in way too deep with all five of them, I needed this pact gone so that there wasn't a constant barrier between all of us. I had no idea how I was going to handle the logistics of five men and one me, but right now it didn't seem insurmountable. It felt like … fate. Like it was always meant to be this way, and it was time for all of us to embrace that.

Rome got off the bed, and as I walked over to him, he wrapped an arm around my waist and lifted me down off the high side. I practically sprinted toward the stairs that led out of the marble room as soon as my feet hit the floor.

"I'm telling the others right now!" I yelled over my shoulder.

It felt good to take some of my power back, to stand up for myself and what I wanted. The gods I had found myself tied to were very intimidating, but they weren't going to kill me. Almost ninety-percent sure. They worked too hard to keep me alive. I was *almost* ninety-percent sure that I could speak freely to them.

The light outside temporarily blinded me as I pushed the door open. By the time my eyes adjusted, I had stepped out into a half-circle of Abcurses, and then I was temporarily blinded for a second time.

"Oh, hey," I said casually, sliding my hands into my pockets.

Except I didn't have pockets, so they just slid down the sides of Rome's shirt. Four sets of eyes followed the movements, before they ran across my no-doubt scruffy bed-hair and swollen lips. They then switched their focus to something above my head. *Rome.*

"We need to talk," I started, but Aros interrupted before I could say anything.

"What did you do?" His accusatory statement was directed over my head.

I waited for Rome to deny what they were all thinking, but he didn't say anything.

"You broke the pact, and I told you what would happen last night." Yael sounded casual, but his stance was anything but.

"Stop it!" I demanded, moving back so that my body was pressed against Rome's. That was the only thing I could think of to keep him safe.

I could have sworn then that Yael looked upset—his lashes fluttered a few times, and darkness washed through his green eyes. I hated seeing him like that, but I also wasn't able to move because I knew that Rome was moments away from being pummelled by his brothers.

"She thinks she's protecting my dick," Rome growled out. "Maybe if you back off a little and listen to what she has to say, we can all get on with the rest of the sun-cycle."

Siret looked even angrier. "Protecting your dick from what?"

For the love of everything Topian—did everyone really *need to keep saying 'dick' so much*? The word barely even had any meaning at this point.

"Rome and I did not break the pact!" I shouted it so loudly that I swear a gasping Jeffrey fell off a nearby floating marble platform. I held out a hand then, toward Yael, and he eyed it for a beat before placing his hand into mine. I pulled him closer to me. The others followed until I was sandwiched in the middle of an Abcurse circle. They weren't all pressing into me, their shoulders were too broad for that, but they were all close now.

"You all made the pact for the sake of the group, right?" I asked, working to lower my tone now that I had their attention.

There were a few grunts of affirmation, and I waited a little longer to see if any of them had anything more substantial to add before I asked my next question.

"And I'm *part* of the group now, right?"

A few more grunts.

"So if the pact is all about respecting the dynamic of the group and stopping fights ... then shouldn't I be included in the whole pact-deciding process?"

Silence was my only answer, until Coen straightened away from the huddle to frown down at me. "You want to break the pact. With Strength. That's what this is about?"

As soon as the words were out of his mouth, the other three pulled away from me as well, and Yael turned as though he might start toward Rome again. I quickly re-captured his arm and rushed out, "No, that's not what this is about. This is about the fact that I should get a say in this as well. I don't want to cause fights or mess up the bond you all have with each other, but you all know that there's more. With me. With us."

I flicked my eyes from Yael, to Aros, to Coen, and then to Siret. Each of them wore distinctly cautious expressions, but the suspicion and anger was starting to fade away. I could feel Yael's arm becoming less tense beneath my fingers, and Coen's fists were loosening by his sides. They weren't jealous of each other in that moment—they were satisfied that I was showing them an even amount of attention and giving them all equal focus. With that thought in mind, I released Yael's arm and stepped more toward the middle of their grouping.

"You're not our brother," Aros finally spoke up, his tone solid, certain. "That's why it's different. You *act* like one of us, but you're not our blood and you're … you. So it's natural that we might develop a different kind of relationship."

"Essential actually," Siret added. "You're special. You're the only person we've invited into our group. The only person who has been allowed to get this close. You're like an outsider who belongs inside, so we brought you further in than we even bring each other, to make up for the fact that you weren't born one of us."

I blinked at him, a little surprised at the emotional analysis. I had no idea that Siret had been thinking so much about my place within their group.

"Whatever the reason," I glanced over Aros's shoulder to make sure Rome was still standing there, "I'm still a part of the group, and there's still *more* to us than a girl-brother friendship. All of us. I know you don't want to cause fights, but *I* don't want to be told what to do with my body and who I'm allowed to do it with—"

All four bodies around me immediately grew stiff, leaning slightly back from me again. I could almost feel the anger emanating from them.

"Who do you want to do it with?" There was a rare frown set into Siret's face, deepening in the lines around his mouth and turning the green-gold of his eyes into a meld of hurt and disappointment.

He didn't need to look over my shoulder at Rome. I knew that they were all thinking the same thing.

"Every person that I've kissed," I quickly answered.

"You've kissed Rome." Siret's serious contemplation flicked over my face.

"I have."

"And Aros."

I flicked my attention to the golden sol for a microclick, before quickly settling it back on Siret's face. I could see where he was going with this.

"All five of you," I told him, "almost."

"Almost," he agreed, folding his arms over his chest. "All five of us ... except me."

I stepped into him quickly, my hand on his forearm. He refused to uncross his arms, so I slid my touch up to his shoulder and then pressed closer to him. I could feel the sudden intake of air that he sucked in; could feel the swell of breath that pushed out his chest. He was nervous, or unsure. Possibly doubting that I really did want them all, though Siret had more than enough experience toying with my reaction to him. He should have known. The idea of me and Rome together had shaken his confidence.

"Are they going to stop me?" I asked, when I was close enough to whisper to him.

He remained still, not embracing me, not helping me to get any closer.

"They think we're arguing." His voice was low, carrying a rough undertone.

"You're using Trickery on them?" I was surprised, but I didn't stop the progress of my hands over the muscles in his shoulders, until my arms were almost looped around his neck. I wasn't quite tall enough to reach the full way without his help.

He began to loosen, just enough to drop his arms and allow me to press in against his chest, though he didn't put his hands on me in any way.

"They don't need to see you flirting with me right now out of pity. And they definitely don't need to see me taking it like I'm starving for the precious scraps you throw my way."

I resisted the urge to groan in frustration, reaching back to place his arm on my spine instead. "This isn't pity. This isn't a scrap."

He rolled his eyes, but his hand stayed where it was, pressing into the curve of my lower back. I lifted up onto my toes and brushed my lips over his: once, lightly, only a whisper of a word that I might still say to him. He chased my lips when I drew back, hovering but not touching, attempting to out-last my control and draw the word out by force of will.

He started to speak against my lips. "If you're going to break the pact, you need to break it evenly. Whatever you give to one of us, you give to the rest of us. Because you want to, not out of pity."

"There's no pity here." The frustration was definitely beginning to leak into my tone. "I couldn't pity you if I tried. You've lived a blessed existence of never-ending food, brain-dead dweller servants, and pranking the gods. I can only pity the poor dwellers who've had to die just to make sure your silk sheets don't have any crinkles—"

"I get the point," he grumbled. Then, a moment later, he grabbed me around the hips and bent my body into his. "You can start evening out the score now."

I lifted my lips to his before he could change his mind, and sighed at the immediate sound of possession that rumbled through his chest. He had been holding back up until now, but something had finally snapped his restraints. He took control of the kiss immediately, digging his fingers into my hips and pulling me up his body so that he could reach my mouth better. I tunnelled my hands into the back of his shirt, pressing into the ridge of muscle that led to the center of his spine. He jostled me once, wrapping an arm around my butt and freeing one of his hands to press against my collarbone, breaking the kiss.

"If you distract me too much, my power will slip." His voice was raw, his eyes more green than gold.

I nodded and he set me down, releasing me with a reluctance that showed in the drag of his hands.

"Okay, this is getting us nowhere," Aros suddenly burst out. "You two need to calm the hell down—Trickery, back off her."

"It's fine!" I quickly threw my hands up when I realised that they were all starting to crowd around me, their postures protective, their eyes on Siret.

He smirked at me, almost back to his normal self. "We weren't fighting. Sorry. Necessary evil."

The change was instant: Coen made a grab for Siret, but Aros grabbed his arm, and he seemed to re-think the decision—but then *Yael* made the same move, and it took both Coen and Aros to haul him back. Siret just stood there, while Rome didn't seem to be moving at all. Only observing.

"It's only fair," I heard Aros saying. "She's kissed the rest of us. He was the only one she hadn't kissed."

"This is how you want it to be?" Coen asked, spinning on me.

"You want to get rid of the pact?" Yael also spun around—Siret seemed to be forgotten in that moment. "You want to try to keep it even between us, instead?" There was a challenge in his eyes, as though he expected me to realise the fault in my thinking and apologise.

That wasn't going to happen, though. There was no fault in my thinking. I really believed that I *could* keep it even; that I could stop them from fighting.

"Let's make a deal." I displayed my palms to Yael, a gesture of peace. "If I can keep you all from fighting about the dynamic, you will stop trying to force restrictions on what I do with my body. Okay?"

Yael frowned, apparently torn, but Aros once again proved himself to be on my side.

"Even," he demanded, pushing past the others to stand in front of me. "Make sure you keep it even, sweetheart, and I won't start any fights."

"If you think you can …" Coen drew my attention, though Aros's hand was snaking around the side of my face. "Then I can do away with the fucking pact."

I sought out Siret, who only nodded at me, but it was enough for now. He had already given in earlier. I had felt it in the way his kiss worked to claim me as much as was possible in the sliver of time that he had stolen. He was finished with the pact.

"That pact is finished," Rome spoke up from behind me, and I felt everyone relax almost as quickly as I felt them all tense up again.

There was still one Abcurse who didn't seem to want to let go of the pact, and it was the one Abcurse who I thought might have serious problems with sharing in any way, shape or form. Yael met my eyes, the challenge still burning in his expression.

"I'll try not to break anyone's dick," he finally announced.

CHAPTER THIRTEEN

I felt … lighter. Ever since I had accidentally-on-purpose overheard them discussing the pact, there had been a pressing weight on my shoulders, trying to tell me how to be and what was okay. I didn't do well with restrictions, clearly, but now I was free again. We all were, and I was determined to keep my part of our new deal. There would be no more fighting over this.

"I'm going to clean up," I announced, an upbeat tone to my voice. Turning to Siret, I added, "I'm going to need some kickass clothes, kickass boots, kickass glov—"

"I get the point," he said drily. "You're going with a theme, and the theme is—"

"Kickass. Yes." I clapped my hands a few times. "Okay, great. Be back soon."

I spun around, accidently causing Rome's shirt to fly up a little—and I probably flashed some thigh in the process, but no one said anything. We were all on our best behaviour. Or at least I assumed we were. I was almost at the top of the stairs when the sound of a throat clearing caught my attention. Tilting my head back to them, I noticed none of them had moved an inch.

"What?" My smile was way too broad for our situation, but happy seemed to be radiating out of me.

I had wanted the pact gone since the very first suncycle of the pact existing, and I had finally won. No one answered me, and I felt my cheeks lower as my smile faded away.

"What?" I repeated, worried now that my one click of happiness was almost over.

Coen was the one to answer me. "Just letting you know that we'll be called to the Sacred Sands Arena in fifteen clicks, and you need to eat. So …"

He trailed off, and I was starting to get the idea of where this was all going. We had just dissolved the pact, and I was heading down to the bather. They wanted to come with me and I wanted them to come with me, but I was pretty sure five and one was something we needed to slowly work our way up to. Besides that, if I wanted to keep the peace, I needed to be careful about keeping things even between them. I needed to delicately work out some sort of schedule.

"I'll be quick." Those words were pretty much thrown over my shoulder as I dashed down the stairs, tripping over the last few and tumbling to the ground.

A huff left me as I lay there. It was really unfair that I got a bunch of Chaos fire power, but I still couldn't manage to stay on my own feet. I was grateful, though, that I managed to scurry up and hide in the other room before any Abcurse came to investigate the thump.

Pulling off Rome's shirt, I folded it haphazardly and put it on a shelf. It probably should have bothered me that I had no real possessions. Hell, I didn't even know where my things were that I had been holding onto. Most likely my fist-rock and the scraps of dress I owned were still in Coen's room. My medical kit and poison antidote—the only things I brought from my village—were still with Emmy. She wouldn't misplace them. No doubt my duffle was sitting neatly on my bed.

I fiddled with the controls on the wall, finally figuring out how to get the water to fall from the ceiling, I considered the reason why I had never bothered to retrieve that bag when I was first soul-linked to the boys. Part of me had never felt like a dweller. It wasn't that I thought I was above dwellers, or equal to the sols. In fact, that couldn't have been further from the truth. I simply hadn't felt that there was a place I belonged. I had never been a proper dweller, and I could never be a sol. I'd always just been me. A weird mess of a being who was determined to prove everyone wrong and live at least twenty life-cycles.

Everything in my duffle had represented a part of my old life. It didn't fit me anymore. I wondered if it ever had. *Or was it that possessions just didn't mean much to me?* I held on to the people I loved, which, before a few moon-cycles ago had only been Emmy. Now I had so much more.

Letting the warm, soothing water wash over me, I felt some of the frantic pace of my mind calm. I was so rarely calm, it was actually a novel experience. No thinking, just enjoying.

"Am I interrupting?"

My eyes shot open and I glared at Cyrus. "Get the hell out, can't you see I'm enjoying my—"

I had been about to say *my alone time*, but his low groan cut me off.

"As much as I appreciate a woman enjoying herself, I need to get this soul-link reinstated between you and the god-squad out there. I'm ... concerned about this little arena experiment that Staviti has cooked up, and I want to make sure they can keep Chaos from overwhelming you."

I reached up and clutched the stone still hanging between my breasts. "I want to keep the link with the stone as well; that way I can have some distance from the boys without killing myself."

Cyrus regarded me for a long moment, his eyes lingering on my chest. I was just rolling my eyes when the door to the bather room slammed open.

"What the fuck are you doing in here?" Rome snarled, crossing the room in a micro-click.

Without waiting for an answer, his fist slammed into Cyrus's face; he had moved so quickly that I had barely blinked before the Neutral god was flying across the room. The problem was, he was flying right toward me, and even though I ducked, he still tumbled into the bather with me. Water splashed everywhere as his body slammed me into the hard base.

"Ugh," I huffed, pulling my head out of the water and trying to get my breath back.

It was made even more difficult due to the fact that Cyrus had his head pressed into my chest.

"This makes us even for the last time, doll."

Right. *Face in penis*. I remembered.

Leveraging my hands under him, I pushed with all of my strength, but he didn't move an inch. I was just lifting my leg to try *knee in penis* when he disappeared—tossed across the room to slam into a nearby wall. I didn't know which one of the guys had done that, and I didn't stop to consider it because I could suddenly feel the strong swell of power in the room, making the air that much harder to breathe.

I scrambled up, letting out a gasp as the rest of the room came into sight. For the first time, I saw a real reason to fear Cyrus as the Neutral God. He was soaking wet, his hair slicked back—defining the hard, gorgeous planes of his face. His eyes were blazing, his shirt plastered across broad muscles. A wispy, white energy was forming around his hands, but the power building in the room had every hair on my arms standing on end. The Abcurses actually looked a little wary—not scared, I'd probably be dead before I saw that expression on their faces—but cautious.

"I came to reinstate the soul-link. I did not touch her." Cyrus's voice was low and rumbly as the walls shook around us. "I should have expected her to be naked ... and I should have waited, so I will not ... pursue this challenge right now. But if you touch me again ..." His eyes were the coldest, soul-sucking pits of hell I had ever seen. I was chilled to my bones just looking at him. "I will not be so lenient," he finished.

Some of the tension in the room eased again, and I blinked a few times as a thick, cream-coloured towel was handed to me. It looked as though my relaxing bather-time was up. I wrapped the huge length of material around myself, securing it tightly before Aros helped me out of the large bowl.

"Are you okay?" he asked, leaning down close to me before reaching out and rubbing his thumb over my lips. He pulled his hand back so I could see. There was a light smear of red across his thumb.

That bastard made me bleed?

Sure, technically Rome was the one who had punched him, but I loved Rome so it was easier to blame Cyrus.

"I'm fine," I said, shooting my best glare at the Neutral God. "He hits like a dweller who's in their fiftieth life-cycle."

Cyrus's lips twitched just slightly, and then he turned that frightening gaze on me. He moved then, his strides eating up the distance between us in no time at all. "You need me, doll. Don't push me too far."

Those low words were hypnotic as they filled the air around me. He lifted his arm, and Siret was suddenly between us.

"I need to touch her," Cyrus growled. "You're making my life much harder than it needs to be."

He seemed frustrated, pulling his hand back to run it through his still wet hair. "My life was perfect, and then one favour for that Chaos asshole, and now …" He trailed off, and from my protected position between Siret and Aros, I saw the Abcurses exchange a look.

"You must have some kind of vested interest in this." Yael crossed his arms over his chest, propping one shoulder against the pole he was standing near. "You're getting all emotional. Who would have thought: *Neutral has emotions?*" He turned to Siret. "You owe me something D.O.D. wouldn't want you to steal. I choose the pantera stone."

"Alright." Siret gave his brother a nod, but then lowered his head and cursed.

Those two had problems. Everything was a competition … especially with Yael. Rome was staring right at me—some of his rage had faded away, but his eyes were filled with turmoil.

I'm okay, I mouthed, knowing that he was kicking himself for sending Cyrus into me. His fists clenched, and I would have crossed to him, but I needed to remain where I was to make sure that Cyrus and the guys didn't try to hurt each other. I also needed to get rid of Cyrus now: he stirred up too much trouble.

"Thank you for helping us." I turned to him, trying to be diplomatic. "I'm ready for the link to be reinstated now."

"Good." He glanced from me to the others, and then seemed to change his mind, striding for the door. "Get dressed and meet me in the next cube. *Alone*. This doesn't need to be a fucking group affair. It's a simple enchantment, and I'd like to keep it that way—*simple*, I mean. The last time I needed seven people to do an enchantment, it was to fix the illusion that *someone* created to convince all the gods that they had woken up with the wrong set of genitals."

"You can't prove it was me!" Siret shouted after him, as Cyrus passed through into the hallways, slamming the door behind him.

The rest of the tension in the room drained almost immediately.

"Cube?" I questioned aloud, choosing to ignore the mention of genitals. Talking about them always seemed to get me into trouble.

"That's what they call the marble residences," Coen informed me, almost in an off-hand manner. He seemed to be distracted as he moved to the door, grabbing Rome's arm as he passed. "Siret, put some clothes on her before it's too late and she gets called to the arena without the soul-link intact. We've done enough fucking around." He opened the door, motioned Rome to go ahead of him, and then turned to glance at me over his shoulder. "We're going to have a quick meeting in Trickery's cube—we'll see you out on the platform after you're done with Neutral."

I felt like questioning his suddenly brisk and almost sterile attitude, but closed my mouth and nodded instead. I thought I understood already: we had an unprecedented arena match to prepare for, but instead, we were fighting like we were in the thirteenth life-cycle. Well, the *rest* of us were fighting. Coen was apparently being responsible and acting his age—whatever that was.

Yael and Aros followed him out, leaving me with Siret, who placed his hands on my shoulders and shook his head at me.

"Your Chaos is a force to be feared, Soldier. Only you would end up in a bather with a Neutral god *completely* by accident."

"Now that I know about the Chaos ... it's almost unbelievable that I didn't suspect it earlier," I told him, watching his face for a reaction. "I really should have just stopped one sun-cycle—probably after setting something on fire through almost impossible means—and thought to myself: *you know what, there really is only one possible explanation to this. I must be a raceless hybrid with the power of a god.* Because why not? Right?"

He cracked a smile, and I felt the trickle of his magic over my skin as he loosened the towel I'd wrapped around myself. I felt the material drop at my feet, but he kept his eyes firmly on my face, which had me breaking out into a matching smile.

"I think that's a very logical explanation to come up with." He pulled back and looked me over with a nod as I felt the fresh wrap of cloth settle against me. "And with the way you're dressed right now, I would totally have believed it. Now get our damn soul-link restored properly so that we can hear your disastrous thoughts a little more clearly. They've been coming and going ever since Cyrus messed with the link in the first place."

I quickly glanced down at myself—taking in the boots that were definitely the ass-kicking type, and the soft leather pants and tight black top that he had woven onto me like a second skin.

"You're brilliant at this." I could feel my smile widening as I turned to walk backwards toward the door—an admittedly dangerous endeavour, but it was hard to drag my eyes away from his tousled hair and the bright focus in his eyes. "Thanks, Five."

"Don't let him touch you," Siret warned me, becoming serious again. "Not any more than necessary."

"He's not exactly a horrible pervert who preys on rogue dwellers." I reached for the handle and pulled open the door with a flourish, because the ass-kicking boots were giving me some serious confidence. "I think he just likes to tease me. And I don't think he's *interested* in me—I think he's interested in what I represent."

"Rogue dweller?" Siret was grinning again. "Is that what you represent?"

"No." I pulled my head up a little in defence of my title. "I represent a flaw in the drive for perfection."

Both of Siret's brows shot up, and he took a few long strides to the doorway, until he was looking down on me from a height again. He compensated by lifting my chin and bringing my eyes to his.

"You've thought about this," was all he said, his tone wiped of emotion.

I tried to nod, but his finger on my chin prevented the movement. "I have. A little. I mean … I didn't write a sonnet about it or anything, but yeah I thought about it."

"Tell me what you thought," he demanded quietly.

I was starting to get embarrassed now, so I quickly forced the words out before I could stumble over them. "You're all *Original* Gods—even more original than the others because you were created as children, and you grew up on Topia. They were created, too, but as adults. As beings that were already fully formed. You five are different. *Topia* formed you, and from what I gather, the magic of the gods isn't so much in the gods, but in Topia itself."

I paused when Siret's mouth dropped open, but he quickly wiped the surprised look off his face and tapped my chin again.

"Keep going," he urged. "Tell me the rest."

"Well …" I averted my eyes, so that his reaction wouldn't put me off my theory. It had sounded like a good theory inside my head, but I was starting to second-guess it now that I was spilling it all out into the open. "You five are almost perfect. The perfect beings. You never allow anyone into your perfect circle, and that is accepted because the gods prize perfection. It's what they're driven toward. It's why they make everything from marble; it's why they wear only pure colours, and they don't mix those colours; it's why they strip the humanity from the dwellers to allow them to serve; and it's why they banish the old servers and bring in the new servers so often. It's all in search of perfection. But you five found me, and accepted me, and haven't let me go. I'm as far from perfect as a being can get, and *that's* what has Cyrus so interested in me. I'm a kink in the system. An irregularity. Something unexplainable."

Siret fell a step back from me, and his laugh was sudden and loud, shocking me to the core. I thought that he was laughing *at* me until he suddenly stopped, grabbed my face, and forced my lips to his in a hard kiss.

"Perfect," he muttered. "You're perfect."

He released me almost as quickly as he had grabbed me, and turned without another word, striding down the short hallway and back into the main room. I followed, but he had already left the cube by the time I managed to shake off the paralysis that his kiss had put me into.

It was going to take some getting used to, these new rules.

Not that I was complaining.

I stopped by the small table in front of the fire, because it had been freshly laid out with food again—by means as mysterious to me now as they were the first time. I was beginning to suspect that there was another magical panel in the wall—one that somehow delivered food, just like the one that delivered water into the bather. I glanced up to see if I could spot anything, but it was just pure, unblemished marble. I grabbed an apple and made a sandwich from the selection of meats, cheeses and breads that had been set out, eating as I walked to the next cube and knocked on the door.

"We have manners, all of a sudden?" Cyrus questioned, pulling open the door.

"Just have my hands full," I replied, waving the sandwich before his face and nudging past him to get into the room. "I had to knock with my elbow. Let's get this done, shall we?"

Cyrus seemed to be trying not to frown at me. "Do you want to finish your sandwich first?"

"Why?" I asked, pausing before taking another bite. "Will it not mix well with the magic? Is this like that swimming rule that Emmy is always telling me about just in case I stumble out of Blesswood and into the river that surrounds the place, like some kind of out-of-control cart with broken wheels? Am I not allowed to have magic performed on me with a full stomach?"

"I'm sorry I brought it up in the first place," Cyrus muttered lowly, before his voice rose to a normal pitch again. "Just … never mind. I need to touch you now—are you going to scream for one of your boyfriends and have them smash me into a wall? Or can we handle this without the drama?"

"It was nice of you to let him do that," I smiled politely. "I really appreciate it, and I'm sure they did too."

He sighed, rolling his eyes up for a moment. "Answer the question."

"No, I won't scream. Unless you have to touch me in any inappropriate places—and if you *do*, then I feel like your job as a rule-enforcer should be taken away because that's an abuse of authority."

"You're right." He narrowed his eyes on me. "I'll make a complaint as soon as I'm done here. There has to be *someone* around here to handle complaints and deal with them accordingly."

"They really don't do any quality-control on you, do they?" I asked. "They do quality-control on the dwellers all the time; making sure they do their jobs and are still loving the gods and the sols with every fibre of their beings. Someone really needs to quality-control you."

He groaned, grabbed the apple out of my hand, and shoved it so hard against my mouth that I had to bite down on it out of reflex.

"Make sure you bring breakfast every time we speak," he said. "It was a great idea. Now hold still, and don't scream."

I tried to say *I can't scream because you shoved an apple in my mouth*—but it turned out that I also couldn't do that. Because I had an apple in my mouth. Cyrus seemed to find my conundrum funny, because his lips twitched upward into a self-satisfied smirk, and then he had his hand against my chest, right over the semanight stone. The smirk faded away almost instantly, and he closed his eyes.

He's doing the intention *thing*, I thought, watching the focus on his face. Was that something they taught in the sol schools? And if so, who taught the Original Gods and the Neutrals?

They'd never had any reason to teach 'control over god-given powers' in the dweller schools, because they were too busy teaching things like 'how to cook and clean and worship things.' I hadn't succeeded in many of my cooking endeavours, because objects and ingredients kept sneaking into my recipes that weren't supposed to be in there. I also hadn't been very good at the serving lessons, because I seemed to naturally repel order and cleanliness. The worshipping lessons I had actually *excelled* in, because genuflecting to a statue with my forehead against the floor had turned out to be a very comfortable sleeping position.

"You're thinking very loudly right now and it's hard to concentrate," Cyrus complained, his forehead creasing in frustration.

"Sorry," I muttered, after dislodging the apple from my mouth. I pulled it back up to take a bite. "It's all in the *intention*, Neutral. Just a tip."

"Thanks, doll. That's really helpful." He popped his eyes open again and wrestled the apple off me, attempting to shove it back into my mouth.

I managed to knock it out of his hand, but that unfortunately sent it bouncing to the floor. I watched as it rolled beneath a decorative side-table, and then I turned to the rest of my sandwich instead. Cyrus was already back to ignoring me, and I paused with my mouth half-full as pain fissured along my chest, sending a flood of darkness to the edges of my vision.

I quickly swallowed the bread that was trying to fuse with the back of my throat, and tried to muster the words to warn Cyrus that I was about to black out, but it was already happening.

Great, I thought, as my eyelids started to flutter. *Try to fall forwards, not backwards.*

I teetered for a moment, on the edge of luck and balance, before the forces that drove my life eventually won, and I started to tip backwards.

CHAPTER FOURTEEN

CONSCIOUSNESS returned, and with it came hurried whispers. "There has to be a way to keep her out of this fucking game." Yael's rage was palpable. "They're doing this to punish us. I think we should just war against the gods."

My throat was dry and my words were raspy when I said, "Bad idea. Gods are bastards."

I managed to prop my eyes open then, to find myself staring up at a familiar wooden ceiling. Five faces filled the space above me, looking down from an impossible height, and as I struggled up, multiple hands reached down to assist me. I looked around to confirm what I had noticed upon waking. We were in the lower level of the Sacred Sands arena. Off to the right were the stairs that would lead us up into the main arena.

My hand reached up and clasped onto the necklace, feeling some reassurance that it was still in place. I wondered if the rest of the link had been reinstated. *I have boobs!* I sent that thought out, and when five heads jerked in my direction, I knew that my soul-link was back, and still as strong as it had been before.

I struggled to my feet, somewhat steady as I reached out and wrapped my arms around Aros. My body relaxed as tension I hadn't even realised was there disappeared altogether.

"Ahh, my soul-link is back!" I cheered.

Aros laughed as he pulled away, his eyes locked onto my face. "*You have boobs*? That was the thought you decided to share?"

I shrugged, stepping back from his warmth. "It's a fact. Facts are important."

His eyes lingered on my face before slowly dropping to my chest. "I agree."

"If you're all done screwing around, it's time for us to deal with the current situation." Coen was still all business-like, which was annoying.

With a whoosh, a small fire sprung up on the bench I'd just been sitting on. All six of us turned to stare at it. No one said anything for a click, before Coen spoke again. "They're going to call us at any moment. We need to draw our rounds out so that there's a good show, that way Willa will have no pressure on her to entertain."

"What order do we go on in?" I asked.

Coen's broad shoulders shifted uncomfortably. "I have no idea. They're doing their best to keep us in the dark."

The heat at my back was growing more intense, but still no one bothered to mention the small fire in the room. I wasn't sure anyone thought anything of it anymore, since it seemed to happen so regularly around me.

"So I'm allowed to use my Chaos powers?" I wanted to know the rules; I couldn't have anyone else getting punished because I didn't listen this time.

Rome nodded. "Yes, you can use anything at your disposal. Don't forget that your opponent will probably be a gifted sol, so they'll also have abilities."

I heard a small shriek then, and spun toward the sound. A blonde, male dweller had just dashed around the corner and was staring with wide eyes at the six-foot flame right behind us. He started gasping and flapping his hands in the air above his head before he turned and ran off again. I looked behind me, making sure there was nothing else going on that I had missed. *Nope, just a little fire.*

"I love the way you keep saying *little fire*," Aros said, laughter in his tone. "It's singeing the ceiling, sweetheart."

Sure, there were a few black marks spreading across the ceiling, but it didn't look that bad. A barrage of footsteps echoed through the area, and then at least a dozen dwellers dashed down the stairs and hurried to where we were standing.

They all bowed low, before multiple sets of flapping hands were waved at us. "Please leave this area," one said in a rush.

Another leaned closer and whispered, "There's a fire behind you."

My lips twitched, but I fought the smile back. "Thanks, but it's fine. It's just a l—"

"*Little fire,*" Aros said.

I glared at him before letting out a ragged breath. "Okay, maybe it's medium-sized now, but I've seen worse."

None of the Abcurses looked surprised by this, and I resisted the urge to stick my tongue out. Half of the dwellers were still bowing to them, so I figured that was punishment enough. One even hit the floor in an attempt to get as low as was possible. They weren't going to stop until we left the room, so to save everyone time, I reached out and laced my right hand with Yael's, and my left hand with Siret's. "Come on, we might as well wait over here."

I dragged them toward the stairs, knowing the others would follow. When we were near the bottom step, an announcement rang through the room.

"Calling to the arena: Coen Abcurse, gifted with Pain." There was a slight pause, and then the announcer continued. "He will face Leonard Fitzwilliam, gifted with Ember."

I tilted my head to the side and met Coen's gaze. "Ember?" I asked.

"His hands can create fire. Not like you do. He has to touch something to use his power."

I nodded. That wasn't so bad. That was no match for a God of Pain. Only … Coen wasn't allowed to use his powers. My heart was pounding with heavy, rapid beats as I gulped in air—but I didn't have time to panic before my hands were released and strong arms wrapped around me.

"I'm going to be fine, dweller-baby," he murmured into my ear. Some of my panic dissipated at the sound of his familiar, grumbling voice. He'd been so business-like and serious, and it had bothered me.

I wiggled my arms free and wrapped them as tightly as I could around his neck. "Don't die, or get burned, or kill the sol." My strangled words had him chuckling.

"Anything else?" He pulled back so he could stare into my eyes. I shook my head rapidly.

"Nope, that's all."

Still looking amused, he lowered me down, and then turned to go up the stairs. I must have made a distressed sound, because he let out a low growl, spun back around, reached down and hauled me up with ease. His lips pressed firmly to mine, and all of the air fled my lungs in a rush. Everything inside of me curled closer to him, my body overcome by the instinct to climb his massive frame and press myself as tightly to his body as I could. Tingling shocks ran along my arms, before continuing down to … other parts of my body. His touch was literally electrifying.

"Pain!" The snap of his name seemed to break through the kiss, and he shook himself as he handed me across to Rome.

"Watch her, don't let her out of your sight," was his last order before he reached out to Siret.

Without a word, Siret gripped his arm, and full body armour materialised over Coen's clothing.

"How will they stop you from using your powers?" I asked, my voice breathless.

His solemn gaze met mine. "By threatening the only thing in the worlds that we give a shit about."

He walked away then, the body suit making him look huge and intimidating. I didn't tear my eyes away until he disappeared out into the arena above. To distract myself, I looked around at the charred back of the room. The dwellers had cleared out at some point, after putting the fire out. I couldn't sit still, knowing that Coen was out there, and I couldn't even see what was happening.

"I need to see him," I blurted. "Can we go somewhere to observe?"

The guys exchanged a look, but no one argued. Siret led the way, taking us from the stairs and down a small, dark hallway. There was another set of stairs at the end, and I was positioned between Siret and Yael as we marched up. Arriving on a small platform, I moved closer to the railing, only to realise we were looking down on the huge arena.

"This used to be a viewing platform for lesser gods; those who weren't permitted in the box," Aros explained.

I nodded a few times, my eyes still locked on the two figures standing down on the sand. There were no obstacles this time, just a huge expanse of free area. The stands, from what I could see, were full. No one would want to miss out on this spectacle.

The announcer's voice sounded close. "Prepare yourselves, competitors. We are putting eight clicks on the timer. The last contestant standing will be named the winner of the round. Sols, this is your chance to impress the gods: do not waste it."

A timepiece went into the sky. It was huge, very clearly displaying the arms as they clicked around. Eight clicks ... I doubted Coen would need a quarter of that time.

The sol looked wary—*who could blame him, really*—as he sized up the male across from him. He stood just below Coen's shoulders, and I could have sworn that he wore lifted shoes.

"You'd think they would have at least searched for someone who might stand a chance?" Yael shook his head, before crossing his arms over his chest. I would have replied, but I was too busy freaking out.

It had begun.

An arm draped over my shoulders and pulled me closer. "Relax, Soldier," Siret said. "It'll all be over in a fraction of a click."

Coen, clearly sick of watching Leonard circle him, let out a visible exhale before he started to move. He wasn't god-fast, clearly obeying the rules, but he was still fast as his long legs ate up the distance between him and the sol.

Leonard turned and ran away. His scrawny legs were pumping as he launched himself up the side of the arena, clinging on like a small bug of some kind. I absolutely did not blame him. Coen charging at him like that would have been all kinds of scary. Hanging from the wall wouldn't end their fight, though. I knew that from experience. Coen went ahead and scaled it with the same ease as running across a completely flat surface. Neither of those things were easy for me, but he made it look so simple. When he drew even with the terrified sol, it appeared that they were having some sort of conversation, and I could see Leonard nodding his head with a frozen look on his face.

Suddenly, Leonard let go of the side, and without doing a thing to break his fall, plunged right into the sand below. The crowd let out gasps, and I heard some jeers. Leonard wasn't making any sounds at all. Leonard wasn't even moving. A set of doors at the base of the arena burst open, and a bunch of dwellers rushed out to scoop him up and drag him away. Coen just launched himself off the side of the wall, landing gracefully. He strode with a casual arrogance back toward the exit from the arena.

"He didn't even touch him!" I sputtered out, my voice a half-screech. "How did he get Leonard to knock himself out like that?" I looked between all of them.

The rest of the Abcurses all wore blank expressions, but I could read the dark twinkle in Siret's eyes.

"What have you five done?" I demanded. "You can't use your powers; you're going to get into trouble!"

I might have hated Staviti and Rau, but that didn't mean I wanted another god fight to break out. Rome patted me on the head, and I would have kicked him in the shins, except his pat soon turned into a soft caress across my cheek. "Don't you worry. We've been getting around the rules of the gods for a long time."

I was starting to get a sneaking idea of what they had done, and if it was true, then he was … pretty smart, actually.

Some of the shock wore off in the crowd, and the announcer's voice sounded again. "Next to the arena is Aros, gifted with Seduction. He will be competing against Jewel, also gifted with Seduction."

Well … *shit*.

I turned to the golden god and before I could think it through, both of my hands were clenched around the material of his shirt, pulling him close to me. I was already up on my toes, but he had to lift me even higher so my lips could reach his. The kiss burned through me like a ray of sunshine. His goldenness seeped into me, and I felt warmth in every single inch of my being.

He pulled away before I could completely lose myself. My breathing was harsh and heavy as I said, "Barely even rolled me that time."

He grinned, that beautiful, perfect grin, and I slumped forward, catching myself against his hard chest. "Don't let her Seduction you," I murmured. "I'll come out there and accidentally punch her on purpose. You know I can do it."

I was set back on my feet as another hard kiss was pressed to my lips. "Don't you worry, sweetheart, she won't even get a chance to open her mouth."

His eyes flicked to Yael, and more of my suspicions were cemented. They were somehow borrowing powers from each other. That way, whoever was in the arena wasn't using their power, it was one of the other gods.

How were they doing that?

Aros disappeared out of our secret viewing station, passing Coen on the way in—who had to duck his head to get through the door, before he crossed over to join us.

I reached up and patted one of his biceps. "Great job, One. Wasn't worried for a moment."

He just shook his head at me, but I edged a little closer. "When you said before that they threatened the only thing you guys gave a shit about … well, what did they threaten?"

I was wondering if their mother had returned: maybe they were using her against them. I doubted they could threaten Abil. Their father seemed to be able to handle himself. Four sets of eyes in varying shades of green were locked on me, and that was when it hit.

"Me? They threatened *me*?" I smiled broadly. "I knew you all liked me. No point in denying it any longer."

Yael's brow furrowed and he looked like he was in a great amount of pain. "How can the fact that gods are threatening you almost every sun-cycle not be bothering you?"

I shrugged. "It's really not a big deal. My teachers and fellow dwellers in the villages used to threaten me all the time too. I'm more than used to it."

I returned my attention to the arena as Aros took to the sands, walking out into the middle of the empty space and spinning in a small, graceful circle. There was no sign of his opponent. I shifted from foot to foot, growing more anxious by the moment, but Aros seemed to be completely relaxed. He walked a short distance. Stopped. Returned, and did another small spin. He settled his eyes on the god-box, quirked a brow, and his lip tilted up just slightly at the corner. The people in the stands started to fidget, a hushed murmur carrying through them.

Eventually, Aros threw out his arms. "Am I not an appealing opponent?" he called out, his voice carrying across the space clearly.

The stands shook with nervous laughter, and Aros eventually grinned, his perfect features almost mischievous as he faced the god-box again. The laughter faded away as the nervous clearing of a throat filled the arena. It was the announcer.

"The second Seduction sol has … withdrawn from the fight. A new contestant has been chosen."

A louder wave of murmuring swept through the arena, and several of the rows of waiting sols jumped to their feet, craning over and around each other to spot who the new contestant was. I didn't bother looking— my attention was all on Aros. The mischief in his face had been chased away by annoyance, and he was staring our way, as though sharing his annoyance with us. It was nice of him to share and everything, but I had no damn idea what was happening. I apparently wasn't a part of their team-effort secret plan.

"That wasn't supposed to happen," Yael muttered.

He didn't sound alarmed, but the other Abcurses had gone quiet, their attention on the sands.

"What wasn't supposed to happen?" I asked. "And actually ... what *was* supposed to happen? You can tell me what's going on. I'm great with secrets. I once didn't tell Emmy that her dress was tucked into the back of her underwear for a whole sun-cycle. Okay—to be honest, I never told her. Mostly because I didn't realise she wasn't doing it on purpose. I thought it was a new fashion statement, the first one from Emmy that seemed fun in any way. Long story short, she got sent home from school with a warning for *exposing herself*."

I could feel the heat of four sets of eyes focussing on me, all giving me that look that I was growing used to by now. That *here we go again* look. I ignored them all to finish my story, because I wasn't going to let them intimidate me out of it just yet.

"My mother was the one in charge of punishing Emmy, and she—" I squinted at the form walking into the middle of the arena, toward Aros.

"She what?" Coen prodded, almost begrudgingly.

I squinted harder, even though I could see perfectly fine. I just ... couldn't actually *believe* what I was seeing. My eyes darted over the wild mess of blonde hair, and the familiar, stumbling walk. I couldn't see the woman's face ... but I didn't need to.

"Your mother *what*?" Siret demanded.

"My mother is about to battle a god of Seduction," I found myself saying, my own tone sounding completely dull and emotionless. "She's about to battle *my* god of Seduction. In a fight. With powers. Here. Now. She's here. Now. In the arena. About to battle—"

"Fuck," Yael cursed. "Someone grab her before she—"

I had no idea who he was talking about, because I was already slipping away from them. I *intend* to beat them to the arena. I *intend* to beat them to the arena. I *intend* to beat them to the—

"Gods-dammit, Willa!" Siret shouted from behind me. "That's not how it works!"

I pumped my legs harder and gritted my teeth, focussing with everything I had, until the sunlight broke out across my forehead and the surface beneath my boots gave way to sand.

I spun immediately, holding both of my hands up to the four gods appearing directly before me, murder in their eyes.

"One more step and I'll take my clothes off!" I warned them. "I'll get naked and use it to cause Chaos everywhere and then I'll steal my mother and … and kick Three in the ball—"

"We'll stay," Coen cut across me. "Go and fetch your mother. It's clearly what *they* want, otherwise they would have never brought her out here."

I nodded at him, and cast a quick glance to the others, just to make sure they weren't going to fight me on the decision, before I spun and ran toward the vision from my not-so-distant past. Aros was staring from me, to my mother, and back again. Maybe he could see the resemblance, or maybe he was just reading the look of panic on my face. She had stopped moving toward him, but she wasn't turning—she was focussed. I skidded to a stop right behind her, and reached out hesitantly. I was a little put-off at how still she had become, and the feeling only increased as she turned and I met her eyes. I could feel my stomach sinking, a heavy dread settling there, mixed with disbelief and hysteria. It edged up, working its way through my body.

"Mum?" I squeaked out, the word catching on a sob.

"That is not my name," she replied, her voice formal and metallic-sounding. "I am called Donald."

"*Mum*?" I screeched, much louder this time.

"My observation is that this Sacred One is broken," she announced, turning to Aros and pointing at me. "Should I call for a healer?"

Aros was at my side in a blink, his arms winding around me from behind, tucking me in against his chest. I wasn't sure whether he was restraining me or comforting me. I was too busy trying to process what was standing in front of me, and what it meant. The announcer was speaking again, but the buzzing of panic was too loud in my ears to make out what the voice was saying. Out of the corner of my eye, I could see a door opening at the base of the arena, beneath the god-box, and several bodies moving through onto the sands.

"Willa ..." Aros was whispering my name, his arms tightening around me.

I still couldn't focus properly. The woman before me wavered, and I could feel a tingling at the base of my skull, a darkness creeping into the edges of my vision.

No! I couldn't let the Chaos take over right now. I wrangled with my focus, trying to direct it back to my mother, but the swarm of bodies spilling into the arena was growing larger with every passing moment, until I was forced to turn and confront the scene. Tears were spilling into my vision but I swiped them away, and suddenly the bodies weren't just bodies, but servers. And they weren't just swarming, they were charging. Most of them were armed with weapons: not the rudimentary kind that you would expect them to have, but the fancy, ornate kind that you would expect the gods to have.

I stumbled back a step and grabbed onto the arm of my mother—Donald—*the server*. She glanced to my hand on her arm, as though surprised, but then seemed to forget about me as the other Abcurses appeared, slowly forming a shield around us.

"You need to get out of here!" Coen yelled over his shoulder. "The gods want to punish us, and they've finally figured out how. You need to leave—" He paused to wrestle an axe from the hands of a server that had tried to swing in the general direction of his torso. He threw the axe aside, raised his fist, and brought it crashing down on the server's head. I watched as the poor man dropped immediately to the ground, and then as Coen took down another four of them.

"You need to leave because these servers aren't going to stop." Yael was shouting this time, throwing aside a spear. "They'll attack all the sols and dwellers at Blesswood until they can get to you. We can't protect everyone here unless you're already safe."

I considered arguing, but they were right about one thing. The others needed protection, and that included my mother and Emmy.

"I'll get carriages and pull them up outside the arena!" I grabbed my mother's arm and pulled her toward the entrance of the arena, almost surprised to see that the path was clear ahead of me. The gods had thought that I would stay and fight ... and they were partly right. I had every intention of coming *back* and fighting, but I needed to take care of Emmy first.

"You need to obey me, right?" I asked my mother, pulling her up to the first row of seats at the very back of the arena.

All of the students were staring, almost climbing over each other to see into the arena, but some had taken their attention away to watch my progress.

"Yes, Sacred One. Of course. Anything you des—"

"Good." I pointed at the stand before us. "I need you to help evacuate all these people."

"Where should I evacuate them to, Sacred One?"

"Back to their dorm rooms."

She nodded, and then began to walk off, shouting out orders to evacuate. I watched her for a click; I was frozen, unable to continue in my task. She was shouting, but her voice was still cold and ineffectual. It didn't sound like my mother's. And my mother certainly wouldn't have been able to follow such a simple task without falling over herself or being bribed to do it in the first place.

It's still her, a voice tried to whisper in the back of my mind. *You can't think away the reality. That's your mother. They've done something to her. She's a server now. That means ... that means ... she must have ...*

"Everyone needs to evacuate!" I yelled, as loudly as I could. I needed to drown out the voice of reason in my head. "Evacuate back to your dorm rooms! It's for your own safety! Everyone please evacuate!"

Only a few of the sols followed my order, but once people began to move from the stands, more followed their lead, and soon everyone was standing and shuffling toward the exits. After a few clicks, they started running, a panicked rush of noise swelling around me. I could see some of the servers climbing the walls on the other side of the arena, knives between their teeth as though they were specially-designed assassins sneaking into a building full of tokens. I had no idea what a group of servers would do with a building full of tokens, though. They would probably just end up cleaning them all and then stacking them neatly, before sneaking right back out the way they had come.

I turned to the barrier behind me and placed my hands against it, leaning over a little to see the wall beneath. Sure enough, the servers had started to swarm there as well. They still looked so cold, so inhuman, but there was something frightening about them now. A being created for the sole purpose of blindly following the orders of the narcissistic gods *really* shouldn't have been allowed to handle knives. There were two right beneath me: one of them had a wicked-looking spear that he poked up in my direction, while the other had what *used* to be a spear, but was now a broken-off, wooden staff. She must have lost the pointy end in the fighting down below.

I swiped out haphazardly for the spear that was still intact, but one of the sols behind me knocked into my back, sending me further over the barrier than I had intended to lean, and I was so busy scrambling for balance that I simply grabbed onto the only thing my fingers could reach, and yanked it back up over the barrier with me. There was a little resistance at first—the server was having enough trouble as it was trying to climb the wall—but they eventually gave up their war with the spear and I jumped back from the barrier. I spun around, turned the spear in my hands, and aimed the pointy end at the hand that had just slapped against the surface of the barrier. A face soon followed: female, expressionless, bald.

"You have taken my designated Order Stick," she told me.

"Your Order-what-now?" I replied, glancing down at the tip of the spear. It was the broken one. Of course it was a broken one. It looked like a splintered broom-handle.

The server pulled her torso over the barrier, and then swung herself up, swinging her legs around and dropping to her feet in front of me.

"Order," she said, making a stabbing motion as though she still held the spear. "Order. Order. Order. It is an Order Stick."

"Ohh …" I drew out the word, trying to tell myself that I wasn't stalling.

I really didn't want to hurt any of the servers, even though it looked like the Abcurses were taking them down by the dozen in the arena. It wasn't the servers' fault. The gods were using them to punish … us? The Abcurses? Me? *Every gods-dammed being in Blesswood?*

"What do you call those?" I asked, using my broken spear to point at the axe that had just appeared over the top of the barrier, a server's hand gripping it as he lifted himself up.

"Those are the Silencing Sticks, Sacred One."

And then I realised that she wasn't trying to attack me just as much as I wasn't trying to attack her. I watched in confusion as the server with the axe cleared the barrier, looked right at me, and then jumped up over the first row of seats without so much as pausing. Two more armed servers cleared the barrier, and still nobody attacked me. I watched the man with the spear land next to the female server whose weapon I had stolen, and I wondered if we had somehow gotten all of this wrong.

Maybe this wasn't what it looked like. Maybe they weren't trying to hurt us. Maybe they were trying to escape—

"Oh my gods!" I yelled, as the man with the spear reached around me, stabbing one of the sols running past right through the shoulder. "What the fuck are you *doing?*"

"Order," the woman-server reminded me, making another imaginary stabbing motion.

"Stop!" I made a grab for the man's spear, surprised when he easily released it to me. "No more order! Stop it!"

The sol was clutching his shoulder, trying to stem the bleeding while he stumbled away from us as quickly as he could move. He wasn't going to fight the servers. Maybe there were too many of them, or maybe the look of utter horror in his eyes was because he thought the gods were angry at him, too. Hell, maybe the gods *were* angry at him. I had no idea what was happening. I only knew that the servers apparently weren't attacking me—just everyone else.

"We need you to come with us now, Sacred One." The woman-server reached for me, but I scooted back quickly, stumbling over the seat behind me before jumping up and over into the next row.

"Ah, sorry, Order Lady. I can't right now. I need to do some things. Maybe later, okay?"

"The Creator has requested you be brought to him," she insisted, her voice rising in some semblance of panic. It was a little off, though, as if she didn't actually feel the panic that she displayed.

"The Creator can just … like … create another time for us to meet then." I waved at the server and then took off, following the wave of sols to the edge of the arena seating.

The server that used to be my mother was standing outside the entrance to the arena, calmly instructing people to evacuate, even though they rushed past her—clearly already intent on *evacuating the hell out of there*. I grabbed her arm as I ran past, and pulled her after me.

It was time for a little family reunion.

CHAPTER FIFTEEN

I found Emmy just outside the back entrance to the dorms. She was standing on top of a bench, slightly off to the side from where the crowd was pushing each other to get into the building, craning her neck in an attempt to examine their faces. Maybe she was looking for me, or maybe she was looking for one of her boyfriends.

"Will!" she called out, catching sight of my face as I separated from the rush and drew toward her. "Holy shit, is that—"

"Donald," I interrupted. "Why don't you introduce yourself to your other daughter."

"Greetings, peasant-dweller," my mother said pleasantly. "My name is Donald. I am the personal server to Staviti, our great and humble Creator. The Father of our Realm. The Benevolent. The Wise. The first and final Creator—"

"T-that … is t-that …" Emmy seemed unsteady, barely able to balance on the bench that she was standing on, and the image of grief tearing across her face fissured a crack through the hasty wall that I had constructed to hold my own grief at bay.

I could feel it trickling through my brain then, like cold water, numbing me to the panic that surrounded us and leaking from my eyes.

"Yeah," I croaked, before clearing my throat and blinking a few times to clear my vision. I needed to get a grip. I couldn't break down yet. Not yet. It wasn't the time. "The gods are pissed. They've sent an army of servers into the arena—I don't even know how. It's like they opened some kind of doorway from Topia directly onto the sands. The guys are still fighting; we tried to evacuate everyone."

"You need to leave," she cautioned immediately, pulling herself together in the same way that I had. "The Abcurses, too. These sols are terrified—I heard some of them saying that they were being punished, and that the gods had sent their ancestors down to discipline them for something."

"For *what*?" I asked, frustrated. "This is too far, even for the gods."

"They're going to blame it on the dwellers," Emmy predicted, shaking her head.

She still hadn't taken her eyes off my mother, and I could see a tear slipping down her cheek un-checked, but she had reeled in the majority of her grief. "They're going to say that they couldn't keep the dwellers in line, and that the gods are punishing them for all the uprisings and disobedience. I know it."

"You're right." I gripped my mother's arm, pulling her into my side. "But why would they *really* do this?

Just because The Abcurses broke their rule not to kill anyone?"

"Well it was their only rule," Emmy reasoned. "And from what you've told me, those boys have spent their time in Topia and Minatsol doing whatever they like. They aren't punishable. Even in exile, they didn't follow the rules. Stav—*the guy in charge*—" she quickly corrected herself, casting a quick look at the sols pushing into the building. "He can't kill them, he can't take away their powers—despite the pretend threat that he can—he can't do anything to them because they're the only beings in that world that he *didn't* create."

"Not the only ones," I corrected, thinking of the panteras. "But you have a point. So this is him being tired of not being able to punish them?"

"No." She shook her head. "This is him finding a way, finally, to get to them."

I frowned, looking at our mother, who stood obediently by my side, calmly watching our exchange. Staviti had left her hair. She still looked almost exactly the same—the only difference being the absence of life that had once flopped half-heartedly in her eyes, and the emotion that had once twisted her features was gone. He had wanted me to recognise her.

"He's going to punish me, instead of them," I surmised.

"Exactly. And it's a double win, because hurting you hurts them. Come on." Emmy grabbed my arm in typical bossy-girl fashion, forcing me to form a clumsy chain, with our mother dragged along at the end.

We rounded the side of the building and started moving back toward the arena, though she swerved off to the side before we could get to the gates again. There was a bullsen-pen around the backside of the arena, with an attached stable and a feeding bay. Emmy released me once we got to the stables, disappearing inside and appearing again a moment later with a harried-looking dweller in tow. He wasn't a young dweller, and I had begun to notice that most of the older dwellers were given jobs within the academy ... but outside the actual academy walls. They preferred to have the younger dwellers inside, serving the blessed-sols-who-apparently-didn't-like-wrinkles.

"Miss," he greeted, glancing at me. "You're the one needing the bullsen? Seven bullsen?" His voice hitched on the last word, indicating that the request was going to be a problem.

"No," I quickly assured him, casting a look toward Emmy. "I don't think we really need to take so many. You don't have any carts available?"

"They're strictly for the use of the sacred sols, Miss."

He just looked confused now, his eyes flicking up over my shoulder to take in the last few sols that scrambled down the path from the arena to the dorms. Several of them appeared to be injured. "A tough arena match this sun-cycle? I could hear the screams from here."

"That's what we need the carriages for," Emmy insisted. "Several of the top sols are injured, and I've been directed to organise their transport to Dvadel, as the Blesswood healers are overrun. Please don't make us wait any longer, or the repercussions will not just land on us."

He nodded, jerking his eyes away from the arena. "Of course, Miss. Wait right here, I'll prepare the carriages. Will two be enough? I only have one spare driver—"

"These two women have been asked to drive," she quickly intercepted, nudging my mother to stand behind me. Luckily, the dweller hadn't paid much attention to her, yet. "The dweller committee felt it best that our representatives travel with them, as the families of the sols will need to be notified of their healing progress in a … diplomatic manner. You know how these sol families take failure in battle …" She let that trail off suggestively, while the dweller nodded a few more times.

"Of course." He hurried back into the stables and we both turned in complete synchronisation to face my mother.

Her expression didn't change, but her eyes moved quickly from me to Emmy, and back.

"Who sent you here?" Emmy asked.

"Staviti," she replied. "Our great and humble Creator. The Father of our Realm. The Benevolent. The Wise—"

"We get it," I muttered. "Why did he send you here?"

"He said: Donald, I would like you to stand in the arena when they call your name. Try not to fall over."

"That's all?" Emmy pressed, apparently frustrated.

"He said I was not to injure the Sacred One," my mother added.

"Which sacred one?" I puffed out a breath. "There are so many."

"You, Sacred One."

"Oh. Cool. Why can nobody hurt me?"

"He would like to meet with you. He does not like when people bleed on his rugs. He was very clear that creating rugs was a chore he liked to avoid, so if I could prevent people from bleeding on the rugs—"

I placed my hand over her mouth to stem the tirade of unhelpful explanations. "He clearly hasn't told her anything important. I can take her with us. Are you going to come, or stay?"

"You know I need to stay." The expression on Emmy's face was sad, but her shoulders were squared, determined. "The dwellers need a leader—someone steady that they can trust, someone who can help to rally them. I won't leave them in this mess. Especially with Evie still injured. Once you and the Abcurses leave, the sols are going to try and take back control of the academy. They're going to send the dwellers so far into the ground that we'll forget what sunlight looks like. I need to stay and help."

Evie. I had forgotten about her. I shouldn't have forgotten about her considering I was part of the reason she got burned. Cyrus was most of the reason, but it was still my Chaos, and I needed to accept my role. There was no time to ask more about her, though. Not right now. "I should stay and h—"

"You *need* to leave," Emmy insisted, lowering her voice as the dweller began to lead one of the carts out. "The longer you stay, the more everyone here will suffer the fate of Staviti's punishments for you. You need to get as far away from all of these innocent people as you can."

Her words would have probably filled me with pain and guilt, if I hadn't already shut myself off to everything. I continued with my very practical, analytical train of thought. "You're right, and I think I know a place. Will you watch mu—Donald? I need to get the guys out of the arena so we can leave. Before things get even worse."

"I'll watch her." Emmy pried my fingers from our mother's arm, and opened her mouth to speak, but the dweller was now directly behind us, fiddling with the bullsen reins. She waited a click, until he returned to the stable, and then quickly rushed out: "She'll be safe with me. I promise. Go!"

I wasn't going to wait for any more encouragement; I spun and ran back toward the arena entrance, searching along the ground for where I might have dropped my broken spear. I didn't see it anywhere, of course, but it didn't matter. I could maybe use Chaos. Probably. Hopefully.

"Found her!" a familiar voice shouted out, and I noticed Aros standing right beneath the arena gate, two stolen spears gripped in his hands and blood smeared up his arms.

"Gods." I lurched to a stop before him, reaching for one of his arms. "Is this yours?"

"No." His eyes were heavy on my face, trying to dig into me, to measure how I was feeling. "Sorry, Willa. We had to hurt some of them."

I turned to the arena, where the others were still fighting, though Siret was now breaking free from the centre of the death-circle, swiping servers out of his way. The bodies were piled up all around them. And … they were still fighting.

"Where the hell are they all coming from?" I asked, flinching as Siret kicked another server out of his way.

"Don't know," Aros grunted, shifting one of his spears to a holder at his back.

I could see Rome in the center of the mass, trying to knock people away from him without doing any serious damage—and mostly failing. I could see Coen, too, causing people to crumble around him, their screams of pain echoing over to me.

"Where's Yael?" I shouted, as Siret drew closer, kicking away another server.

"Went to find you. Figured we'd need to send Persuasion to convince your ass to stop being a hero."

"Ah. Well, I have returned. Just in time to rescue you."

Aros snorted, using his second spear to tap me on the shoulder. "We could have been done with this fight half a rotation ago—figured you wouldn't want us killing too many of them, though."

"Thanks, Three." I wanted to pull him into my arms and wrap around him, but I had to fight the urge off. I was forcing *all* of my emotions away. I needed to.

"Found her!" The shout came from behind me, but I didn't have time to spin around before two arms locked around me, drawing me tightly against a broad chest. "There's a dweller-Emmy outside the arena with Willa's mother and a couple carriages. Apparently, Willa is trying to rescue us."

"That's what she said," Siret confirmed, before turning and running halfway back to the death-circle. I could hear his shout still, from where I stood. "Hey Pain! Strength! Willa would like to rescue us now!"

"Now?" Rome bellowed back. "Can it wait a bit? We have a bet going!"

"What a bunch of shweeds," I muttered, before summoning an internal reprimand to project into all of their heads.

We need to get the hell out of Blesswood before Staviti tears the place to the ground in his attempt to punish us.

"She has a point!" Coen yelled across the arena. "Be there in a click! I've almost beaten his body count!"

"Ye-ah," I drawled sarcastically, rolling my eyes toward Aros. "They're trying *really* hard not to hurt anyone, aren't they?"

"Let's um ... go and see the carriages?" Siret reached forward and grabbed a hold of my shirt, attempting to pull me out of Yael's arms.

It didn't work; Yael only tightened them around me, lifting me up off the ground.

"Mine," he grumbled. "Let's go *see the carriages*."

Siret's eyes narrowed, and I started to realise that they were possibly all a little riled up from the fighting. I tapped on Yael's arm, and wriggled a little until he loosened them, allowing me to stand again. We didn't have time for a god-brother-fight, so I reached out and caught Siret's hand, and led them both from the entrance. Aros followed behind, a small smirk on his face as though he found my intervention a little bit funny.

Outside, the pandemonium was continuing to die down as the final few stands of people fled the arena. I wondered if the sols were finally starting to re-evaluate their burning desire to become gods. I would have been thinking twice if my perfect, benevolent, wonderful gods had sent a bunch of warrior-Jeffreys down to try and wipe me out.

It didn't matter if it had all been meant as some sort of message or punishment for me and the Abcurses. In a way, being nothing more than unimportant collateral was probably even worse.

"There they are!" I pointed toward Emmy, who was wearing a frustrated sort of expression.

She was staring at my mother, who stood before the two carts, two bullsen tethered to the front of each. I barrelled forward, dragging Siret and Yael with me, Aros keeping pace with no effort. Emmy's head snapped up as I reached her side, and I saw her swallow hard. "Is … Donald okay?" I asked, my voice hesitating over the name.

She nodded, blinking rapidly. "Fine. Donald is perfectly content and fine and in love with Sta … the gods."

I was the one nodding and blinking now, up and down, my movements mechanical. "Wonderful. Donald is really making someone proud." *Not us, but someone.*

I couldn't bring myself to look at her—at the face that was so familiar. Bodies pressed against me, sinking in on either side, with Aros stepping up behind me. They didn't have to ask: they knew my pain as well as they knew me. They didn't say a word, but when I tilted my head back to take them in, their expressions said a lot. There were flames burning in Yael's eyes, like tiny pricks of green ember. Siret wore no smile, and for him that said everything. I couldn't find much humour in the situation either, but I needed to continue pretending that everything was okay, otherwise I would break down completely. Just another sun-cycle in the life of Willa Knight.

Aros's chest expanded, the scent of burning sugar drifting across to me. He seemed to be burning up or something, as heat burned from his body, radiating through my spine.

"You okay?" I asked him, his reaction the most potent.

He seemed to tear his gaze from my mother with reluctance. "Are you okay?" His voice lowered, his hand pressing into my cheek as he tilted my head back to meet his molten gaze.

I tore myself away before he could make me cry, and practically threw myself into the cart. Of course, the step was higher than I had expected, so I tripped and head-butted the bullsen instead. The beast kicked out, and if a strong grip hadn't wrapped around my middle and yanked me back, I would have probably lost half my face to a bullsen hoof. Siret's arms were so warm and familiar; his energy tickled against my senses in a calming way, but I didn't allow myself to stay in his arms for long. There would be time to fall apart, but that time wasn't now. For now, I would keep my barrier erected. I would deal with the situation at hand.

"Into the cart, Donald," I ordered, pushing myself off the broad chest and turning with a deep breath.

"As you wish, Sacred One."

She clambered up with ease, her gait still robotic, but capable.

"See you soon, Em," I murmured. "Stay safe."

She nodded, and then in a flash she wrapped her arms around me, yanking me in with her crazy strength and squeezing me too hard before she let me go and ran off toward the nearest building. Back to her job as the dweller-saviour of Blesswood.

I attempted to climb into the cart again—a hand on my butt making sure that I actually made it this time. "Thanks, Five." I didn't bother turning my head; I knew it was him.

Why I had chosen the same cart as my mother, I had no idea. Maybe I wanted to punish myself, because everything that had happened was because of me. Not that I had been the one to actively *do* this to her. That was all Staviti: the asshole who liked to play with dwellers and sols and even gods as though they meant nothing.

"Do you want to move to the other cart, Willa-toy?"

I shook my head at Yael. "No, my moth—Donald is my responsibility. I need to keep an eye on her."

My mother was across from us, sitting upright on the seat, staring around. Siret settled in next to her as Yael sat on one side of me and Aros on the other. I was directly facing Siret, his twinkling eyes locked on my face.

"Will Staviti try and bring her back?" I asked him. "Can he just poof her out of here or something?" The whispered words rattled from my chest, my eyes flicking to my mother's blank face.

Aros lifted his arm over the back of our bench seat, settling me in against his side. Yael had his hand on my thigh, his hold somewhere between gentle and firm. Siret was the one to answer me.

"No," he said. "She'll only leave if she receives an order from him, or someone who ranks higher than us. If he didn't give her instructions to return, then she'll wait until she gets them."

A heavy weight dipped the cart—knocking me forward a little—followed by a second, even heavier dip.

"Coen and Rome are driving," Aros murmured in my ear as we started to move forward. "I think you got a little carried away trying to save us, sweetheart. We only need one cart."

He was right. The five of us fit just fine in the back, with the two biggest bodies up the front. Apparently, I hadn't counted everyone right … but there was no point in admitting that out loud.

"It was *actually* a preventative measure," I told him, as the others sat in tense silence. "I told the dweller working in the stables that I needed the carts to transport injured sols. It made more sense to ask for two."

"Lie," Siret muttered from the other seat. "She crinkled her nose."

"I saw it too," Yael added. "Definitely a lie."

Aros grinned at me. "You were so busy saving us you overreacted a little, huh?"

I chose to ignore him, turning away from Siret as well—which left only my mother to look at. She stared at the window, oblivious to our conversation as she watched the scenery. Except … her eyes weren't moving. She wasn't really watching the scenery. She was simply staring. Sitting. Part-way existing. I couldn't bring myself to look away from her, all the while wishing something else would happen as a distraction. I would have gladly dived back into a discussion about the number of carts I overcompensated with, but everyone was staying silent.

As if he'd heard my desperate mental plea, Aros tightened the arm which was still draped behind me, before spinning me to face him, finally tearing my gaze from my mother.

"Sweetheart," he murmured, his sugary scent washing over me.

I snuggled in even closer, pushing my body into his, and his hands slipped around me, helping me further. I somehow ended up on his lap, facing him, both of his hands pressed into my back.

"This isn't your fault," he continued to whisper, the words meant solely for me.

I bit my bottom lip to stop it from trembling. "I know."

That didn't change anything though. Even though I hadn't been the one to kill—*change* my mother, it still didn't reverse the fact that it had been done. I couldn't even mourn in a normal way, because there was nothing normal about this. She was technically gone … but she was still right there. She even still had her hair. I thought that she maybe even smelled the same, but that was possibly only because the chemical scent of the guardian's cave wasn't so different from the strong alcohol scent that had always clung to my mother's clothing. Aros tilted his head and pressed a kiss just below my ear, followed by another, closer to my cheek.

"Close your eyes," he said, and I immediately obeyed, caught up by him.

He wasn't blasting me full-force with his power, but he was certainly slipping me low, intermittent doses. A few more pressed kisses, the final one ending at the corner of my mouth and I became completely boneless.

Another hand joined Aros's at my back, and I knew from the possessive way it hooked into the dip of my waist that it was Yael. No doubt I should have been embarrassed by what they were doing in front of my mother, but I knew they wouldn't take it too far, and I needed the contact. The distraction.

Or ... maybe I was just a terrible decision maker, and they brought out the unthinking worst in me.

Yael's hand hooked in tighter, tugging on me, and Aros released me almost without a fight. They were working together, for me, because I needed them.

"Relax, Rocks." Yael's rich voice slid over my skin, and unlike Aros, he was hitting me hard with his gift.

Darkness hovered on the edge of my vision, and even though I could have attempted to fight it—I wasn't *that* far gone yet—I didn't want to. I wanted to give in to them. I wanted them to look after me, even if it was just this once and I had to spend the rest of my life pretending to rescue them.

Just this once ...

Arms tightened around me, and then his persuasive voice filled my head.

"Sleep, Willa-toy."

The rhythmic movement of the cart stopping was the first thing my subconscious registered, and I didn't linger any longer in my escape. It was time to face the music. My face felt a little numb, like it had been pressed to a hard surface for a long time, and when I finally pried my eyes open, I realised why. I was still on Yael's lap, his arms banded tightly around me, my face pressed into his chest.

"You drool," he said.

"And snore," Siret added.

"Do not," I protested, my voice a little raspy. "I sleep with you guys all the time. You can't try telling me that now."

I lifted my head from the soft material of Yael's shirt, which did appear to have a small wet patch on it.

Whoops.

"Learn something new every sun-cycle," I allowed.

They chuckled, and I looked around for my mother. She wasn't there.

"What happened while I was asleep?" I asked, swallowing down the panic at having her out of my sight. "Where's my mothe—Donald?"

"Why do you keep calling her Donald?" Siret asked me. "That is just a stupid server name that Staviti randomly picked."

"I ... don't want to hear her correcting me," I choked out.

I stumbled up off Yael's lap, my legs wobbling under me as I tried to get the blood pumping through them.

Siret was watching me closely, his expression hard to read. "We're stopping here for the night. The bullsen need to be watered and rested," he finally said, when I got my footing.

"Just like the dweller," Yael added with a smirk.

I punched him in the arm, mostly because I tripped while trying to slap him, but it all worked out in the end. He just grinned, before palming either side of my waist, and setting me firmly on my feet.

"Sacred One!" The unfamiliar mechanical gasp had me spinning around, until I remembered that my mother now sounded ... mechanical.

I moved toward the doorway of the cart, trying to see what was going on. I still couldn't see her, but at least I could hear her.

"Yes?" I finally asked, a dose of caution in my tone.

"Sacred Staviti has asked me to report all acts of violence perpetrated against you. This will not be tolerated. He does not like bleeding on his rugs. Or his artefacts."

"Just a love tap, right Willa?" Yael's grin got broader, if that was even possible.

I narrowed my eyes, judging the distance as I tried to figure out if I could *love tap* his face. Harder, this time. More like a love-punch. A love-black-eye-and-possible-broken-nose.

"This is what happens when soldiers become heroes," Siret announced to the group, as though we had all gathered just to hear his opinion. "The power goes to their heads; suddenly, they're changed; suddenly, they start beating up their—what would you call us?"

He directed that question to me. "We're not your friends, so you have to pick a different word. Maybe ... boyfr—"

"Princesses," I inserted.

"Not where he was heading with that," Yael inserted blandly. "But go ahead and explain."

"If I have to run after you five, rescuing you all the time—that makes you the princesses in the story."

"When you finally get around to rescuing us, we'll revisit nicknames." Yael smirked at me.

I prepared to launch myself at him, but Siret materialised right in front of my face, bending over to fit in the back of the cart. "Come on, Soldier." He was trying not to smile. "No time for more violence. Besides, you don't want to break a Staviti rule, right Donald?"

"Correct, Sacred One."

Irony didn't register with the servers, but it registered with me, and I appreciated it. No one broke more rules than the Abcurses. I took two steps toward the exit, only stopping because my mother's head was still poking through—that mess of blonde hair taking up a lot of space.

"I ... uh, need to get out," I told her.

She gave me a blank look and a nod, before backing out. I took a fortifying breath, mentally preparing myself as best as I could, before I ducked my head out. It was twilight, just a shadowy light remaining to illuminate the forest area we had stopped in. I slowly descended, scanning the surroundings so that I could find Rome and Coen. Two huge shadows looked to be moving a few yards away, but I couldn't tell if it was them. Of course, if it wasn't them, then this was probably not the best place to be sleeping for the night. They were *very* big shadows.

Three Abcurses pressed in close behind me. None of them seemed concerned about the area we were in, so I would adopt some of their confidence.

"I have set the cave up for you," my mother said, standing off to the side. "As requested."

I levelled a glare at Siret, then Yael, and finally Aros. "Stop ordering her around. She is not our server."

I didn't care if she gasped like all the other servers and used all the proper nouns like all the other servers. Whatever Staviti did to make her this way didn't matter—she was still my mother. A sharp sting of pain travelled up to my head, and I quickly shook the thought away. I couldn't dwell on it right now—Yael wouldn't be able to use his Persuasion on me every time the pain got too much, so it was better if I just focused on what we had to do.

"Can you please show us this cave?" I did my best to make that sound like a request, and not an order.

My mother's spine was suddenly ramrod straight, a sense of purpose filling that blank face. "Of course, Sacred One. It is my honour."

"Can you call me Willa?"

The words slipped out before I could stop them. It was a stupid thing to ask, because I knew the servers were programmed, and they would never call me just Willa. And sure enough.

Gasp. Mouth open. Hand flapping.

"No worries," I said with a wave. "Sacred One is fine."

Donald calmed herself then, before spinning around and marching off into the woods. I hurried after her. The boys moved a little slower, but stayed close. Donald was heading for the shadows, and within a click or two, the distinct shape of two more of my Abcurses came into sight. They looked to be arguing at the entrance of the cave. I strained to hear what they were saying, but the sound of rushing water nearby muffled the conversation. By the time we were close enough, they had quit whatever they were doing, instead turning to watch us approach.

I sensed their eyes on me, and I wanted nothing more than to drown in those stares. But I couldn't. The Abcurses made me feel too much, they always had. They penetrated the bubble I had lived most of my life in, the bubble that protected me from any kind of emotional overload. Because life was hard. Really hard.

I dealt with it in my own way, but I still felt the pain of it.

I always had. Over the life-cycles I had developed a pretty useful shielding technique ... only that shielding was pretty much fucked now. Fucked, because five beautiful, arrogant, asshole-gods had fallen into my life, and I was pretty sure they crushed my shield on their way down. Best sun-cycle of my life, really. But now, with my mother, I was desperate for that shielding to return. I needed it. I wasn't going to survive this otherwise.

"Dweller-baby?" Coen's concern hit me in the chest; I forced a smile to my face.

"Yes, One?"

"Are you ok—"

"Fine, no worries at all. Got any food? This dweller needs to be fed and watered."

The silence after I interrupted was heavy, but no one pushed me again, so I just strolled into the cave. My mother said that we were sleeping in the cave, and sure enough, inside, a fire was blazing in a natural fire pit near the entrance, and there were some blankets and coats laid out in makeshift beds. I had no idea how she'd managed to get them there, but it probably also wasn't that big of a mystery. No doubt, the carts had an emergency storage of camping supplies in the event of broken wheels or flooding. Even though I'd slept most of the journey there—wherever *there* was—a deep-seated exhaustion was tugging at my centre. Pulling me down and making my thoughts hazy.

A sliver of my brain was aware that it was likely grief, an exhausting sort of emotion, but I ignored that part and pretended to just be tired. The Abcurses filed in one by one, each picking a spot on the floor, their long legs spread out in front of them as they rested back against their arms. Donald remained standing near the entrance, keeping an eye on everything. No doubt waiting for an order.

The silence felt ... tense. Unnatural. No one really knew what to say or how to put into words everything that had just happened. Eventually, though, I couldn't handle one more moment, so I had to talk.

"What are we supposed to do now?" I asked. "Staviti ... he's not going to stop until I go to him." My eyes darted to my mother. "He's not going to stop hurting people I care about."

Panic froze my vocal cords, before I managed to force a single word out. "Emmy."

Why didn't I insist that she come along, I mean ... my mother was one thing, but Emmy was so much more. I couldn't survive losing her.

A male voice cut through my freezing terror. "I'm keeping an eye on Emmy; she's fine."

CHAPTER SIXTEEN

THE voice didn't belong to any of my guys, and by the time I turned my head, Rome and Coen were on their feet, both of them blocking Cyrus from entering the cave. I stood, unable to see him through their bulk, but I needed answers, so I made to push through Rome and Coen. They both caught each of my hands at the same time.

"We can't trust any of the gods right now," Coen said, his voice terse.

I swallowed roughly. "I need to hear what he has to say."

"You can hear from right there," Rome countered.

With a loud exhalation, I stopped trying to move forward, and stopped attempting to pull my hands free. If I was being honest, I kind of needed the support anyway. Cyrus was relaxed, standing with ease; his bright eyes observing us all closely in the same calm and unaffected manner that he usually displayed. The disconcerting expression made me uncomfortable, and I didn't even know why.

"Why are you keeping an eye on Emmy?" I asked.

He shrugged, his white robe lifting and shifting across broad shoulders. "I have a theory about how all of this plays out. I'm not going to ruin that by letting the dweller die."

That made ... no sense. *Asshole*.

Siret let out a low laugh from behind me, and I knew that my thought had been heard.

For now, I'd accept that Emmy was under Cyrus's watch, and when he changed his mind about that—which no doubt he would—then we would deal with it accordingly.

"Why are you here, Neutral?" Aros bit out. He had moved close to my back, working with Rome and Coen to close me in.

Cyrus stepped to the side, revealing a crate sitting at the entrance to the cave behind him. It was made from wood and a golden, glittery metal: it was finer and more ornate than any storage crate I'd ever seen.

"I heard about what happened in the Sacred Sands Arena," he announced. "Thought I would drop off some supplies and information."

"Information first," Yael demanded.

He was his usual, bossy self again, and there wasn't a hint of the worry in his voice that I was sure he felt. I knew him well enough now to see the tension in his tight jaw and the muscles in his arms that were starting to stand out starkly against the dark tan of his skin.

Cyrus's eyes flashed and his own casual geniality disappeared. "Staviti wants Willa. He is not going to stop until he gets her, and he doesn't care how many dwellers and sols he has to destroy to make it happen."

I'd already deduced most of that from what the servers had told me, but hearing it put so bluntly hit me like a punch to the chest.

"What does he want with her?" Rome was practically vibrating next to me, his huge body seeming to swell even larger as his voice boomed out.

Please don't say kill me. None of the servers had attacked me. No Order Stick had been used on me, but maybe Staviti was waiting to do it himself. Maybe there was something specific he wanted from me before he did it. Maybe he wanted to turn me into a server like my mother, so that he would have a matching pair. No, that couldn't be it, servers were made from dead dwellers. So what the hell was it?

Cyrus met my gaze full-on, his pupils burning through me with their intensity. "She is too powerful already, and will become the Chaos Beta when she dies. Rau has been trying to rally anarchy against the Creator, and if he gets the power of a Beta, he might just succeed."

"So … he definitely doesn't want to kill me then." I laughed.

Cyrus's brow wrinkled. "Of course not. If you die right now, you become the Beta."

That was something I was aware of—but not in the same way as I was aware that I had blonde hair and a general lack of balance. It didn't quite seem like a *fact*. It didn't quite seem real.

"What is he going to do with me if he can't kill me?" It was worth asking; being prepared was always a good thing.

"He will weaken you. He will make you wish and pray for death—but he will not let you die until you are too weak to cross into Topia."

Everything inside of me stilled, fear seeming to attack my mind from all sides, prickling along the back of my neck. I fought through it, falling back on my usual coping mechanism.

"He's not very *original* for an Original, is he? Torture and death, blah, blah. He needs a new bad-guy rulebook."

Six sets of eyes locked onto me with matching expressions that I had become used to seeing. They were looking at me as though I was insane. Probably because I had a huge, beaming smile plastered right across my face. Admittedly, smiling in this situation made me pretty damn insane, but if I didn't smile, I would lose it completely, and losing it wasn't something I was ready for.

No one spoke; I wasn't sure any of my guys could get words out from between their clenched jaws, so I tried again. "Maybe one of you should just kill me now? Then I'd be a Beta and it would be too late?"

It had been a random thought, but the moment I said it, it felt like a good plan. A *great* plan, even. Rome and Coen had let me go at this point, so I could turn and better see all of their faces. No one looked pleased by the plan.

"We're not killing you," Siret said. "Even if one of us was capable of doing that to you, Chaos would take you as soon as you became the Beta. That, or Staviti would find a way to end you with one of Crowe's blades. You'd find yourself in the middle of a war. A war we might not be able to save you from."

I pushed out my bottom lip, and for once, I allowed my face to show how troubled I was.

"Are you seriously pouting because we won't kill you?" Rome blinked a few times.

I sniffled, and he threw his hands in the air, before whirling around on Cyrus—except Cyrus was gone, and all that remained was the crate. It looked like he had decided to bail before we started fighting amongst ourselves. My mother had no such qualms: she was opening the lid of the crate to reveal what was inside— from my vantage point, I could only make out the top of a bread loaf.

"Should I prepare some dinner?" she asked, her hands digging in and coming up with a bunch of carrots and a loaf of bread.

Of everything that had happened that sun-cycle, those words were the thing to finally break me. The shield I had erected around my heart shattered, and the pain I'd been trying to hold at bay threatened to burst out of me and send me crumbling under the intensity of it.

"Willa-toy?" Yael noticed, and I swallowed hard before waving him off.

"I'm fine. Just fine. I need to … you know, *girl-stuff*." I stumbled toward the entrance of the cave as I spoke, needing to get away from everything. From my mother, who for most of my life would never have asked to prepare dinner. She was dead. Really, truly dead. "Be right back." I was surprised that I even managed to sound somewhat normal.

Coen called after me. "Don't go far, Rocks."

I waved behind me before continuing on, stumbling only a few times as I broke out into the trees again. It was almost completely dark now, but I wasn't scared. I was already full of grief—there was no room left inside of me for fear.

Hot, salty tears were making a slow trek down my cheeks. I didn't wipe them away. More would come: the absolute soul-crushing pain that clenched my chest and had shooting pains crashing through my mind was too much. The tears wouldn't stop for a long time. I had so little in my life. There had hardly ever been anything that I could call my own.

Except my mother.

She had been mine. My mess to clean up; my dweller to complain about. My memory to leave behind …

A damaged piece of my life that Staviti had no right to touch. Especially not before I had a chance to go back and say goodbye. Or go back and say *anything*. A scream built up in my throat, but I choked it down. If I screamed, there would be five pissed-off gods and one confused server out in the woods with me.

I just couldn't handle the way the gods played … well *god*, singular. *What fucking right did they have to meddle in the lives of others, to set the rules that everyone else had to live by—which they broke when they felt like it—and hand out punishments to whoever they wanted, for any crime they determined?*

It had to stop: there had to be a way to stop it.

"Dweller-baby?"

Coen stood beside me. I had been so worked up that I hadn't even heard him approach. His large hands cupped my face, and the pain in my chest increased further, the tears a veritable stream that I was almost choking on. I was struggling to breathe as they filled my mouth and nose.

"Baby, please, just stop."

He was cupping my face, his thumbs wiping the tears away. I lifted my face to him, gasping breaths escaping out of me.

"She's dead," I whimpered. "Gone. Stripped away and reduced to a brainless server."

It was too dark to see his eyes well, but I didn't miss the flash of fury that carved his face up into hard lines.

"Staviti will pay for that," he promised. "We'll make sure that he learns not to mess with us again."

I shook my head rapidly. "No, you can't do that. He's already proven that he can and will punish you five." They needed to stay as far from Staviti as possible. "Promise me you won't do anything to him." I sounded desperate, but I didn't care.

Coen dropped his hands down from my face, running them across my shoulders and wrapping his fingers around my biceps. "I can't promise that, Will. He started this, and we aren't going to let it stand."

I forced myself onto my tiptoes, a brief flash of warmth brushing through me. *Will*. He had used my nickname.

I wriggled closer to him, desperate to get my point across. "If I lose you," I started on a whisper, "any of you five, I won't survive. My mother ..." My voice broke, but I recovered. "My mother is killing me, but I'll learn to live with it. I can't lose you guys as well. I can't lose anyone else."

He dropped his arms lower before lifting me up, so that he could capture my lips. We were both a little out of control, and the kiss was hard and biting. His power licked across my skin, down my arms and across my waist where he was gripping me. The pain-pleasure thing was usually really enjoyable, but right now I had too much pain inside of me already.

I wrenched my mouth back, a salty taste on my lips as I stared up into his shadowed face. "Pain ... I need less pain right now," I tried to explain, and Coen seemed to understand. He dropped me gently to the floor, before pressing a more gentle kiss to my forehead.

"I'll get one of the others," he said, stepping back. I opened my mouth to protest, but he cut me off. "I can't control my Pain around you tonight, but you shouldn't be alone. Tonight, you need one of my brothers."

He didn't sound upset—which was a huge relief—but I knew that Coen was great at concealing his thoughts. Before I could double-check, though, he was gone, striding back toward the cave.

The agony was building inside of me again, now that I was back on my own, so I started walking. I headed toward the sound of water that I could hear through the trees. I expected Coen to send out Siret or Aros, since they were the happiest of the five brothers, and Aros especially had a power more suited to easing pain. What I didn't expect was to see the same volatile duo that had been nominated to babysit me the night before. Rome and Yael appeared on either side of me as I walked, their profiles only just visible in my peripheral vision. They didn't say anything, but kept pace quietly, until we hit the bank of the river that I had been walking toward. It was much bigger than I had expected, and the sound almost roared in my ears, a mist floating up toward my face.

"There must be a waterfall nearby," Yael commented quietly.

It was the first thing that any of us had said, and the sudden sound of his voice shocked me a little bit. I stared toward the inky spill of water churning a short distance below me, and started to cry. It was gentle at first, but soon began to evolve into heaving sobs that crumbled me into a ball on the damp grass. Arms wrapped around me, holding me together as I lost myself to the grief, pouring it all out into the night until my tears ran dry and there was nothing left to give. I pushed myself away from the tangled embrace that I had ended up in—not because I didn't want to be close to them, but because my skin was flushed, my face and neck were uncomfortably soaked in tears, and my hair was matted to the damp skin. Suddenly, I wanted nothing more than to tear the clothes from my body and submerge myself in the cool, churning water before me.

"Do you guys know how to swim?" I asked, taking another step closer to the water and feeling the bank give way a little beneath my feet.

"I don't see how that question is relevant when we all know that you definitely *can't* swim, which would mean that we're definitely *not* going swimming right now," Yael answered cautiously.

I almost smiled at the hint of trepidation riding his tone. My hands were already playing with the hem of my shirt, so it was barely even a conscious decision when I started to lift it. It was halfway up my torso when Rome spoke.

"It might be dark out here, Will, but we can still tell the difference between a black shirt and a whole lot of bare skin."

"Oh good," I answered, quickly pulling the shirt all the way off, and then slipping my fingers into the waist of the kickass fighting pants that Siret had made for me. "If you can see me, you can stop me from drowning."

"Not going swimming." Yael sounded disgruntled—as though he already knew that he had lost this particular fight.

"Want me to start crying again?" I asked.

He released a heavy breath, and I almost started to feel bad for him, until the breath turned into a curse as I slipped the pants the rest of the way down my legs and stepped out of both my pants and my boots.

"Maybe we should just let her get naked," Rome said quietly. "It seems to make her feel better."

Maybe he was right; maybe taking my clothes off *did* give me some weird sense of freedom. Maybe it was all a by-product of living a smothered, rule-bound existence, or maybe it was just my way of preparing for the inevitable naked accidents that came about as a result of my clumsiness.

"Don't even pretend you're doing it for her," Yael snorted.

I ignored them both, stripping my underwear off and stepping away from the discarded items. I crouched down a little, trying to get closer to the water, but the dirt along the side of the bank wasn't so much dirt as it was mud, and I didn't so much *walk* down the short incline to the water as fall directly on my ass and *slide* down the short incline to the water.

"Now we actually *have* to go swimming," I announced, as Rome and Yael cleared the slope-of-death and landed beside me in what I assumed would have been a lithe and graceful way, if I had been able to see it.

"Are you okay, Rocks?"

I wasn't even sure which one of them had asked. It was too dark for me to see much of anything clearly, which was probably why neither of them had been able to catch me—the way they usually would have—before I went down.

"I'm fine," I huffed out, as hands plucked me up and held me out so that I was dangling somewhat. They turned with me so that I ended up further out into the water, but facing back toward the bank. "I just have mud in places that mud should never be," I admitted, as the hands carefully set me down again.

My feet were lowered into water this time, instead of mud. It was something they appreciated.

Yael chuckled, and judging by the proximity of the sound, he was the one to have picked me up. "We can fix that. Can you stand right here without falling over, drowning, stabbing someone or setting the forest on fire?"

"Not going to make any promises." I sniffed.

I could hear Rome's low laugh, then, and I turned to the side to try and make him out. It was dark, but he had been right about what he said before: it wasn't too dark to be able to tell the difference between our arena clothing and the sudden expanse of bared skin as he swept his shirt off. I swallowed as I stared at what I could make out of the muscles lining his torso, and then I had to quickly blink and look away as he pushed his pants off and threw them toward the bank with his shirt and boots. Yael had taken a step back from me, and was pulling his clothes off, too … and now I was starting to realise why they overreacted every time I got naked.

It was … *a lot* to take in.

I turned in the water, my heartbeat trying to rip out of my chest, and took a hesitant little step further in.

"I said not to move," Yael cautioned me, his voice muffled behind the clothing he was pulling off.

"How'd you even see that with a shirt over your face?" I complained. "I barely moved!"

"I just figured you would try as soon as I wasn't holding you back anymore."

I grumbled in response, digging my toes into the riverbed. There was a strange combination of soft sand and sharp little rocks beneath my feet. It wasn't unpleasant, but each small prick of discomfort was enough to keep me feeling alert. It wasn't the sort of river that you could lay down and doze off in, or the sort of river that you could lazily float through while you basked in the sun …

"You couldn't do that in *any* river," Rome announced, suddenly appearing right in front of me as he spoke to the thoughts in my head. "Why do we need to keep reminding you that you can't swim?"

"Maybe I can," I countered, taking a step further into the water again—this brought me directly into contact with him, and before I could stop myself, my hands were on the bare skin of his stomach.

I could feel his muscles contract at my touch, and I could hear the deep breath he pulled in above my head.

"Maybe all beta-sol-dweller-hybrids can swim …" I continued. "Maybe it's a secret skill of mine, just like disappearing people's clothes and starting little fires."

"I have a bad feeling about this," Yael sounded from directly behind me.

I couldn't see the evidence that they were both completely naked, but Rome was pressed tightly enough to my front for me to be able to feel it, and when Yael's heat draped across my back, I knew that they had both stripped down. *Did they do that for me? A show of naked solidarity?*

"You like being naked," Rome said, answering my thoughts yet again. "And you threatened to cry. We thought this was the safer option."

I laughed—the sound sudden and light. I hadn't laughed that easily in a long time, but I found his statement *hilarious*. There was nothing safe about the three of us standing naked in a river, with mud stuck to places on my body that would need to be washed sooner or later. *Nope*. This was not my version of a safe scenario. As though catching on to what had set me off, Rome started to chuckle along with me, and then Yael was laughing, too. That made me laugh even harder, until I was slumped against the hard chest in front of me and the laughter naturally died away. It was almost a relief, being able to laugh as much as I had just cried: I tilted my head up to the sky, trying to catch sight of the stars hiding behind what seemed to be a dense cloud cover. I stayed that way while the other two quietened, pulling in deep breath after deep breath. I felt like an open box: my emotions spilling out everywhere. All I wanted was to be submerged in the water, to cool the burn of intensity that seemed to be leaking out of me in a constant stream.

"Can I swim now?" I asked the shadow that loomed over me.

"Yeah, Will." Rome looped an arm around the small of my back, pulling me up off my feet as he stepped further back into the water.

He drew us out into the middle of the stream and I saw Yael's shadow following us—I could also still feel him close by. It seemed that they had both forgotten their rivalry, at least for the moment. They were putting aside their own needs to take care of mine. It warmed something inside my chest, and I looped my arms around Rome's neck, pulling my legs up around his waist. I had intended to wrap myself around him in a hug, but his sudden grunt and the way his hands slipped down to my butt was enough to make me pause and re-evaluate the heat of something huge and hard pressing between my legs.

Whoops.

"Just ignore it," Rome growled, "or this is going to be a very short ... swim."

"I don't even want to know what *it* is," Yael spoke up, only sounding a little agitated.

"Wouldn't it be a him?" I asked, before I could stop myself. "I mean ... an *it* has no gender, right? So wouldn't it be a him? Wait ... wouldn't it be a *you*? Shouldn't it be a *you*? But if it's not a *you*, then does it have a name or something to separate itself from you?"

Okay, yes. I was rambling. It wasn't like I was completely inexperienced; there had been that one boy in my seventeenth life-cycle. But ten clicks of fumbling, pain, and an inevitable disappointment did not compare to me now having a god's *thing* pressing right against my *thing*—

"Please stop," Yael interrupted my thought. "Firstly, we don't want to hear about you and a fumbling—soon to be dead—dweller. And please say the words, at least. That was one of the most uncomfortable inner monologues I've ever heard from you, Willa-toy. I mean it. Say dic—"

"*Whoa!*" I tried to twist out and hit him, but I only managed to push my torso back from Rome and create enough momentum to fall backwards. I might have flopped into the water if Yael hadn't stepped up and caught me between the two of them. "That's enough of that conversation," I squeaked, once I was secured.

I didn't even want to think about what I was now feeling pressed against the base of my spine.

"You're still thinking about it," Yael complained softly, his voice in my ear.

"I can't help it." I tipped my head back, letting it fall onto his shoulder. "It's right there. *He's* right there? *You're* right there? Someone needs to help clear up the personal pronoun issue."

"It's a dic—" Yael tried again, but my knee-jerk reaction this time was absolutely no different to the last time.

I swivelled around to hit him again, and somehow ended up unbalancing us all. My sudden, swinging lurch was enough to tip Rome backwards, and I was forced to twist off to the side to avoid falling on top of him. I sank into the river, the cool water rushing over my head and the sharp little rocks biting briefly into my skin. Luckily, the water wasn't very deep, so my head still broke the surface when I found my feet again, or else this might have been a very different night. Different, because I would have drowned.

I slicked the hair away from my face, glancing back and forth between the two big shadows standing near. Neither of them were reaching for me, even though I could see the bunching of their arms in the darkness— a sure sign that fists were being clenched.

"You really need to stop doing that," Rome warned me. "We don't know what might be in these waters, and if I can't stop you from drowning, I can't let you in the water."

"But I *can* swim," I protested. "I'm doing it right now! Look!" I spread my arms out, pulling my hands from the water so that they could hear the trickle of water dribbling back to the surface from my fingers.

"You're standing, Willa-toy." Yael sounded amused. "That's not swimming."

"Let's agree to disagree." I took another step backwards, and they matched it with a step forward. "How long do you think the others will let us stay out here?"

"Long enough," Rome said, avoiding the question.

"I think we're in the middle of the stream right now—it might not get any deeper," I noted. "Do you think we could walk a little further up?"

"You want to see the waterfall?" Rome asked.

I nodded, before realising that they couldn't see me. "Yes." My voice was faint—smaller than I had intended.

I was standing there naked, in the dark, with two completely bare Abcurses and too much emotion for my *rogue-dweller* brain to handle. I felt vulnerable. Exposed. More exposed than if I had stripped and paraded my naked self in front of the entire academy and all of the gods. This was a different kind of openness. I was letting them in, inviting them into my grief and asking them to understand something that I couldn't even explain.

"Of course we can walk to the waterfall." It was Yael who spoke, his voice soft and understanding.

My mouth dropped open and my stomach flooded with warmth all at once. *An understanding Yael? Wow. They really needed to stop surprising me.*

"Lead the way, Will." That had been from Rome.

When had they started using my nickname? I wasn't sure, but I liked it. A lot. I turned from them and waited until the slow push of water against the back of my legs indicated that they were directly behind me. They weren't going to go in front, or pick me up, or force me to get out of the water—they were going to follow behind and simply be there if I needed them. I started walking with a small smile curving my lips, and by the time the spray of the waterfall was raining over us, the smile had widened into something full of happiness. I laughed, again, and waded through the stream until the water was almost up to my neck.

"Am I swimming yet?" I called out, trying to be heard over the sound of the waterfall, even though they were both directly beside me.

"No," Rome answered. I could hear the same low chuckle from him as before. "You're still standing. Your feet aren't allowed to be touching the ground."

I pushed up from the riverbed, looping one arm around Yael's neck, because it was easier, before using that leverage to pull my other arm up and around Rome's neck. They helped to tug me up the rest of the way, their hands settling either side of my waist naturally, and I kicked my legs a little through the water.

"There." I knew I sounded satisfied. "Now I'm swimming."

"Now you're *hanging*," Rome clarified.

"You know what." I turned toward his face in the darkness. "This is why I don't ask your opinions on things."

He grinned—I could see the white flash of teeth against the tanned skin of his face, and then, suddenly, I couldn't take it any longer. I needed to be closer.

I needed more.

CHAPTER SEVENTEEN

I acted without thought, tightening my arm around Rome's neck until he had to bend down closer to my face. I could feel his breath against my lips and the contracting of his hand at my waist. I wasn't thinking about the consequences any more, or about my mother. I didn't care about Staviti, Cyrus, Rau, or any of the other asshole gods. My mind was full of Rome and Yael—the warmth of their skin, the hard press of their muscles, and the cool water that licked between us. I wanted to stay there forever ... but instead, I would settle for something that might help me keep the memory of my first swim forever.

The pact was broken and I was ready for this.

"Willa—" Rome started to warn, but I wasn't listening.

I pressed my lips up against his mouth, swallowing the sound that grumbled out of him. He resisted for a fraction of a click, but as I opened my mouth and flicked my tongue out to caress it against his, I felt his will crumble. In a flash, my body was shifted around. I wasn't sure who helped me to face Rome, or when I had wrapped my legs around him again—with no barriers between us, I couldn't stop from rocking against his hard length as our kiss became frantic.

There were hands everywhere, breath everywhere, and my brain was scattered from the feeling of his tongue pushing into my mouth. Yael was behind me again, pressing so close that I could feel him all the way down my spine. His hands wrapped around my front, his fingers brushing across my stomach. I could feel the pressure of his touch as it continued lower, sliding across damp skin, until it dipped down, almost level with my hips. With a low moan, I pulled back from Rome, trying to push up into the touch.

"Are you okay with this?" Yael's voice was only a growl. "I can't leave. He won't leave. It'll have to be both of us."

I didn't really know what that meant—I knew what it *meant*, but I didn't know how it was possible. I nodded anyway, because right now I needed both of them. Yael's fingers slipped lower, until he brushed across my centre, touching me right where my body ached. I moved against his fingers, and he groaned into my shoulder. Rome stole the sounds that I might have made by taking my mouth again. The kiss was wild, almost desperate, and I started to wonder if I might be in over my head.

There was a lot of build-up in our relationship. A lot of need and frustration and desire—I wasn't sure how I was going to handle *one* of them in this state, let alone two of them. I pulled back again to voice my concerns, but then Yael's fingers slid inside me, and I decided I really, *really* didn't care anymore.

I pushed up into his touch again, my hands gripping onto Rome's shoulders as a tingling sensation built inside of me. Starting low and spreading through my body until I couldn't take any more; everything welled up, exploding out in a sudden detonation that left me shuddering and falling against the expanse of Rome's chest. He was breathing hard—almost as hard as me—his entire body clenched beneath mine as Yael pulled his hands back, setting them at my hips again. Rome pressed into me then, his hardness sending another shockwave through my body. His growl of possession had me clutching at him, Yael still supporting me from behind.

"Still okay, Will?" Rome's voice was a rumble of need, and I could do nothing but nod and hold him tighter.

I needed this, Yael's magic fingers had only left me craving more. Rome must have read that need in my eyes because he shifted my body slightly, and then that impressive length of his was pushing inside of me. Slowly, allowing my body to adjust as he filled me.

I groaned. Rome was big. Almost too big. I wasn't sure I could take any more of him.

"*Relax,*" he tried to tell me, almost through gritted teeth. "Breathe, Will, relax. Please. *Fuck.*"

Somehow the sound of my nickname growled out of him was enough for me to relax, and then suddenly I was full, complete, and almost coming apart again already.

Pleasure overwhelmed me; it felt incredible, better than I could have imagined. That feeling of being surrounded by two of my boys. Of being able to touch them the way I was and have them both touch me in the same way.

Hands gripped me everywhere, brushing across my nipples, sliding along every sensitive part of my body. It was hard to believe that there were only two of them there. Yael was warm and hard against my back, and I couldn't help but lean into him while Rome gripped my hips, sliding in and out, his pace increasing as we both lost control. I found Yael's mouth, and reached behind me to wrap my hand around his length.

I had no idea what I was doing. Two sun-cycles ago, I would have panicked at the thought of having two Abcurses come apart in my hands, but now it felt almost empowering. Empowering enough that when Rome pulled me down onto him one more time, his teeth sinking heavily into my shoulder—and the orgasm ripped through me with enough force to kill a regular dweller—I could have sworn that some kind of *actual* power swelled up inside me, exploding outwards and vibrating through the water. Yael shuddered behind me, pushing himself into my hand and groaning, and then we were only a mess of limbs and gasps and shock.

What. Had. Just. Happened.

"What the fuck," Yael groaned, almost repeating the thought that had echoed through me. "That wasn't supposed to happen."

Rome only grunted in response, his chest and arms were shaking slightly as he stared down at me. I groaned again as he lifted me up, slowly sliding out of my body, before he pressed a kiss onto my lips. Just a gentle press of skin, and then I was being passed into Yael's hands. I was glad that he hadn't set me on my feet, because I was pretty sure I couldn't stand.

I may not have even been able to walk.

Maybe I needed one of those wheeled chairs that some of the older dwellers used when they hurt their backs after too much labour. *Oh gods ... how was I going to run away from Rau next time if I was confined to a wheeled chair? How was I going to explain being confined to a wheeled chair to Emmy?*

"Calm down, Will." Rome sounded partway breathless and partway amused, a rough tenor still carrying in his tone. "You just need a few clicks. Your body will ... readjust."

I buried my head into Yael's neck, making an embarrassed sound, but really, my entire body was too satiated to feel any proper embarrassment.

"How am I going to tell the others?" I muttered against the sweat-dotted skin of Yael's shoulder.

"Just keep it even," he murmured. "That's the only thing that matters."

I nodded, and then I was being passed back to Rome again. He bundled me up against his chest, one arm hooking beneath my knees and the other banding across my back.

"Hold on," he warned me, a micro-click before he was ducking beneath the water and taking me with him.

I closed my eyes and held my breath, loving the feel of the cool water rushing over my flushed skin, and then we were breaking the surface again. I pushed my hair back, opening my eyes to the shadow of Rome's face that was now a little more visible. Either my eyes had adjusted better to the darkness, or else the moon was peeking out from behind the clouds overhead. He met my gaze, and stilled, his lips pulling up in a smile that matched the one I hadn't even been aware I was wearing.

"I love you," I found myself saying, before turning to look at Yael. "I love you both."

And ... I really need to start thinking about things before I say them.

I quickly closed my eyes and sucked in a breath. *Oh, gods. This was about to get awkward.* Surprisingly enough it hadn't been awkward to this point, even though I had expected Rome and Yael would be the least okay with sharing—

A slight touch against my lips had me peeking up through one half-open eye: Yael's face was close to mine, his thumb against my lip.

"I love you, too, Willa-toy. I don't know what I'd do without you. Life—immortality—none of it meant anything until you tripped in and started setting things on fire."

I opened both of my eyes only to close them again as his lips pressed to mine, soft at first, and then harder. His tongue only barely brushed into my mouth before he was pulling back, and I was being shifted in the arms that held me. Rome's face loomed over me, his lips pressing once against mine. He didn't seem to care that Yael had just been kissing me.

"I love you, Rocks. Never doubt it."

It was all too much for my heart. I pressed my lips to his again and then quickly twisted out of his arms, barely managing to land on my feet. My head only just poked out of the water, and I glanced up at them both from my height disadvantage.

"Am I swimming yet?" I asked, to dissipate the tension.

Yael rolled his eyes. "And she's back."

"Never left, Four."

"One."

"Four."

"On—"

"Alright, brat," Rome interrupted, tugging almost playfully on a lock of wet hair that was hanging down over my face. "Let's get you back before Cyrus shows up again and gets another eyeful of something he's not supposed to see."

I cringed, leading us back downstream—I moved closer to the edge, so that I would be able to spot the dark outline of our clothes against the bank, and then we were out of the water and dressing ourselves again. I felt a strange mix of lingering foreboding, grief, and pure happiness: and the volatile mix of emotions was starting to make me feel a little sick. I thought about my mother back in the cave, cooking food with the supplies Cyrus had left, and another tug of grief pulled at me.

"She never would have been caught dead cooking me an actual meal," I told the others, surprised that I was suddenly willing to talk about my mother. "Emmy used to do all the cooking—and before that, she would just bring back leftover scraps from the tavern."

"We're going to make him pay," Rome promised quietly. "Whatever he wants from you, he's not going to get it. He's been trying to mess with us for decades—"

"Decades?" I broke in. "How old are you all, exactly?" It felt almost absurd to be asking that question after everything we had just done.

"Almost a hundred life-cycles," Rome answered. "And for almost a hundred life-cycles, Staviti has failed to take us down. He's about to find out that it's just as hard to reach you as it is to reach us."

"He's about to find out that you're not just a tool to hurt us," Yael added. "You're one of us."

"He's about to find out what it feels like to have my knee in his Sacred Balls," I tacked on.

"That's our girl," Rome grunted, clearing the entrance to the cave and stepping aside for me to go in first.

Coen was sitting against a rock, his back up against the wall of the cave and his hands folded behind his head. His eyes levelled on me as I came in, flicking over my wet clothing and the loose pieces of grass stuck to my damp legs. His examination extended out to Rome and Yael for a moment, but quickly returned to me, his face remaining expressionless. I felt a small tug of guilt, but I wouldn't let it gain any traction. That would ruin us. I needed to focus on keeping things even. I walked up to him, positioning myself directly between his legs, my arms looping around his neck as I wrapped him in a soft hug.

"Thank you," I whispered, just for him.

He returned my hug, pulling me into his body, and I could feel the tension draining out of him, as easily as that.

"You should eat," he finally said, pulling back.

I glanced around, searching out my mother; she was standing by a fire that she most definitely had not built—unless Staviti had also reprogramed her with basic wilderness survival skills—and she was stirring something in a small, cast-iron pot. Siret and Aros were sitting close to the main fire, their heads still leaned a little toward each other as though they had been in the middle of a private conversation when we had walked back in. They both watched me, their expressions as careful as Coen's had been. I walked over to them while Rome and Yael moved to the crate, rummaging around inside it for what looked like several bundles of coloured robes. That spurred me a little faster in Siret's direction, and I quickly seated myself between the two of them. I had a feeling that Cyrus had only packed god-clothes in the crate, and if he thought that I was the

Chaos Beta, then he would have definitely packed red robes for me, and there was no way that I was changing into a pair of red, Chaos robes. *Nope.* No way.

"What's she making?" I whispered, as Siret and Aros seemed to relax a little more, planting their arms behind them, their palms flat against the blanket they were sitting on, so that an arm from each of them crossed behind me, forming a wall of muscle for me to lean against.

We all turned toward my mother, who was still happily stirring away.

"Water, by the looks of it," Aros whispered back.

"What?" I asked, a little too loudly.

My mother looked up, noticed me for the first time, and then went back to what she was doing. *Well now that was a little more like the old mum.*

"She poured some water in there, propped it over the fire, and she's been stirring it ever since," Siret informed me, a small smile on his lips. "I don't think she knows how to cook."

"What about all the ingredients?" I asked, glancing over at the crate again. "Didn't Cyrus send over a bunch of food?"

Siret shifted, reaching into his jacket as Rome and Yael approached the fire—now dressed in coloured robes.

"Here," Siret sounded apologetic. "That's all we could salvage. She ate the rest."

He was holding out half a carrot and a small chunk of bread with a little wedge of cheese stuffed inside.

The cheese actually still had teeth-marks in it. I looked from the food to the robed Abcurses, and couldn't seem to decide which image was funnier. Rome was dressed in a deep, royal blue, a hint of his massive chest left bare as he spread out another blanket and sat on the other side of the fire, his glittering eyes locked onto me. Yael was in a dark, forest green—a shade darker than his eyes. His wet hair had been pushed haphazardly back from his face, but a few strands were still falling forward into his eyes.

"Do you both wear those things all the time in Topia?" I asked, trying to keep the amusement from my voice.

"Try not to be too impressed," Rome grumbled.

"There's a robe in there for you, too," Yael told me, ignoring the question completely.

"Is it red?" I asked, finally taking the food from Siret and nibbling on the end of the carrot. I was starving, but there was still too much frazzled energy bouncing around inside for me to be able to easily digest any food.

"Yes." He glanced up, the fire flaring up between us and momentarily obscuring the look of wicked amusement painted across his beautiful features.

"Figures." I sighed, stuffing a whole bite of the carrot into my mouth and breaking it off. "Cyrus has one hell of an agenda. I won't be wearing it, by the way. In case you were wondering."

Aros grinned, before tilting his head toward Siret. I was just worrying about what those two had cooked up when Siret reached out and touched my arm. I felt the familiar ruffle of clothing being changed. The material that had been slowly drying against my skin was being replaced by a slide of silk, a burst of gold flashed before my eyes, and when Siret removed his hand, I was dressed in a beautiful golden creation.

Jumping to my feet, I did a quick spin, taking in the entire outfit. The hem was all different lengths—not as long as the dresses from Siret and Yael, but still past my knees. In fact, it seemed as though the entire dress had been made up of different lengths of silk. It was comfortable, smooth, soft. I could have slept in it just as easily as I could have fought in it.

I *loved* it.

"It's time you wore my colour," Aros said smoothly, his eyes running down the length of me.

When I stepped closer, he reached out and gripped a section of delicate silk from the top of the gown, tearing it off in the blink of an eye. I dropped my head to see what he'd done, surprised to see a band of bare skin poking through the top. The dress was so free and flowy, it was almost as good as being naked.

I leaned in closer and pressed a kiss to his cheek. "I love it."

CHAPTER EIGHTEEN

AFTER my meagre serving of dinner, I had to convince my mother to stop stirring her pot of water. She'd been at it for several rotations and wasn't showing any signs of letting up.

"Mu—Donald?" I sidled up to her, peering into the pot. Most of the water had evaporated by now. "Do you think we could maybe stop stirring now?"

Siret and Aros were still sitting together, talking quietly—they had first 'watch' over the cave, while the others were trying to catch some sleep. I glanced over to them while my mother paused in her stirring, and Siret looked up and winked at me. I tried not to smile, but it was pretty hard to *not* laugh at the things that Siret found funny.

"It hasn't turned into soup yet, Sacred One. We must wait. Patience is an acceptable trait in such lowly beings as those tasked with serving the Great Staviti, our benevolent and wise Creator of All Things."

"You lost me at soup," I admitted. "When you speak too formally like that I tend to give up in the middle somewhere."

She stared back at me blankly.

"Oh-kay." I drew out the word. "Let's try this again: can you *please* stop stirring?"

"The Sacred Ones do not wish to have soup?" Cue small, mechanical-sounding gasp.

I gestured around the cave. "Most of the Sacred Ones fell asleep half a rotation ago."

She stopped stirring completely then, her spoon clattering against the edge of the bowl. "I see. I will now become Silence."

I blinked. "You'll what?"

She didn't reply, but turned and walked back to the crate. She lowered herself to her knees, folded her hands neatly in her lap, and closed her eyes.

"Hey." I walked over to her, waving a hand in front of her face. "Donald? What the hell?"

She was as still as a rock; there wasn't a single twitch behind her closed eyelids, and there was no rise and fall of her chest to indicate breathing of any sort. I wasn't actually sure whether the servers still had those functions, since I'd never actually thought to check … but it was clear that my mother didn't have them—at least in that moment.

"What happened?" Aros asked, appearing beside me, his eyes on my mother. He didn't look surprised.

"What's she doing?" I asked him. "What the hell does *becoming Silence* mean?"

"It's their version of sleeping," he told me, now looking mildly uncomfortable. "They kind of … shut off. I don't know how else to explain it. Most of the gods don't allow their servers to go into Silence unless they're upset at them."

"Why?" I frowned, looking back to the pot that she had abandoned by the fire. *Was she punishing herself?*

"Because there's always a chance they won't wake back up again."

I blinked, my head whipping back to my mother. I was on her in an instant, my hands grasping her arms, shaking her almost violently.

"Wake up!" I was almost screaming, so it came as no surprise when not only did her eyes pop open, but there was a flurry of movement and the swell of big bodies suddenly surrounding me.

"Greetings, Sacred One," my mother announced, before shifting her focus to Aros. "Greetings, Sacred One." Her eyes shifted again. "Greetings, Sacred One." Another shift in her gaze. "Greetings, Sacred One—"

"The others are fine," I quickly interjected. "We can just assume that the first greeting was kind of a 'blanket' greeting, okay?"

"As you wish, Sacred One."

"I'm not okay with that," Coen spoke up. "I want to be greeted."

My mother turned to him as I rolled my eyes.

"Greetings, Sacred O—"

I quickly placed my hand over her mouth for the second time that sun-cycle. "He's just *One*," I told her quietly, "Not Sacred One."

"Greetings, One," she corrected herself.

"And I'm just Willa." I attempted to push my luck with the name again.

"Greetings, Sacred Willa," she said, turning to me. How she was still wearing that blank expression was beyond me.

"If I hear *greetings* one more time, I'm going to put her back into Silence," Yael announced.

I gasped, whirling on him as my mother hung her head a little. She almost looked dejected—oh, *nope*, she was just plucking a thread from her clothing.

"I wouldn't *really*!" Yael had his hands up, hoping to ward off an attack from me—but I was now slightly distracted by the fact that my mother was wearing normal, dweller clothing.

"Why does she still have hair?" I asked the others, running my eyes over her again. "And why is she still dressed in her normal clothes? Where's the perverted little skin-suit thing? And … come to think of it … aren't Staviti's servers a little … younger-looking? There was a guy in the outer rings who picked me up in his cart and he said that the guardians didn't like taking dwellers as servers after a certain age—"

"What guy?" Aros demanded, his hands on my shoulders spinning me around.

"Picked you up in his cart?" Coen added angrily. "What the fuck does that mean? Is that dweller-slang for something dirty?"

"Define dirty?" I asked, thinking back to the dead bodies packing the cart.

The five brothers seemed to swell then, gathering so much temper about themselves that even my mother took a hasty step backwards. She covered it up by bending to the crate and pretending to rummage around inside it for something. She came up a micro-click later with what looked like the broken handle of a serving spoon, and stuck it in her mouth as though it was a breadstick. She tried to bite it, frowned, sniffed it, and then tried again.

"That's not for eating." I sighed, reaching out and confiscating it off her before turning back to my guys. "What's the problem? I forget his name; it was Zane, or Gary, or Zac—or something. He was pretty nice, I guess. Lonely. Wanted a friend. I wish he'd have put me in a more comfortable position—it was super cramped, pressed up against the little window that looks out to the driver's seat of the cart—"

There was a flurry of activity then, and more than one curse slipped out as five angry gods began to jostle into motion. Rome seemed to be storming toward the entrance to the cave, but Aros grabbed the back of his shirt and managed to haul him back to the others. Coen picked up a nearby rock the size of a bucket, and tossed it toward the back of the cave. I heard the sound of cracking stone, and then suddenly they were huddling around in a circle.

"We need to find him," I caught Yael muttering, "And we need to kill him."

I could feel my mouth dropping open, and I tried to ignore the dull thud of panic that was starting up in the back of my skull. I pushed forward, inserting myself into the middle of their circle.

Suddenly, I was at the center of five *very* angry sets of eyes. *And was that ... disappointment? What the hell?*

"Someone needs to tell me why this is such a big deal," I demanded, my voice only a little bit shaky. "It was just a cart ride. Without him, I would have died."

"*Just* a cart ride?" Siret was the one to speak, and I registered confusion in his face. I nodded, and his frown deepened. "But you just said it was code-speak for when dwellers did dirty things to each other."

"Things that should not have happened after you became one of us," Yael added.

If I thought my mouth had dropped open before, it was nothing compared to now. "I …" I was actually speechless. I opened and closed my mouth a few times, before managing to get a few words out. "I … did *not* say that."

"I'm pretty sure that's what she said," Yael argued. "Pain asked if it was dweller-slang for something dirty, right, Pain?"

Coen nodded—and while it was great to see them all working together as a team, it was *not* great to be on the wrong side of that team.

"That's right, Persuasion," he confirmed, as though we were in a dweller court-of-commons, and I had been sentenced with the theft of a very valuable loaf of bread. "Instead of denying it, she asked for clarification on the level of dirtiness."

"And then she admitted that it was very dirty," Rome added.

"And said something about being pushed up against a window." Even Aros was on their side.

I let out an exaggerated breath. "It was dirty because of all the dead bodies. And before you *even go there*, the answer is *no*: we were not doing dirty things with the dead bodies, honestly what the hell is wrong with you five?"

"Tensions might be a little high at the moment," Aros murmured, sounding defensive.

"So you didn't have sex with a dweller named Gary or Zac or something in the back of a cart?" Siret apparently needed clarification.

"No," I growled, pushing against his chest.

"Oh, well, in that case. Back to bed!" He spun on his heel and sauntered back to his blanket, completely ignoring the daggers that I was staring into his back.

"Um ... yeah, I'm going back to sleep, too." Yael took a step back to match Siret's, and then he was turning and retreating to another blanket: typically, he was the only one not sharing a blanket.

Coen had fallen asleep on his rock, leaning up against the wall—and that was where he returned now, soundlessly, as though he wasn't quite sure how to take back the whole dweller-sex-cart incident. He had his feet resting on a blanket, though, and that was the blanket that Rome returned to now. He could only fit his torso and head onto it, while he stretched the rest of his massive body out onto the rock, folding his hands up behind his head and closing his eyes.

"Wake me up when it's my turn to be on watch." His soft grumble echoed through the cave, rousing my mother from her position by the crate.

"Yes, Sacred One!" she called out, scrambling to claim the task as her own. I think she felt better having a task, so I decided to give her another one.

"Why don't you take the last blanket and try to catch some …" I paused, wondering if the servers actually rested at all. If they had a thing called Silence, then probably not, and I really didn't want her to mistake my order and send herself back into a weird comatose state that she may or may not wake up from again.

"What would you like me to catch, Sacred Willa?" she questioned. "Some of my usual catching tasks include: Greg, the other lowly being under the command of Staviti the Great, Wise, and Benevolent. Our master likes to tell Greg to run, and tell me to catch. It is one of his favoured pastimes."

"He sounds like a joy," I replied dryly. She only returned my sarcasm with a blank stare, and I let out a sigh. "Okay, well … forget the catching. Why don't you just find somewhere comfortable to sit? Maybe that blanket right there?" I pointed to the blanket hanging over the side of the crate. "Maybe you could lay on it? And maybe you could close your eyes but *not* send yourself into Silence? Can you do that?"

"As you wish, Sacred Willa."

She moved obediently to the blanket, lifted it from the side of the crate, and shuffled over to the side of the cave opposite Coen and Rome. I didn't blame her, after their recent show of anger—even though they were pretending to slumber now like the giant, gentle beasts that they weren't. I watched as she spread out the blanket, stared at it for a moment, and then lowered herself onto it, face-down, her arms awkwardly outstretched to either side.

"Am I doing it right, Sacred Willa?" she called out, her voice muffled by the blanket.

I had no response for that. I stared at her, shaking my head, while Siret and Aros tried to control their laughter by the fire. They were the only ones not pretending to sleep. Probably because it was still their watch duty.

"Are your eyes closed?" I called back.

There was a pause, and then another muffled reply. "Yes, Sacred Willa."

"Then you're doing it ... right." I struggled to say that without laughing myself, or cursing, or groaning out in frustration and throwing a giant rock at the back wall—but *some* of us had to show a little maturity. Clearly, my mother wasn't going to do it.

༺♡♡♡♡♡༻

I was roused awake when Aros shifted to my right. He was standing, but that meant that the warmth I had been sleepily snuggled into was leaving—my yellow dress, while extremely comfortable, was not very warm—so I reached out for his arm, trying to pull him back. He fell back down beside me, his eyes tired as his hand slipped around the side of my face.

"I need to wake Coen and Yael up," he whispered. "They're taking the next watch shift."

"I'll take over the watch shift," I murmured back, pushing myself into a sitting position.

Siret was on my other side, and his arm slipped from my waist to my lap. I thought that I had woken him, but he only made a small grunt and slipped his hand into my dress, settling it against the warm skin of my hip. Aros's touch against the side of my face shifted, and then he was turning my head back to him and pressing his lips to mine. It was a sleepy acknowledgement.

"Wake someone up if you get tired," he said, before lowering himself back down. He knew better than to fight me on staying up.

I was one of them. Part of the team. I needed to pull my weight.

Even if pulling my weight turned out to be really, really, *really* boring. Several times, I thought I saw a rock move, but it was just the flicker of the dying fire making patterns on the cave wall. I wasn't sure how long I sat there for, but when footsteps sounded at the entrance to the cave, I was almost relieved. I disentangled myself from Siret and Aros—who had both somewhat curved around me in their sleep, their hands claiming part of me to hold onto—and reached for the knife that someone had left on the rock beside my mother's cooking pot.

I was *so* ready for a fight. Or anything, really. Anything but more wall-staring.

Unfortunately, the god who appeared was more of the scary-but-still-annoying kind than the attacking kind.

"Cyrus," I said, a little disgruntled.

"Doll." He was speaking almost in a whisper, though it still managed to carry the derisive tone that always underlined my nickname. "We should speak outside."

I glanced back to my sleeping Abcurses, and nodded. He was right—if they woke up and found him standing right in front of them, there was no way that they would go back to sleep after that. There were only so many interruptions they would be able to handle before they gave up on the whole idea of 'rest' and decided to find a different cave to hide away in while we worked on a better plan.

I followed Cyrus out to the cave's entrance, and then hugged my arms around myself as he kept going, further and further, into the cover of trees. It wasn't warm and balmy as it had been earlier in the night: the air had a snap of cold to it now, and I started to wish I was wearing that stupid red robe after all.

"What do you want?" I asked, when it seemed like Cyrus wouldn't stop moving.

He did, then, spinning around to face me. "So many things," he replied thoughtfully, cocking his head as I drew level with him. "I want a change. A new system.

I guess you could call me a revolutionary—but I also want to survive, and revolutionaries generally don't have a great history of surviving."

I had no idea what he was talking about, but I didn't have much of a chance to argue before a flash of red in the trees caught my eye. I craned my neck to get a better look, panic starting to swell up in the base of my stomach. Flashes of red were never a good sign: especially out in an isolated, dark place.

"If you scream," a grating, high-pitched voice announced from the trees, "I'll make sure those boys of yours don't wake up at all."

"Rau," I hissed, moving around Cyrus to face the cloaked man as he strode from the trees.

I pulled my knife up, holding it out in front of me with both hands gripping it tightly. I still had no idea how to use a knife in self-defence, which seemed like a substantial oversight given how often I ran into perilous situations. I thought about screaming through my mental link for the guys, but I wasn't sure just how well Rau would be able to follow up on his threat. *Could he really defeat them? Maybe he isn't alone …* I glanced into the trees to see if I could spot any more flashes of colour, but Rau was moving toward me quickly, forcing my attention back to him.

He reached into his pocket and pulled out a knife—eerily similar to the knife I held in my own hands. *Wait a click …* it wasn't just similar, it was the same! I glared down at the blade I held, feeling as though it had betrayed me in some way, only to find that I was clutching a short, smooth stick. It wasn't even sharp at the end.

"What the hell?" I threw it aside, the panic inside me growing to an overwhelming point. "I didn't know Chaos could do stuff like that," I said, hoping that maybe if I started talking, Rau would stop moving toward me.

I glanced to my side, at Cyrus. I was almost surprised to see him still standing there, but then it dawned on me that maybe he had drawn me away from the Abcurses on purpose.

"Chaos can do most things," Rau told me, that voice of his rubbing up my skin the wrong way. "There's a potential for Chaos in almost every situation. You just need to know how to use it. But I can teach you."

His eyes were gleaming, and I cast another look at Cyrus. *Why wasn't he saying anything?*

"Did you set this up?" I growled out at him, taking a subtle step backwards.

Rau had stopped moving, finally, but he was still too close. I could see the spots of precipitation marking his robes from the damp grass, and the way his eyes flickered in constant appraisal of both myself and Cyrus, along with the environment around us. He couldn't seem to keep his attention on one thing long enough to even identify what it was, before he was moving on to the next thing. I would have thought him distracted and skittish, except that his posture was braced. *Ready* for something.

"This might be a little bit my doing," Cyrus admitted, as Rau's hand suddenly flicked, and the knife that he had been holding sailed through the air toward me.

I flinched, lurching out of the way as fast as I could, but Cyrus had already reached out. He plucked the knife from the air only an inch or so away from my face.

"That wasn't nice," he said—the words directed at Rau.

I was shaking, my eyes on the blade. *What the hell was going on?* I thought Cyrus had betrayed me, but there he was, saving my life. I fell back a few more steps, trying to control my urge to turn and run away from the situation.

"I can't protect you if you're standing all the way over there," Cyrus told me, though he hadn't actually taken his eyes off Rau—who, in turn, still hadn't taken his eyes off me.

He didn't even seem shocked that Cyrus had foiled his death-by-flying-knife plan. He was simply staring at me. Waiting for something. I moved closer to Cyrus, stepping partway behind him. If I couldn't wake the Abcurses up, he was the best chance that I had, and if he had saved me once, then maybe he would do it again.

"What do you want?" I asked Rau, my voice almost steady despite how much I was shaking.

"I want you to *die* already." It was almost a whine. "Why won't you just *die*?"

"I ..." I didn't really know how to answer a person who was actually *whining* about the fact that I wouldn't up and die. "I'm not ready?" I finally replied. "I guess?"

"You're ready when I say you're ready." He drew up to his full height, crossing his arms and ceasing the flickering movement of his eyes—resting them solely and heavily on me. "Do you know why?"

I swallowed. I had that feeling that I sometimes got when I knew that I was about to be told something that I really didn't want to hear.

"Why?" I finally gritted out, when it didn't seem like he had any more secret knives hidden up his sleeves and Cyrus didn't seem to be handing back the one he had thrown.

"Because I am the God of Chaos, and you, little girl, are my Beta."

Cyrus turned, then, and I only got a flash of the apology in his eyes before he was shoving the blade toward me. I felt the shock of something piercing my skin, pushing past the barrier of my ribcage and searing through me with an agony that seemed to go beyond pain. It was ripping me apart from the inside out. I tried to scream, but the sound died off in my throat as a hand wrapped over my mouth. I lifted my arms, trying to fight off whoever was restraining me—but even the slightest movement seemed to twist the knife deeper, and I started to tilt toward unconsciousness.

The image of the trees wavered before me, and I would have collapsed, if an arm hadn't wound beneath my neck, cutting off my air supply. The space where

Rau had been standing was empty—only Cyrus was still visible to me, his eyes swimming in front of my face.

I couldn't tell if he still looked apologetic or not, because the tears were blurring him out.

"Die." A high-pitched whisper sounded, directly behind my left ear, and the arm around my neck tightened. "Why won't you *die* already?"

CHAPTER NINETEEN

PAIN.

Suddenly, it was everything I knew.

My limbs felt like they were burning and my head was aching with the memory of pain ricocheting through my entire body. My stomach cramped violently, and I opened my eyes, attempting to sit up.

Everything was white. The ceilings were white; the wooden furniture had been painted white; the sheets wrapped around my body were white; and my rage, when Cyrus came into view, was white-hot.

"I'm going to kill you," I announced, my voice croaky and weak. I cleared it, and tried again. "I'm going to kill—" this time the words died off on a cough that seemed to seize through my whole body.

Dying was *hard*.

Wait a click—

"You stabbed me!" I pointed a finger at his entirely too-neutral face. "How am I still alive? Was it a trick? Is Five here? Was it an illusion? Why did he have to make it so damn *painful*?"

"It wasn't an illusion," Cyrus answered carefully, "and I did stab you—*but,* before you kill yourself all over again trying to murder me out of revenge, you should probably ask *why* I stabbed you."

I could feel that rage again, and I knew that some of it spilled into my tone when I answered him. "I don't think the *why* is really so important in this scenario. I think a stabbing is still a stabbing and should be treated as such. Where are the Abcurses? Why aren't they torturing you right now?"

"They did," he admitted. "I healed. They're waiting in a secure place. I gave my word that I would send for them when you woke up."

I frowned, glancing toward the open doorway leading out into Cyrus's living room. I recognised his secret little hidey-house. What I didn't understand was why he would bring me here.

"Did you say something about me killing myself all over again?" I asked, my tone going completely flat. Surely he hadn't said ...

"Yes, Willa Knight. You're dead."

"I'm dead," I echoed, still completely toneless. "Like ... died and ascended to Topia?"

"More like murdered and smuggled into Topia, but you can tell whatever version of the story you want to all your new Topian friends. *If* you manage to stay here that long."

"*Where else would I go?*" I almost screamed, starting to sound a little hysterical now. "I'm *dead*, Cyrus!"

"There are ways to kill the gods, just as there are ways to weaken the sols so that they never become gods. Really, there's a way for everything. You just have to find it: and now *we* just have to find a way to keep you here, and keep everyone from knowing that this is where you're hiding."

"But Emmy … my mother …"

"Donald is in the living room. It seems that Staviti was a little … lax, in his orders with her. You were supposed to be captured at the arena and brought to him, and Donald was supposed to be the distraction that stopped you fighting long enough for one of his servers to grab you."

"Why didn't he just tell Donald to grab me?"

Cyrus smiled then: a crooked, humourless grin. "Donald isn't very good at following orders."

"It runs in the family," I admitted, and if I was going to be completely honest … I was a little proud.

He shook his head at me, stepping back toward the doorway. "You can go and fetch them now," he called out. "She's awake."

"Yes, Sacred One." I could hear my mother's robotic-sounding reply, and I clenched my jaw a little too tightly, my eyes flicking to the open doorway.

She wasn't even going to come in and see me.

She wasn't even happy that I was awake—alive— *going for Round Two?* I wasn't sure how to describe my current state.

"What would you call this, exactly?" I asked Cyrus, glancing beneath the sheet that had been draped over me.

I was dressed in white robes—I preferred the yellow dress so much more. I would have thought that they were Cyrus's robes, except that they fit me perfectly. I frowned, plucking at the wispy material before drawing the sheets away completely and holding up a section of the skirt toward the light, sticking my hand beneath it.

"What in the name of Topia are you doing?" Cyrus asked, following the movement of the skirt with his eyes.

"Checking to see if it's transparent," I muttered. He closed his eyes, and I caught him shaking his head again, but I wasn't going to let him avoid my question, so I dropped the skirt and met his eyes again. "I don't feel dead. I definitely feel like I've been *stabbed* by an *asspit*, but I don't feel dead."

"Did you just say *asspit*?" His brow was a little scrunched, as though such high and mighty beings as the Glorious Gods of Topia didn't say things like *asspit*.

"What of it?" I asked defensively.

"What *is* it?"

"An asshole was too … small a word to describe you. You're an asspit. An asschasm. An asscrater—"

"Wow," he interrupted, holding up a hand. "I think I get the picture. Unfortunately. Thanks for that. And to answer your question: whether you feel dead or not, that's what you are. We made sure of it. Welcome to godhood, doll. Try not to stop the world from turning in the right direction."

"That's something I can do?" I finally managed to pull myself out of the bed and stand, my legs threatening to collapse beneath me. I pressed a hand to my ribcage, right between my breasts. There was a scar: thick, long, and raised. I could feel it through the flimsy robe.

"Honestly …" Cyrus glanced at where my hand was pressing, his frown matching my own. "I have no idea what you can do."

"So why the fuck did you kill me?" I growled out, getting a little agitated that the Abcurses had left me alone with him after he had stabbed me.

"Rau was convinced that you were the Chaos Beta—hell, even I was convinced. His curse had been centuries in the making, a concoction proven to alter powers—alter allegiances. He had been using it for a long time on the sols, because Staviti wouldn't allow the Chaos power to be cultivated in Minatsol. The curse that hit *you* was different. It was powerful enough to alter a god: powerful enough to kill a sol. And you, a dweller, survived it—*absorbed* it, as though you were a god yourself."

"I actually tripped into it," I told him. "Didn't mean to do any absorbing or anything."

"Of course not." He sighed. "You have always been a dweller. Rau guessed that you had formed a soul-link with Abil's sons and we both assumed that the soul-link was the reason you had survived. It made sense. He had tailored the curse for Abil's bloodline, and when the curse splintered you, the pieces of your soul that fractured apart were drawn to the beings around you that the curse had been intended for."

I frowned, leaning back against the side of the bed. It was a nice theory and everything, but I was failing to see how any of it justified stabbing me to death while Rau whispered sweet, creepy nothings in my ear. I opened my mouth to tell Cyrus that much, but he was already continuing with his story.

"So that's what we thought, but when I joined your soul-link and channelled your power, I noticed something strange."

"Only one strange thing?" I quipped. "Because I remember a cart full of bodies and a server-creation-farm. That's at *least* two strange things. And Fakey making out with Mountain Man counts for five points, so that's seven strange things."

"I have no idea who those two people are, but the strange thing wasn't to do with what was happening around you, it was your power. Your Chaos … wasn't actually Chaos."

"What are you talking about? You set a building on fire and disfigured a bunch of people." I had meant the statement to come out sounding matter-of-fact, but the image of Evie flashed into my mind as I was speaking, and it ended up coming out as an accusation.

"It was pure power," he told me, his expression openly curious. "I have been the Neutral God since before Abil's sons were born—believe me, I know what Chaos feels like. Your power is not it."

I blinked at him, trying to process that information. "But I do have a power? I mean … Topia isn't going to realise that I'm not a Chaos Beta and kick me out, right?"

He grinned, but once again, the motion was without any real warmth. "I felt your power. It was connected directly to Topia. You belong here more than all of us."

"Is that why you shoved a knife in me and let Rau give me a death-cuddle?" I was back to my biting tone as I narrowed my eyes on him. "Because I *belong* here?"

"No." The answer hadn't come from Cyrus, but from the doorway. Coen was standing there, staring at me. "Apparently, Rau had planned to hit you with another curse, like a back-up curse, just in case the first wasn't enough to make you strong enough to enter Topia. He had embedded it into the knife he tossed at you, and Neutral was supposed to make sure that the knife hit you in the exact same place as the previous curse." Coen strode further into the room, stopping beside me, his hand raising to my chest and pressing against the scar through my robe. "Instead, Neutral pulled the curse into himself and gave you the knife without the enchantment."

I stared up at Coen, who wasn't meeting my eyes, until another figure appeared in the doorway. Siret. He was staring at the place where Coen still touched me, and I watched as one-by-one, the rest of my Abcurses appeared. None of them approached me, or even looked at Cyrus.

They're still in shock, I realised.

"We didn't know if you would wake up," Coen whispered, so low that I almost didn't hear him.

My head snapped back to him, and I quickly pushed his hand down from my chest, wrapping my arms around his neck and pulling him down far enough that I could hug him properly. He wrapped his arms around me softly—too softly, as though he thought I would snap in half if he squeezed any tighter.

"I'm here," I assured him, loud enough that the others could also hear me. "I'm not dead, I'm just on Round Two."

"Technically, it's your final round." Cyrus spoke from the other side of the room. "There are no rounds after this one."

"I refuse to die," I snapped back, still angry that he had stabbed me. "I'll have as many rounds as I want. And you still haven't explained yourself properly. Why the hell do you care if I die from Chaos, die from a knife, or not die at all?"

Coen released me, almost reluctantly, and I turned as the others moved to surround me. Aros linked his fingers through mine, and Siret claimed my other hand, while Rome planted himself almost directly in front of me and Yael moved beside Coen. I could still see Cyrus, even though Rome was probably trying to block him out—and he looked annoyed.

"We tortured him for a really long time," Aros murmured to me, somehow sounding seductive even though he was talking about torture. "And we eventually listened to what he had to say—but if you want us to do it all over again so that you can watch, just say the word, sweetheart."

"How sweet," Cyrus noted dryly.

I squeezed Aros's hand, but shook my head in a little *no*, my lips curving up at the corners.

"Why do you care?" I repeated, flicking my eyes back to Cyrus.

"I felt the power," he explained. "If that amount of power became too absorbed in Chaos, it would destroy both worlds completely. You could say that I was just in it to save myself, or you could say that I was in it to save every single person or creature that you hold dear."

"I'll go with the first option," I returned. "So if Rau thinks you helped him, then why isn't he here, demanding I destroy the worlds with Chaos?"

"Because of us," Rome announced, his voice booming around the room. He was still pissed, apparently. "Neutral didn't tell us his plan, so we stormed out of the cave and started raining hell. Apparently, that was the plan all along. That was why Neutral didn't tell any of us that this was going to happen. He wanted it to be *believable*."

I broke away from Siret and Aros, moving in front of Rome and standing before Cyrus, looking him over very carefully. There wasn't a single hair out of place; not a single wrinkle in his robe.

"You took on Rau's curse?" I asked for clarification.

He nodded: his only answer.

"And you took what I'm assuming was a very major beating from these five?" I nodded my head toward the Abcurses.

"Yes." This time, Cyrus's lips twitched in a smile.

"So why do you look like you've been spending the sun-cycle luxuriating in a bathing chamber?" I asked suspiciously.

"Because he's the damned Neutral." Yael said the words like an accusation. "We can't destroy him. The bastard just kept healing himself. It was a nightmare. Eventually, we were too exhausted to keep killing him, so we listened to what he had to say."

Well, now I was a little bit terrified of Cyrus.

"You know I can't stay hidden in here forever, right?" I walked away from them all, feeling the eyes following me.

The Abcurses were anxious. They wanted to touch me, to reassure themselves that I was really there, really *real*. I wasn't sure how I knew that, I could just feel it. Just as I could feel their reluctance to reach for me with Cyrus in the room.

"It's a temporary solution." Cyrus sounded somewhat disgruntled. I supposed that was understandable, considering that he had just absorbed a curse and been tortured a whole lot, just in the name of saving *possibly* the universe but *probably* just himself.

"How close are we to finding a permanent solution?" I asked. "One where I can see Emmy, and check on Evie, whose face you almost burnt off, in case you don't remember. I also wouldn't mind punching Dru in the ballbags. And it would be nice to get my things from Blesswood."

"I already brought them," Aros spoke up. "You've been out for quite a few sun-cycles now. I checked on dweller-Emmy, too. She wanted me to give you this."

He came over to the doorway where I had stopped, and handed me a small, cracked timepiece. It had been a gift for Emmy, from our mother. She never remembered birth-dates—or any dates, really—but that sun-cycle had been special. It had been one of the rare sober times, and she had returned home with a cracked timepiece and a wide-brimmed farmer's hat with a hole in the top of it. She had told us to choose which present we wanted, and Emmy had chosen the broken timepiece, because she was never late to anything anyway. I had chosen the hat, because I could widen the hole in the top and pull it all the way down over my head, so that the wide brim acted as a catching-plate for all the food I dropped at dinner time. Emmy had *hated* my genius contraption, and it only lasted through seven dinners before it mysteriously disappeared.

I smiled at the memory, turning over the broken timepiece in my hand. There was now a chain looped through the top of it, and I turned without a word to the others, approaching my mother in the living room.

"Hi mu—Donald." I held out the time piece. "I have something for you."

She had been sitting on one of Cyrus's white couches, her back ramrod straight and her eyes fixed steadily, unblinkingly ahead. She jumped to her feet when she heard me speak, and then bowed twice in short succession.

"Greetings, Sacred Willa."

She stared at the timepiece—obviously not recognising it, and then reached out and took it from my hand, raising it to her lips. I blinked, confused, as she tried to bite down on it.

"Oh my gods." I quickly stepped forward and snatched it out of her hands. "Why are you always trying to eat everything?" I looped the chain quickly around her neck, and then stepped back again. "You're supposed to wear it."

She looked down at the timepiece, and then back up at me. There was no emotion in her face, but for some reason … I was strangely okay with it. Maybe I was deluding myself, but I refused to think of her as simply a server: something separate to me and the life I had lived. She was my mother, no matter what form she took. No matter how drunk. No matter how forgetful. No matter how … dead.

"Thank you, Sacred Willa," she said.

"Just Willa," I tried again, turning away from her with a small sting of disappointment.

"Thank you, Willa."

I paused, my head snapping up. The Abcurses were all standing in the entryway to Cyrus's room. I met Siret's eyes—because he was a little further in front of the others—and I could see that he was just as shocked as I was. I spun, slowly, but my mother was already back to sitting on the couch and staring blankly. I assumed Cyrus had probably told her to do that. Maybe she had started trying to eat his furniture. I glanced behind the guys as I walked back to them, seeing no sign of Cyrus.

"Where did he go?" I asked as I stopped in front of Siret. He didn't reach for me, but I could still feel the pull in our soul-link that ached for closeness.

"He left—off to another of his secret lairs. Said we could have a few sun-cycles here to ourselves. Rest. Recover."

I nodded, and cast my eyes toward the bed. Apparently, that was all the invitation they needed. Rome was already moving over to it, kicking his shoes off as he went.

"I could sleep for a whole life-cycle," he groaned, picking up the mattress and sliding it from the bed frame.

I blinked, watching as he dropped it on the floor and sank onto it with another groan. Movement from behind me had me turning around before I could ask what the hell he was doing, and I noticed Coen walking into the room with another mattress dragged behind him. He dropped it beside the first mattress, and then kicked his shoes off, walked over to me, and pulled me right down beside him. I crumpled to the soft surface, my white robe fluttering around me, and he stretched me out until I was laying partially on my back and partially on my side, with him curved around me.

I've died and gone to Topia, I thought, as Aros tugged off his shirt, kicked off his boots, and dropped to the mattress on my other side, pulling my hands to his chest and tossing a heavy leg over my thigh. Yael and Siret claimed the rest of our makeshift bed, and I relaxed just enough for my body to sink into the heat that surrounded me.

"Does anybody know what I am?" I hadn't really directed the question at one of them in particular, and so none of them answered me, at first.

"You're perfect," Aros told me.

"Ours." Coen's voice was low. Exhausted. "You're ours."

How long had they spent trying to kill Cyrus? Hopefully it wasn't the whole time I had been unresponsive.

"Stubborn," Yael added. "You're also really fucking stubborn."

"You're never allowed out of our sight again." Rome seemed to be half-asleep when he answered, his voice a sleepy grunt.

Heard that before.

"You're Willa-damned-Knight," Siret told me, his familiar voice wrapping around me in a way that had me smiling into Aros's chest. "And so much more."

TO BE CONTINUED...

ALSO BY JANE WASHINGTON

Curse of the Gods Series
Book One: Trickery
Book Two: Persuasion
Book Three: Seduction

The Seraph Black Series
Book One: Charcoal Tears
Book Two: Watercolour Smile
Book Three: Lead Heart
Book Four: A Portrait of Pain

The Beatrice Harrow Series
Book One: Hereditary
Book Two: The Soulstoy Inheritance

Standalone Books
I Am Grey (coming soon)

ALSO BY JAYMIN EVE

Curse of the Gods Series
Book One: Trickery
Book Two: Persuasion
Book Three: Seduction

A Walker Saga
Book One: First World
Book Two: Spurn
Book Three: Crais
Book Four: Regali
Book Five: Nephilius
Book Six: Dronish
Book Seven: Earth

NYC Mecca Series
Book One: Queen Heir
Book Two: Queen Alpha
Book Three: Queen Fae

Supernatural Prison Trilogy
Book One: Dragon Marked
Book Two: Dragon Mystics
Book Three: Dragon Mated

Supernatural Prison Stories
Broken Compass
Magical Compass

Hive Trilogy
Book One: Ash
Book Two: Anarchy
Book Three: Annihilate

Sinclair Stories
Songbird

CONNECT WITH JANE WASHINGTON

inquiries@janewashington.com

WEBSITE:

NEWSLETTER:

FACEBOOK:

FACEBOOK GROUP:

AMAZON:

GOODREADS:

CONNECT WITH JAYMIN EVE

jaymineve@gmail.com

WEBSITE:

NEWSLETTER:

FACEBOOK:

FACEBOOK GROUP:

AMAZON:

GOODREADS:

Printed in Great Britain
by Amazon